THE BODYGUARD
& THE MISS

Lotte R. James

To my friends, and first readers, Val and T.
To those on Twitter who have kept me sane, made me laugh and
supported me.
And as always, to my mother, BB.

CONTENTS

I.

Miss Angelique Marie Claire Fitzsimmons had always had a very clear plan for her life. It was the plan her parents had crafted for her; the same plan many parents like hers made for girls just like her. Girls of good breeding, and good fortune. The little darling debutantes of society; the future wives and mothers of the most important men in the kingdom. This plan was inordinately simple and immutable: catch a good husband, bear him sons, be a beautiful, flawless reflection of his power and standing.

Make the best match you can, and settle down into a life of comfort and purposelessness.

Angelique had never questioned the plan, never dared to dream of anything else. For how could she dream of more when all she had ever been shown, all she had ever been taught, every word, every gesture, every choice of ribbon and bow was made to ensure the success of the grand plan.

Not even the romantic books and plays, not even the tales of adventure and passion she had happened across occasionally stirred her as they did others. She had never read a book of dashing heroes and fair desperate maidens, and thought, *oh were my life such.* She enjoyed them, as sure as her peers, but she'd always seen them for what they were.

Pretty words; and nothing more.

Life, Angelique knew without the shadow of a doubt, was not as it was in books or on the stage. Life was a desperate race for survival, even among those of her rank and prosperity.

Life was being strapped into stays too tight for one to breathe in, and starving oneself so one could wear the current fashions. Life was listening to one's mother fret and scream when one handled a teacup wrong, and life was pretending to be friends with the right people so that society would forget about your eccentrically absent baron of a father, and remember instead that you were worth twenty thousand pounds.

Life was days and nights of pushing through debilitating nerves, and smiling through feet blistered from hours of dancing with eligible men in the hopes of catching their eye. Life was gritting your teeth until you thought they might fall off whilst landed lords touched you in places you didn't want them too, so that they might be tempted just enough to offer that elusive, coveted contract in exchange for your body and soul.

Life was only that; a collection of insufferable memories.

The knowledge, that more would come in future, as numbing as those from the past.

Nothing good, nothing beautiful.

Only an anxious mama and a fear that would never leave you.

And one lived with it, *lived it*, because there was no other way.

When one ran away from home, things did not end as they did in storybooks. They ended with despair, destitution, degradation, and death in ditches. So to avoid such fate, one did as they were told. One caught the best husband one could, and lived the best one could, and that was it.

At least, that was what Angelique had believed, until four years ago.

And now, as she stood before the back entrance of the Shadwell brothel, about to run away from home, she knew with absolute certainty that her life as it was before, was over.

As she raised her fist and knocked on the forbidding black door, in the symphonic cacophony of voices and sounds that made up this part of town, she could almost hear that great master plan, or rather, what little remained of it now, being torn to shreds and tossed to the chilly spring breeze that smelt of humanity, and of the river.

Good riddance.

Angelique wished the Devil would take that plan, as surely as he had crafted it. It was not hers anymore, if it ever had truly been and not merely that which her mother and society had convinced her was her *duty*. Her lot. The only option. *'The only way, my dearest,'* Lady Fitzsimmons had been wont to say on many an occasion. Daily, in fact.

The only way to what? Subjugation and misery? A lifetime of fear and idleness?

No more.

Once, the idea of running away had seemed so terrifying. She had fantasised about it on occasion, in crowded ballrooms and during dinner parties that made her nauseous and dizzy. Only, even as she had, she had seen that dream as a thing which would inevitably lead to death, and misery. Now however, it seemed the only option to avoid such things.

Or at least, to meet them on her own terms.

By her own choice.

Taking a deep breath, Angelique pushed it all away, and tried to focus on the current task, namely, running away. Only, it was hard to concentrate when your body still shook like a leaf in autumn, not from the damp chill, but from the fear, and your heart was pounding so that it was all you could hear, even over the fracas of this place, and all you could see were those eyes...

The door before her was thrust open, sending a wave of perfume-scented warmth towards her. She blinked, her eyes adjusting to the dim light of the corridor beyond that seemed then as bright as the sun in the darkness of the alley. Clutching the greatcoat tightly around her, she raised her head so the guard could see her face beneath the shadow of the cap she wore. The new, bored looking bruiser that filled the doorway eyed her carefully, but showed no emotion as he compared her delicate features to the worn men's clothing she sported.

Most likely not even the strangest thing he's seen this evening.

'I need to speak to Miss Lily,' she said, as confidently, and authoritatively as she could, considering her current state.

'I know ye,' the guard asked in a menacing growl.

'No,' she said, taking a step forward. 'But Miss Lily does.'

The guard glanced over her shoulder, though what he could see in the pitch beyond, she wondered.

Perhaps he could see like a cat in the dark.

His eyes returned to her, and she stood tall, as tall as she could considering her small stature and the fact that the man was quite literally twice her size, and returned his stare, unflinching, as dear Mama had taught her. Only the lessons had not been for such occasions, and Lady Fitzsimmons would surely faint if she knew how her lessons were being used.

If she knew anything of what you'd been up to these past years…

After a long moment studying her, the bruiser nodded, and moved aside so she could enter. Angelique stepped into the plain corridor, all white washed walls, simple brown carpet, and tin sconces; all a far cry from the plush, colourful, and lush public ones she was used to.

Forcing herself not to shiver, to enjoy the warmth she could barely feel now, she waited as the man closed the door behind her, and tried to convince herself the sound of it loudly clicking shut was good. Closing the door on her past. Not as ominous or foreboding as it felt.

The beginning of a new chapter.

'Name,' the bruiser asked, almost bored.

'Of no consequence to you.'

'Ye stay here,' he growled as he passed her, forcing her to plaster herself against the wall to make room. 'And don't touch anything,' he said, pointing a lumpy finger at her that looked to have definitely been broken more than once. In fact, most of him looked to have been broken more than once. 'I'll see if Miss Lily'll come down.'

Angelique nodded, having absolutely no intention of going

anywhere, and the giant continued his way, taking a sharp right a little ahead as he made his way up the back stairs towards Lily's rooms.

It wasn't that Angelique had any fear of this place; after all, it wasn't her first time here. In fact, it was her fourth, or perhaps fifth, though admittedly, her first time here alone. She'd come to see what Lily had built, curious after hearing of the project from one of Percy's workers, his wife Meg's friend Sarah, who ran the meal house at the wharf in her stead, since Meg was a viscountess now.

Countess, actually.

The lighterman's daughter would be a countess now, much to society's dismay; now that Percy's father had passed, and he had become Earl of Brookton.

A mere four days ago. How he must be -

Don't think on him. It will only make this worse.

Regardless, countess or lighterman's daughter, still, Meg protested Angelique's *flights of fancy*, such as visiting this place. Everyone who knew of those *flights of fancy* had protested them, particularly her visits here, exclaiming loudly at the scandalousness of her desire to visit a brothel. No matter their pasts, they couldn't see past the visage of innocent youth painted on her, see past what she *should* be, to who she really was; whoever that was.

And truth be told, she wasn't entirely sure at whose door that fault lay.

Hers, or theirs.

Or all of ours. Life's.

Even Lily had taken issue with her visits at first, though her objections hadn't been born from fear of impropriety. Rather, because she had been quite sure Angelique was one of those well-intentioned, well-bred women intent on spreading the word of the Lord to her girls, to save their souls. But in truth, Angelique had merely wished to see what the woman who was surely not much older than herself, had built with only her wits, and will.

What a woman had built, for other women. Regardless of their occupation. Just as Meg had built the meal house and the foundling home. She had not judged Meg because of her occupation, so why should she judge Lily, nor any of the other girls, nor anyone. At least, not anymore.

Her entire life, she had done just that, as she'd been taught to. So swept up in the plan, her own anxiousness driving her, she had judged, and gossiped, and selected friends as one did jewelry, and wielded information as one wielded a sword. Only to quickly learn how very terrible it was to do so.

And how liberating it was now to simply get to know people, whatever their origins. To get to know them, for who they truly were. Even if they were *beneath you.* Even if they served you no purpose, not even friendship. For when one got to know people, one got to know themselves, and the world they lived in.

When Lily had realized that Angelique saw what she'd done, how she'd built a strong business, and given the girls a safe and healthy place to work, she had warmed to her. Just as Angelique had. They had become unlikely acquaintances, not quite friends, for some lives could never intersect to that extent no matter how much one wished it so.

So she had returned, spent time with Lily and her girls, learned more of them, and their lives. Shared meals, and song, and drink, and blissful moments with them. Much to Percy, Meg, and Will's dismay.

She tried to push away thoughts of them again, but it was not so easy. Inevitably, they returned to the forefront of her thoughts, and a little shudder crept through her. At the thought of her friend and perennial self-appointed guardian who would be after her as soon as her disappearance was noted. She'd thought... But with his father having just passed, and his accession to the earldom... With his wife expecting, all his business...

Besides, he could never understand. None of them could.

Which was why she'd come here. Why she couldn't let more people know who she was. Let more people witness her flight.

Both for their protection, and her own. This was it. Her one shot. And she would *not* muck it up. Be the incompetent ninny so many thought her.

Or back to the prison you once called home it shall be...

The sound of footfalls tore Angelique from her mired thoughts, and she turned to find Lily coming towards her, the giant behind her.

Tonight, Lily looked particularly beautiful, sporting a sinful burgundy and purple silk creation that looked more like veils twisted and swept around her body than an actual gown. It was gorgeous, and shocking, and entirely appropriate considering her position. And besides, the rich burgundy set off her pale skin, and blonde curls so like Angelique's own, that were untidily, and yet, perfectly, swept up onto her head. The purple meanwhile complimented her golden eyes that normally twinkled, but tonight were full of concern.

And not just for me I think...

'Come,' Lily said gravely, whatever she'd seen in Angelique's face enough to alert her to the seriousness of the situation. 'Bob, watch the door. You never saw her.'

Bob the giant nodded, not that Lily could see, but Angelique sensed the woman always knew when orders were obeyed or not.

And how to ensure they always were.

Nodding at him as he passed her again and resumed his post, Angelique went over to Lily, and found herself immediately wrapped in her deceptively strong arms. She wasn't entirely sure if she had launched herself there, or if the young madam had pulled her into the embrace, but she didn't care. She found the tears she'd been fighting all night, indeed, all her life, came immediately, springing forth and soaking the woman's silk gown.

Lily stroked her head for a few moments, murmuring reassurances, holding her tight, before slowly disengaging.

'Let's to my office,' she said kindly, taking Angelique's hand and turning back towards the stairs. 'I feel we've a lot to discuss, and not much time to do so.'

Nodding feebly, Angelique followed, her heart already a little lighter.

I can do this.

No more prison.

No more fear.

∞

'So,' Lily sighed, settling behind the enormous mahogany desk she called her own moments later, as Angelique dropped into one of the thick leather armchairs before it, a glass of gin in her hands. Lily's office was so much like her father's study, it was odd. Only this place was actually used, not a shrine to a man she'd not seen in years. Only here, the bookshelves lining the room, magnificent marble hearth, thick blood-red curtains, and plush Persian rug felt warm and comfortable rather than... *Dark and terrifying.* 'What brings you here in the middle of the night, *alone*, Miss Fitzsimmons?'

'Angelique, please,' she said, for the hundredth time.

But tonight, Lily nodded as she took a healthy gulp of her own gin.

'Angelique. What the Devil are you doing here?'

'I need to disappear,' she said, hoping the desperation in her voice, which she was unable to conceal, would help her case. She knew what she was asking; what the woman risked if she agreed. But she somehow knew she could trust her; that she was perhaps the only person in the world that she *could* trust. 'Quickly. I have money, I've been hiding bits of my pin money for years,' she stammered on, needing Lily to know that though the timing may seem rash, but months before her majority; the idea wasn't new. 'I thought I could do it on my own, I want to go to America, but the truth is, I have no idea how to... Be safe, and not found. I just, need to get where I'm going without anyone being able to track me. Without Will being able to track me.'

Lily grimaced and reached over to pour herself another gin.

'Why,' she asked flatly.

'It's… Complicated.'

'Are you in danger,' the woman asked, concerned, her eyes hardening. 'Has someone hurt you?'

'Yes. No. I don't know,' she sighed, before downing her own gin and holding the glass out for more.

She would take courage, in whatever form, liquid or otherwise.

How to explain this without explaining? How to put it into words so the woman would help her, and not truss her up and send her back home with the recommendation she be committed to a mad-house?

It felt like she was in danger, constantly, but from what, or whom?

Certainly not whoever Percy was worried about when he hired Will.

That much at least, she knew. For she'd been afraid, for far longer than that. Only, it was difficult to explain, that feeling, low in the pit of her stomach, the one she lived with, a constant state of…

Dread.

And then there were the nightmares, a recent and terrifying addition to her life.

'This isn't just a bored little miss off for an adventure,' Angelique said earnestly. 'I need you to know that. And there have been no… Direct threats, or misadventures. It's… I know, in my heart, that something is horrendously wrong,' she admitted. Speaking the words aloud, it felt freeing. Not as she had thought it would; not as if she'd brought the invisible threat to life. Made it somehow more tangible by speaking of it. *It is already too real for that.* 'That if I don't disappear, tonight, something terrible will happen to me.'

Sipping her gin, Lily studied her carefully for a long moment, the gold of her eyes darkening to amber.

Angelique willed all she felt to shine in her own eyes, to

convince Lily to help her.

'I just want to find somewhere I can live my life,' she pleaded.

'I will help you,' Lily said quietly, examining the bottom of her glass pensively. 'Tell you where and how to travel, give you clothes that'll make you invisible. From what I hear, you already know how to defend yourself, so that's good. You'll need to. And you'll need be patient. The Ghost'll be after you come morning, I'd bet my own life on that,' she laughed, referring to Percy, the mad viscount - *earl* - who'd taken up the vigilante's mantle when he'd come to Shadwell himself all those years ago.

Not that he knew Angelique was aware of that side of him; the man thought he was so talented at keeping his secrets.

She and Meg had many a laugh regarding that. Though deep down, it hurt that he didn't feel he could share all of himself with her. That he didn't really share much of himself or anything at all with her really. Even after all they had been through together, he still saw her as a child, a weak, small, female thing to be protected, not trusted.

As everyone does.

'And naturally that bloodhound you usually trail.'

Angelique nodded grimly.

Of all who would come after her, somehow Will was the one she both minded, and feared the most. She got the feeling the man would follow her to the ends of the Earth.

I suppose we shall find out if that is true soon enough.

'It ain't about being quick, it's the opposite,' Lily warned, her voice slipping further into its original, broader tones. 'It's about runnin' them ragged and keepin' them guessin' as to where you're headed until it's too late for them to follow.'

'I understand. And thank you. I know what I am asking. As I said, I can pay -'

'Don't insult me,' she said with a disgusted look. 'I know what you're asking. And what you're after. And I know you wouldn't come askin' here if you had another choice. So I'll help you,' she stated. 'And I'll keep your secret if they come sniffin', which they're bound to. Every woman deserves a chance to make her own fate.'

'Thank you,' Angelique said softly, tears burning her eyes again.

Though she forced them back down with the next gulp of gin she swallowed.

'Now,' Lily said with a mischievous grin and determined look as she rose, and came around the desk. 'Let's get you ready. You've a long journey ahead.'

That, I do indeed.

At least, I pray I do.

II.

The scream which tore through the house before dawn's first rays had Will bolting upright amidst a tangle of sweat-soaked sheets. It wasn't her scream. He knew her screams, all too well now; knew they signalled no villains bursting through locked windows; only invisible demons of the mind. Those screams awoke him, but not as this scream had.

With dread in your heart.

Without a second's hesitation he was up, throwing on his breeches as he tore out of the butler's cupboard, willing the fear to awaken and sharpen his mind. If anything happened to her, he was dead. So he needed to be as always alert, and in full possession of his wits. Not... *Concerned.* Which he wasn't. The fear he felt now as he tore across the house, knocking in walls, and nearly taking down countless priceless artefacts towards Angelique's rooms, it was fear for his own survival. Fear for his position, and plans; it wasn't fear *for* her.

No.

That was simply the remnants of his dreams taunting him. The faded memories of an unlived life lost, of damned cottages and cows, mingling with his current state to produce something...

Useless.

Mentally shaking himself, focusing on the task at hand, he prayed someone had merely burned themselves on hot embers or stained a favoured gown or something as benign and meaningless.

Surely it was nothing. Over a year he'd been posted at the little gremlin's side, and nothing. No danger to be found, save for that she created for herself.

And - enough.

It was true, she had been acting… Odd, lately. Well, odder than usual. More… Removed. Less playful, and engaged, flitting about like the society darling she was. Instead, she'd seemed increasingly worried. Anxious. And she had been paler, prone to more *attacks of the nerves* as Lady Fitzsimmons was wont to call them, and there were those shadows beneath her chartreuse eyes, which themselves had been without their usual mischievousness and lustre.

Lustre, really? Get a hold on yourself.

Which he did, as well as on the door frame to Angelique's rooms, not even needing to force his way in to see what had happened, for it was open; open onto the worst sight imaginable.

Emptiness.

The dark, disgustingly delicate and floral room was devoid of a Miss Fitzsimmons. There was the scullery maid, currently sobbing into Mrs. Landry, the housekeeper's shoulder, but no Ange - *Miss Fitzsimmons.* His heart dropped down to his boots, and his gut churned.

No…

'Wake the mistress,' he ordered the housekeeper coldly as he strode in without preamble. Telling the lady that her precious daughter was gone would not help matters, the woman was an excitable shrew on the best of days, but it had to be done. *Prepare for an attack of nerves…* 'Get the men to search everything, and the grounds, *carefully*, and send word to Brookton House. Tell the earl he's needed here immediately.'

Without a word of protest, Mrs. Landry tucked the maid into her arm, and swept out.

She knew as well as anyone what his true purpose was here, and who his employer was. It was the only reason he'd been allowed such liberties since he'd come here. Sleeping in the butler's pantry rather than the servant's quarters, trailing the annoying young miss quite literally everywhere, bursting into her room half-undressed in the early morning...

And now it seemed, all he had done, all he had worked for, had been for nothing.

Will raked his fingers through his hair as he prowled around the room, noting everything to make sense of what had happened.

Bed unmade, but barely slept in for usually it is worse than your own. Tangled, and mangled -

Window open, though she always sleeps with it closed and locked, no matter the heat.

No broken glass, scrapes or any other signs of forcible entry.

No dresses or shoes missing, but - damn. Men's clothes stash missing.

Will bet that if he went down to the garden, he would find her little footprints through the patches of mud in the garden, leading all the way out back to the mews.

So she hasn't been taken.

He let out a breath he hadn't been aware he was holding, and stopped at the window, gazing out into the darkened twilight.

She ran.

Why, he couldn't say. Certainly not, why *now*. The girl would reach her majority in a few months, and likely have all she needed to buy or force her own freedom them. Regardless, the truth of *why* and *why now* mattered little.

He had to get her back. Quickly, and quietly.

Christ.

Of all the society misses in the goddamn city, it had to be this one. The annoying, thrill-seeking, clever, indomitable, spoiled -

Focus.

Yes. Too late for regrets now.

Now, he had to get on the road. And track her down before it was too late.

I made a promise, little gremlin.

And not you, not God nor the Devil himself will prevent me from keeping it.

No, nothing would. For that promise, was his life.

And nothing was worth what little he had.

∞

'Oh Egerton thank God you're here,' Lady Fitzsimmons cried, launching herself into the newly minted Earl of Brookton's arms as soon as he appeared at the drawing room door. Egerton had no choice but to brace himself, and take the woman in his arms, patting her cotton capped head as she continued her sobbing and whimpering in the folds of his coat.

Will had been dealing with her for the past twenty minutes, and by dealing, he meant standing at the mantel, rubbing his forehead as he tried to formulate a list of all he had to do whilst the woman wailed and muttered incomprehensible nonsense about her husband and debts, and who knew what else.

Not he, for he had managed to stop hearing her after about five minutes, though every once in a while a shrill scream of his name brought him sharply back to the room.

'It's happened, oh dear God, Egerton,' the woman cried as the earl, who looked as Hellish as Will felt right now, carefully pulled her away from him and guided her back out to the foyer to presumably set her into her maid or the housekeeper's capable hands. 'I knew this would happen, I just knew it!'

'There there,' he said soothingly, shooting a glance over his shoulder at Will who simply shrugged, impatient to get started. 'All will be well. We will take care of this.'

'It's him, I know it's him, my husband -'

'We will find Angelique, I swear it. Now, you must rest, and keep strong for her.'

Rolling his eyes, Will waited for Egerton to reappear, which he did seconds later, Lady Fitzsimmons' cries echoing through the house as she was returned to her rooms.

'What the Hell happened,' the earl shouted once he'd closed the door, heading for him with murderous intent in his eyes. The man was definitely not to be trifled with; but then again, neither was Will. '*How* could this happen?'

'She ran,' Will said starkly, pushing off the mantel, and standing his ground squarely.

Egerton stopped, gaping wordlessly, his hazel eyes uncomprehending.

'What? How? How do you know,' he finally managed.

'I know.'

'After all we've done to protect her,' Egerton said, shaking his head, and setting about pacing the room, dishevelling the mass of golden curls on his head even more. 'Are you certain it isn't -'

'I'm certain,' he said firmly, knowing the earl referred to the mysterious villain who had come after him the year before, and remained nameless, and faceless.

One of many suspects who might've been in the running had An - *Miss Fitzsimmons goddamnit* - actually been *taken*.

He still wasn't sure if he might've preferred that option to her simply running away from her privileged little life like the spoiled brat she was. Somehow he got the feeling she would be even harder to find; the girl was far from stupid, and knew all Egerton and he would do to get her back.

But I will, little gremlin.

'I don't understand,' Egerton said feebly, dropping onto the sofa, all his anger dissipated leaving nothing but concern and fear. 'Why? Why now?'

Because she is a she-Devil who is continuously seeking the next thrill to chase her boredom away.

'I don't know,' he said instead. 'You know what she's been like.'

'Yes,' Egerton said sharply, his jaw ticking. 'Still, I cannot believe she would just up and leave like this, not after everything. She would've told me, or Meg -'

'No, she wouldn't,' he scoffed. Schooling himself a moment later when the earl shot him a glare to curdle milk. It was difficult sometimes to remember his place; difficult to mind his words when it came to Miss Fitzsimmons. They all saw her as the paragon, somewhat termagant of a paragon, but paragon nonetheless. *Tread carefully now.* 'Even without all that is happening for you right now, she knows you never would have let her go,' he said as conciliatory as he could manage at the moment. *If freedom is truly what she sought.* Which, in truth, it might be. Though she would regret it once she'd had a true taste of the cruel world that lay in wait for her. 'I will find her, my lord. Whatever it takes.'

'This can't get out,' he said, raking his hair again so that he looked about as mad as many believed he truly was, marrying a poor commoner as he had. 'We need to preserve her reputation until she returns.'

Will nodded.

Yes, preserve her reputation.

The most important thing of all to them; what he'd seemingly been doing rather than protecting her from unknown enemies for the past year.

'And I cannot leave... I have so much to attend to with my father's death,' he sighed, and not for the first time Will detected some bitterness in his tone at the mention of the man. 'I'll make enquiries here, make sure you're right.' Will clenched his jaw, but Egerton pinned him with another stare. 'I won't lose anyone else. I trust your judgement, but even so. If she's unprotected, this might be the right moment for someone to strike.'

'Of course,' he agreed.

The man wasn't wrong.

This would be an ideal time for someone to strike at her, when she was alone, and vulnerable, and unprotected...

Damn.

'She can't have done this alone,' Egerton said, rising.

'I know,' he nodded. 'I have some ideas as to who may have helped her.'

'You find her, Will,' the earl said, coming in close. 'And you bring her back, safe.'

Will nodded, finding he did not have it in him to offer empty reassurances.

Empty promises.

He would do his best, to bring her back unharmed, but the truth was, he couldn't promise that she would be by the time this was all over.

'I'll keep you informed of my progress, my lord,' he said.

Egerton nodded, and began to make his way out, but stopped just shy of the door.

'As much as it pains me to say it, I think perhaps you know her better than anyone,' he said with a slight frown, and the statement nearly made Will burst out in hysterics. 'I trust you.'

He contained his amusement at the insanity of the earl's words, and simply nodded.

Egerton left, and Will followed not too long after. He was dressed, packed, and atop his mount within twenty minutes, heading straight for Shadwell. The girl might be clever, but she was forgetting that he had followed her around for the past year.

Everywhere.

Perhaps the earl was right after all; perhaps he did know her better than anyone.

Only you do not know me, little gremlin.

III.

A ngelique stood at the edge of the waves, and turned her head up towards the Heavens. Eyes closed, she relished the feel of the light spittle of rain on her face, and the bite of the salty wind as it lashed around her. Though her heart was still heavy, and that fear she had lived with her entire life was still alive in her gut, she felt lighter. She was close now, so close to total and utter freedom, and she could swear it tasted just like this. Just like the salty cold wind of the sea.

It hadn't been easy; in fact this journey so far had been the most difficult thing she'd ever done in her life. Three weeks she had been on the road, weaving and doubling back across the isle. It had been three weeks of stuffed mail carriages, walking, random carts, boats, and roadside inns. Three weeks of changing from governess, to widow, to stern school teacher, always with somewhere to go, and someone to meet. It helped protect her from the nefarious types who travelled the roads in search of easy prey, most of whom she had been able to avoid, and it also left a trail of breadcrumbs to a hundred other towns and cities she would never be.

In the end, it hadn't been all bad actually, she had shared a coach or meal with some interesting enough people, a vicar, some maids, another governess or too, and many a travelling businessman, who strangely were always very vague about what precisely their business was. She had seen some wonderful sights, from the rolling hills of Somerset to the rocky heaths of Yorkshire, and she was safe, and alive.

And so close.

Tomorrow, she would take the ship to Dublin, and then she would travel on to Cork, and then, America. She wasn't entirely sure what she would do when she got there, or even where she would decide to settle, but she had an education, she was willing to work, and America was the land of opportunity. It was where people could reinvent themselves, and make something new; of themselves, and of the world. She thought she might miss England, but standing here in Scotland, on the precipice of the final moments of her journey, she realized that she really had nothing to miss.

Yes, she had friends, and good ones at that. True ones. More so now, than she would've said four years ago. Back then, she'd certainly had rooms full of *friends*, young misses like herself who knew nothing of kindness or loyalty. Only scheming and manipulation; for that is what they'd been taught. What she'd been taught; for that was who she was too.

Back then, she'd helped Effy destroy Lydia Mowbray's life. Lydia, who was meant to be her friend, but who had used her like a pincushion and who she in turn had not hesitated to throw to the wolves. Lydia too had come to Scotland, with the love of her life. She hoped it had turned out well for her, and she wondered for a moment, if they had stayed here, or if they too had moved on, far away; far away from the grasp of the Duke of Mowbray.

At least I do not have a father who will come chasing after me so.
At least I do not have a father guilty of such horrific crimes as he.
For I do not have a father anymore.

The baron hadn't been seen in society for oh... Fourteen years. He dwelled in the family's country seat, doing God only knew what, with whom, or why. Not that she missed him. She couldn't remember him well enough to miss him, and even what little she did remember, fragments, well, it was nothing to be nostalgic about. Overbearing, rigid, steadfast in his pride and rank, cold, and cruel at times...

Certainly not a father to miss, or love. She had never asked what had driven her parents to live as they had; she had wondered, once, some time ago, but never dared ask.

Perhaps it was mama that drove him away.

Oh mother...

This would destroy her. She felt a slight pang in her heart, at the manner of her departure. No matter what her mother was, she was still, her mother. No matter that all she remembered were anxious recriminations and desperate attempts at throwing her into the path of eligible men, she was still her flesh and blood. She was still one of the few people Angelique could say that she loved.

Somewhere, deep down. Despite it all.

Her mother was still the woman who had given her the best life she'd known how to, alone, and despite the precarious position their father had put them in. Angelique could not fault her for doing what she thought best, and maybe, once she arrived in America, she could write her a proper letter. Explain, apologize, something. Find a new way to have some relationship, no matter how tenuous and distant, with the woman who had raised her.

I will write to them all once I am free.

Angelique wondered where they were all now, her mother, her friends. If they were all sick with worry, if Will was lost somewhere in Shropshire searching for her among the sheep. It pained her to cause them such distress, but she couldn't do it anymore. Couldn't just sit there prettily, smile through the pain, and wait.

Wait for whatever terrible thing was coming. And even if there hadn't been that terror looming on the edge of the horizon of her future, she still wouldn't have had a life, of her own. Not even once she reached her majority in July. With no inheritance, no settlement, only little more than she had now to build her life, she would still have had to run away to make what she

21

wished to of herself. No matter that in the eyes of the law she would be a grown, free woman; they would not let her go lest she run. They would continue to foist their own plans on her. And no matter one's love for others, no matter one's love of one's country, one had to have a life of their own to be able to enjoy the land they called home, and the people who were family.

One had to have freedom, of choice, to love.

To live, truly.

So she had run, now, rather than later.

Now, rather than suffer another minute of torture, or fear, of...

Those eyes.

Brushing the loose curls from her face, Angelique turned to face the wind, slipping back on the bonnet she had taken off to fully enjoy the experience that was her little walk by the low cliffs. She took a moment to commit all the details of that moment to memory, just as she had taught herself to do with every moment she truly relished these past years.

So much of her life was unknown to her, disappeared into the blank void of childhood. That, or there were no good memories. Well, very few. But as life had become nigh on unbearable, she had found that memorising the few good moments, and then recalling them, had given her the strength, courage, and hope, to continue.

Some were small; the beaded detailing on her come-out dress. Others, were more important, more vital. The morning she had learnt who Effy Fortescue truly was. The day Percy proposed to Meg in Rotherhithe. The faces of some of the children and babes in Meg's foundling home. The first time she'd shot a pistol. The first time she had -

Nevermind. Only memories now. Time to make new ones.

A small smile appeared on her face, a true smile, with nothing else but contentment to sour it, and it grew on her lips as she slowly made her way by the water's edge back towards town.

She decided she very much liked Scotland. The lush greens, the greys and purples of the rocks and heather, the wildness of it, especially the sea. Today, it was the blue-green that appeared before a storm, vibrant, and ominous all at once. This land, it spoke to her of the past, of ages when all was simpler and no one cared much if you curtsied properly or could embroider. It spoke to her of an age long-gone, of magic, and wonder, and was, she thought, a poetic place to end her journey on this island.

Not for the first time, she wondered what America would be like. She'd heard so many tales, of great mountains, and soaring cities. Of strange, wild beasts, and stranger men, exploring still untouched lands. She had seen drawings and read many books, and it felt as if the land across the sea called to her, whispered to her on this very wind, urging her to come forth and seize her destiny.

So I shall. Very soon.

All she hoped, was that when she at last reached that distant land, the fear would finally disappear.

Please God, let it be so.

As she made her way back to the inn she would call home for the night, she wondered if she would ever know what that fear had been born from. Because if not, she had the suspicion that perhaps not even a new life, not even the Almighty himself, could chase it away.

Chin up. Only time will tell.

∞

After what was perhaps the best lamb stew she had ever tasted in her life, even better for it having been eaten in the raucous, but warm main room of the inn, where sailors and fishermen and travellers ate and laughed and sang together, Angelique headed back out for another walk, this time around the port to watch the sunset. She couldn't get enough of her newfound freedom, of the simple bliss which came of deciding for oneself whether one wished to go outside, or have an extra portion of bread.

The simple bliss which came of not having one's life scheduled and dictated.

She sighed and leaned against the railing surrounding a portion of the basin, savouring each second of the changing view before her. Each shade of orange changing into pink, each purple turning to metallic blue and grey. She savoured the clanging of the sails, and the distant shouts of some late workers on the ships. It reminded her a little of Percy's wharf, of the London docks; though on a much smaller, and nicer-smelling scale.

A gentle pricking at the back of her neck tore her from her thoughts, sending her heart racing as it had remorselessly for years. It felt as if someone was watching. Shivering slightly, she drew her shawl tighter and glanced over her shoulder, careful to maintain a carefree, insouciant air best she could.

There was no one there; at least none but those out for their evening strolls or off to the public house. Nothing sinister at all.

You're only getting a bit unsettled as you are so close to your goal.

Yes, that was all there was to it.

Still, she had to be careful. She was beginning to lose herself in the shining future promised, and not minding herself as sharply as she had her first days on the road.

As she had, in truth, for years before that; though for different reasons.

Her reverie a bit spoiled, but unwilling to let herself be shaken by absolutely nothing, she began walking again, intent on finishing her circuit before turning in for bed. But as she did, she felt it again, that pricking; the hairs on the back of her neck raising. She forced herself to remain as calm as possible, to maintain a steady pace, as she occasionally glanced over her shoulder.

Still, there was nothing. No one even so much as sparing her a glance.

No one. And even if there were, you can scream, and fight, and run.

There are ways out.

Angelique tried desperately to shake off the unease, to enjoy the last of her promenade, but in the end, she couldn't. Halfway around, she turned back towards the inn, resolved to spend the rest of her night behind a firmly locked door, wedged with a chair just to be sure.

Following the edge of the basin, she made her way back towards the main square, then began up the high street, her pace quickening ever so slightly as she passed into the shadow of the greystone houses and shops, another shiver running through her. Turning sharply down the side street that led up to the inn, she looked behind her again, only to find nothing but the same threadbare gathering of evening wanderers.

Nothing. See? Breathe. Get to the inn.

Huffing slightly as she followed the street up the hill, she realized within moments that it was deserted. Her heart fell, just as her palms wetted beneath the cotton of her gloves, and her chest tightened.

And that, is when she heard it.

Footfalls.

It shouldn't be anything to send the fear of God into her, only it did.

And when she turned, there was a figure, there, following behind in the shadows, online the outline of a greatcoat visible.

No.

So stupid, she'd been so stupid and careless, and now that thing that was nothing but a shadow of fear was behind her. There was no fighting it, no matter her training. Hell, she could barely draw in a proper breath, barely think. There was only running.

Run. Move!

Picking up her skirts, she did finally manage to spur herself on.

You can make it. Back to the inn.

And there, she could find help, surely, at least until…

Just run!

But she was no match for her pursuer. No sooner did the

warm lights of the inn appear before her just on the edge of the rise, no sooner did the raucous sounds pouring from it reach her ears, but a hand grasped her arm and dragged her backwards into an alley.

Angelique screamed with all she had, but it was quickly muffled by another hand as she was pulled into a hard chest. She writhed and stomped whenever she could find her footing, shoving her elbow anywhere she could as she tried in vain to get to the knife in her boot.

But it was no use.

Her training was not enough; particularly not when she couldn't think. When all she could do was shake and when she couldn't catch her breath, and screams echoed in her mind. Tears began to stream down her cheeks as she fought with all she had left in her, even as her body began to shut down and her mind froze in terror, for it was all over.

The shadow of her nightmares had come, and there would be no escape from him.

IV.

A ngelique,' Will said harshly, still holding on to her tight. He needed her to hear him, to let his voice break through the haze of utter terror she seemed to be lost in. Of all the things he had expected... It hadn't been that, and it threw him. Perhaps he had gone about this the wrong way, he thought belatedly as he pulled her further into the depths of the quiet alley, far from any passersby who might decide to be heroes tonight. Only, three weeks he had chased her across hill and dale, the girl having led him on a merry chase indeed, and he wasn't about to lose her at the last moment.

He needed her subdued, and compliant before they stepped foot back into that inn.

But when she had looked back at him, her bright green eyes sparkling in the darkness... The terror in them had slashed through him like a knife. Cut through to a place, to a part of himself he didn't know. A place, which *felt*.

Surprise, he had expected. Anger, a little fear, but terror such as this, a terror so familiar he could taste it...

What are you so afraid of little gremlin?

'Angelique!'

She stilled suddenly with a whimper in his arms, and he had the very unwelcome notion that she felt rather nice just where she was, and that she could stay there however long she liked so long as she never looked at him again as she had just now.

If he hadn't needed to keep her quiet and subdued, he might've released her just then. His body warred with itself; one half telling him to hold her close, the other screaming out that he was going mad. He didn't touch people, didn't hold them; and she was the last person on Earth he'd ever want to if he ever did.

Christ. Do not get attached.

Sadly, he found that he'd had to remind himself of that all too often over the past year.

'Angelique,' he repeated, softly now that she could hear him. 'It's only me.'

'*Mweil*,' she sobbed against his hand, which he guessed was meant to be his name.

'Yes,' he reassured her. Everything inside him for some reason seemed to want to reassure her, to promise her she would always be safe, even if he knew that was a promise he could never make. A promise, not for a man like he to make. 'I'm going to remove my hands now, but you need to promise you won't scream or run. Please, you know it's over. I found you. If you want to talk, we can go talk, civilly.' Angelique nodded. 'Promise?'

'Mhm,' she sighed, nodding again.

Slowly, he released her, and she gasped in a deep breath as he did.

In the dimming light, he saw her fight to even out her breathing for a few long moments, then sniff loudly, and wipe her cheeks before turning to face him again.

'I am sorry I frightened you,' he said as gently as he could, which apparently was quite so despite the fact neither gentility nor gentleness were part of his being. 'Who did you think I was? You know I would never hurt you.'

In the physical sense at least.

'No one,' she croaked, shaking her head dismissively, obviously preparing for a fight as she squared her shoulders. 'Some villain or other. You scared me,' she hissed, shoving him back forcefully, so abruptly he was actually knocked a little off balance and forced to take a step to steady himself. 'What the Devil were you thinking, sneaking up on me like that?'

'Me,' he exclaimed.

God, to think he'd felt bad for putting her in such a wretched state.

What of him?

He, who had spent three weeks on the wretched roads across the country, hunting her down like some fugitive? Eating stale bread, and sharing stuffy rooms with odorous strangers? So what if that was nothing to him having survived so much worse? It had been three weeks of riding remorselessly after her, worrying about her -

Not about her.

'What the Hell were *you* thinking,' he growled, focusing on his anger and frustration. 'Running off like that? With no word, just disappearing into the night like some criminal -'

'A miracle,' she exclaimed with bitterly mocking wonder. 'It speaks!' Will glowered at her, and she matched it. 'The fact is, I do *not* have to explain myself to you,' she sneered, turning on her heel and marching back towards the inn.

And there she is again, the haughty little gremlin.

'I suppose that's true,' he admitted with a wry grin, that must've sounded in his voice for she turned and glanced at him over her shoulder, and down her nose as she was so often wont to do despite the fact he was practically two heads taller than her. 'But you'll have some explaining to do when I get you back to London.'

'I am *not* going back,' she declared, turning and pointing a finger at him. There was steel in her voice, and pain too. A flicker of fear in her eyes again that made him frown. 'Not ever. And do not even think of trying to throw me over your shoulder and carting me back, for I swear I will die before I go back there, and then it will be my corpse you cart.'

God forbid.

The resoluteness of her statement rendered him speechless, and he stood there a beat as she continued her march back to the inn.

This is not going to be so easy.

Truth was, he could objectively do just that.

He could parcel her up in the dark, tie her, gag her, throw her on the back of his horse, and take her from here in an instant. She was skilled, and clever, but in terms of pure strength, he outmatched her, no question. Sure, the journey would be difficult, and tiresome, but he could do it, if he truly wished to.

But for some reason, he found he didn't quite have it in him.

Damn it.

He wasn't entirely sure where these vestiges of guilt, and morality were coming from, but truly, it was the worst time they could've decided to make an appearance after a lifetime of absence.

It appeared he would have to find another way to force her compliance.

'Let us have a drink, Angelique,' he said in the most conciliatory tone he could manage with all the frustration and fear, *yes, a little twinge of it at the prospect of potential defeat, only that*, coursing through him. 'And discuss matters civilly. You know I answer to to the earl, and I cannot just pretend I never found you. We must find some way to compromise.'

She threw him a thoughtful look, then slowly nodded.

'Fine,' she said just as they arrived before the inn.

∞

'How did you find me,' Angelique asked, eyeing Will dubiously over the rim of her tankard. They had settled with an ale into one of the quieter corners of the public rooms, into a discreet alcove that nonetheless had a good vantage over the entire room. There was no way she was going to go into a private room with the man before her; away from prying eyes, she was not safe. She got the feeling he wouldn't hesitate to make her eat her words and toss her over his shoulder and haul her back to London. Here at least, she might have some help, though even then she doubted most would wish to involve themselves in strangers' business. 'I mean, I was so careful…'

It was frustrating really, more so now that she could think and breathe again.

The fear had returned to its usual simmering self, and finally her hands had stopped shaking. When he'd taken hold of her… She'd never felt such fear in her life.

Well, other than when she woke from those dreams, the ones with the faceless man. Other than whenever she glimpsed the *other* man; when she saw those eyes.

Other than that night she'd been forced to dance with him; the night she'd run.

Angelique shivered slightly, then forced herself back to the room, and the problem at hand. Will was eyeing her as he always did, a cool, calm, collected, icy penetrating stare. His grey eyes, as sharp and unyielding as stone, never seemed to hold any warmth. None of him did. Though he was undeniably handsome; she had forgotten how much so. Only, his beauty, for it was beauty, really, was like that of a statue. Removed, immovable.

Guarding its secrets.

Yes, with the short, nearly silver hair, longer locks of which tumbled regularly into his eyes, the darker, straight brows, those eyes, a little deep set, but luminous, the strong nose that looked to have been broken at least once, the sharp cheekbones, dimpled chin, square jaw that never seemed quite crisply shaven even when she could still smell the shaving cream on him; with the lush bow-shaped lips that more often than not seemed pressed into a disappointed pout, he was most definitely *beautiful.*

With the tall stature, long limbs, and unconcealable strength of his body; with those hands that could take down a man with a single blow and yet seemed so delicate, and graceful, there really was no denying that fact.

Just as there was no denying that she was drawn to him; had always been, from the first time she'd laid eyes on him. And not because of his looks, she was not one to be dizzied by a handsome face, and she had been tested by her fair share, but because of something else.

Because of the contradictions that he was, perhaps.

Because of something she saw in his eyes; the way he'd made her feel.

Because of something that lurked beneath the aura of detached coolness, even beneath the unmistakable aura of threat and danger and roughness. Something she had sensed from the first, then glimpsed in rare moments after. Every time he had pulled her back from the edge of danger, thwarting this no-good ruffian or that, or when he'd slid just a little closer to her when some dandy or other had tried to get too intimate. It was in the way he watched her, watched *over* her.

Or perhaps she was just being fanciful.

Perhaps it was simply that he was handsome, and from what she could tell, not too far from her in age, though he seemed to have lived a thousand lifetimes, and seen all too much in all of them.

It doesn't matter. He doesn't matter.

Straightening, she forced herself to meet his gaze, and found in his eyes a darkness she'd never seen before, which felt like something akin to questioning, or pity. Neither of which, she needed. Just as she didn't need him, no matter that'd she'd felt a pinch of relief when the fog had lifted and she had realized who found her. That was only because he wasn't a shade come to end her life after all.

Perhaps not, but he has come to bring your flight to an end. And that cannot be.

'You were careful,' he said after a moment, taking a sip of his ale as he leaned back, surveying the room. It was the most relaxed she'd ever seen him; not that she for one instant she believed he was *actually* relaxed. The man was always sprung tight, ready to leap heroically into action. 'You did well. Only, there was a pattern to your dissimulations, and that was not so hard to follow.' After all, she had lasted three weeks, so perhaps she hadn't done so badly. 'She didn't say anything,' Will added, turning his full attention back to her. 'Your friend, the madam. I knew she helped you,' he said, with what looked like the whisper of a smile at the corner of his lips, though that was impossible, because Will never smiled. *Thankfully, for the dratted man is already too damned handsome for his own good.* He never usually spoke either, but that was another matter entirely. 'But only because she protested so much.'

Angelique nodded, not that she doubted Lily; but neither did she doubt how fearsome Will or even Percy could be should they set themselves to it.

The last thing she wanted was for someone else to get hurt because of her.

'So what now,' she asked. 'How do you propose we settle this predicament of ours?'

'You come back with me, to London, willingly, and I do everything I can to persuade them all to let you do as you please. In a matter of months, you'll be a free woman, regardless.'

A burst of laughter escaped her, taking both her and Will by surprise.

Quirking his head, he regarded her in a way she'd never seen, which apparently only added to the whole hilarity of the situation, and his words.

'I told you, I'm never going back,' she said, all her resolve apparent in her tone once she'd calmed from the hysterics. 'And even if we did try your plan, we both know your intercessions on my behalf will not be worth a penny.' Will's jaw ticked, and his entire being hardened, before he bowed his head in silent concession. She hadn't meant it against him, but truly, what stock would her mother or Percy put to his thoughts and opinions? 'So I suggest you come up with something better,' she added gently.

'Let me write to the earl,' he said, after the briefest pause, which meant he'd already thought of this option before proposing the first. *So the man can play chess after all.* 'Let him meet us here. You can tell him yourself that you will not go back, and settle all your affairs.'

'No,' Angelique said, shaking her head, and examining the meagre remnants in the tankard before her. It *was* a solid offer, only... 'Percy will only try to force me back. He won't listen, none of them will. And besides,' she added, tossing her hair back, reminding herself just who she was. *Miss Angelique Fitzsimmons, daughter of Baron Fitzsimmons. And Will is... No one.* 'I have a boat to catch tomorrow. It will be God knows how long before Percy even arrives. I'm not waiting around here forever.'

'Then give me a week,' Will said, almost what sounded desperately as he leaned forward. And there it was, in his eyes, a sort of pleading. Though if it was merely to help him preserve himself from having to drag her back kicking and screaming, she knew not. 'One week. If Egerton hasn't arrived, you are free to go, with my best wishes for your life.'

'Why would you even offer that,' she scoffed, buying time to make the decision. 'There is no way he could make it in time. For a messenger to even make it to London - unless he's already following you?'

'No, he isn't,' Will said, and it seemed the truth. *Though not entirely...* 'One week, Angelique. There is another boat in a week.'

'I...'

Angelique.

He had never called her that. He had never called her anything really, once, perhaps twice, uttered *Miss Fitzsimmons* under his breath in a judgmental, warning tone, but *Angelique...*

Everything else, her past, the present, the dozens of people around them, even the sounds of the world turning seemed to disappear. It was as if she was hypnotized, hypnotized by those dark grey eyes that she couldn't read so well anymore. And yet they were close now, so close...

Had he moved, or had she? She couldn't remember. All there was, was closeness. The black bits of stubble among the dark brown on his jaw. The flecks of black and blue in his eyes. The warmth emanating from him in that instant. The question in his eyes; and that in her own.

All there was, was them. All there was to the world was what was illuminated by the flickering stub of a candle between them. And what a lovely world it was. Safe, and warm, where there was no fear, or duty, or sadness. She felt something shift then, as if his utterance of her name had opened a door, unlocked something, another path, another way. A wall was torn down between them, a bond forged in those precious few moments that deep inside she knew was stronger than anything.

A bond she knew would change everything.

'Why do even want to run so badly,' he asked softly, breaking the silence.

Angelique shook her head and pulled out of the spell, leaning back as every inch of her closed off to him again.

As it should be.

'That is none of your concern,' she said coldly, raising a brow in the haughty manner her mother had taught her.

Some things from her former life would always be useful.

Will sneered as he nodded and leaned back as well. It hurt her a little, to be so blatant in the reminder of their positions again, but it had worked the first time, and she'd not even meant it. The truth was, he would never understand. No one ever would, nor could. Imagining bonds and questions and closeness were the fanciful imaginings of a girl. And she wasn't, couldn't ever be again, if indeed she ever had been.

This, a separation, a barrier, was how it was. How it had to be. These were her demons, her shadows to face and grapple, and yes, run from. And though it was true, that she somehow sensed he *might* actually be one of the only ones who could hear her out and not call her mad, one of the only ones in the world who might believe her, she couldn't do it. They had lived nearly side by side for over a year, yet lived separate lives, and changing any of that now, fostering any kind of intimacy or closeness...

That would be madness.

'One week,' she repeated, and she thought she saw him exhale a breath of relief. Again, something utterly impossible, as the man before her, she was quite certain didn't breathe. Didn't feel. He simply wasn't human. At least, that is what was easier to believe in that instant. 'But you must swear to me, on your honour, that after that, you will not pursue me anymore.'

Angelique thrust out her hand, and he stared down at it, as if he'd never seen anything quite so curious in his entire life.

'You trust my word,' he asked, genuinely surprised.

'Why shouldn't I?' Again, he pondered her words very seriously, that little frown she knew so well making its reappearance. 'Besides, it's not as if I have any leverage to force you to keep it.'

'Very true,' he said, smiling a wry, crooked smile. The gesture took her entirely off guard, and lowered her defences again. It seemed yet again she couldn't quite remember what her troubles were for the briefest second. *Just as - no.* 'On my honour,' he continued, taking her hand in his, which she noted much despite herself, felt entirely as lovely as it looked. 'One week, and if the earl is not here, I will not stand in your way. But you must promise,' he added, tightening his grip just enough to pull her a little closer, and by a little, it was actually enough for her to feel his every breath on her cheek. *To smell every note of -* 'Not to try and run before then. If you do, be sure I will follow you to the ends of the earth if I must.'

'I promise,' Angelique breathed.

Will held on to her hand, searching her eyes for another moment which seemed an eternity, before finally letting go, and rising.

'Then let us retire for the night. You've had a trying day, I think,' he said, offering out his arm.

'Pardon me, what?'

∞

'This is entirely improper, and unacceptable, and unfathomably illogical,' Angelique raged as she paced the tiny square of floor in the otherwise spacious, but cramped room she had rented for the night - or rather now, week. It was more than he would ever wish for, with a spacious, clean and inviting looking bed, two old, but perfectly plush and well-upholstered paisley armchairs and a nicely polished coffee table by the rather large hearth, rug, full-length mirror, dressing table, wardrobe, and set of small windows that overlooked the town and firth, rather than the stableyard.

What she likely considered meagre dwellings, he, and a large majority of the population saw this for what it was: luxury accommodation.

'I gave you my word I would not run,' she continued, pulling him back to her rant as she stopped and pointed a finger at him again. 'I do not see why you need to stay *here* to ensure it.'

'It is bad manners to point a finger at someone,' he said, stepping forth and grabbing hold of the offending thing before she could even register what he was doing.

He carefully twisted her arm around until it was behind her, and she was pulled rather flush up against him.

He was making a point he reminded himself, not enjoying any bit of this. Just as he hadn't enjoyed watching her rage at him since he'd asked the innkeeper for another key to her room, and declared them a runaway couple, thanking the woman profusely for keeping *his fiancée* safe whilst he was delayed on the road to meet her. Just as he hadn't enjoyed one bit all the nonsense she'd put him through since he'd first met her.

For she is a spoiled devil, like the rest of them, and you despise her and them.

'And as I said the first time,' he continued, quite literally looming over her again, intently ignoring the richness of her scent as it surrounded him. *Wool, salt, violets and her.* 'It is for your own safety. Unless that is, you would rather tell me what it is that has you so frightened.' Angelique stiffened, clenched her jaw, and looked away. 'I thought not.'

'Let me go,' she ordered after a moment when he did not release her, though in truth it sounded less of an order, and more of a feeble request.

'You can get out of this hold,' he said, a little smile tugging at the corners of his lips. He never smiled, and yet, he found the urge quite unbeatable this evening. As he often had in her presence. Though it was no wonder really, the girl was a mess. Sometimes, an amusing one, even to someone who didn't even quite know what amusement was. 'I've seen you get out of more complex ones.'

He wasn't entirely sure why he was challenging her like this, or even reminding her of her rather impressive fighting skills.

Only, he felt as if he needed to remind her of her own strength. Her own power; if only so he would never have to see that fear in her eyes again. In a less than fair fight, or even a fair one, she might not be able to beat him, but then again, he'd seen her take down plenty of strong men and women in practice. His brute strength might overpower her, but if she truly wanted, she had the wiles, and courage, to take him down.

But earlier, when he'd grabbed hold of her, it was as if she had forgotten all she'd been taught. Fear had paralysed her. He'd seen it happen, felt it happen himself, but he'd never imagined she would have cause to feel such terror as what had robbed her of her senses. He was curious about that, and wondered if it had anything to do with the nightmares she suffered from.

Not that any of it matters.

'Quite right,' she said simply with a sly grin that told him he was in trouble.

With notable grace, she spun out of his arms, untwisting her own, before she swung back around, her finger still in his grip so that she could twist his own arm enough to make him suffer, and release her. Somehow unsatisfied by the little pain she had caused, she stomped on the arch of his foot with her heel, and punched him in the solar plexus for good measure.

Wheezing slightly, he bent over to catch his breath, and huffed out a laugh as she stomped away.

You did ask for it.

'I am too tired to fight you anymore tonight, Will,' she said, taking her nightclothes from her bag, and setting them behind the privacy screen. 'However let us be clear. You will sleep in the chair facing the door, and you will not at any point, turn it to face anywhere else. When I change clothes, you are out of the room. And should you so much as come within three feet of me, I will cut off some anatomical articles you might miss. You know I can, and will,' she added ferociously.

'As you wish,' he said, adding *little gremlin* in his mind.

With a satisfied nod, she swept herself away behind the screen, and Will made a great show of leaving the room, careful to take both keys with him lest she decide to lock him out. He wandered down the hall, and towards the stables where his mount and bag awaited him, giving her plenty of time to change, and giving him time to ponder his current situation, which was, all in all, not as bad as it could have been.

Not ideal, but not completely desperate either.

One week.

One more week of keeping an eye on her, and then, it would be done.

Perhaps even less, depending on the man's arrival.

Then it would all be over. Well, for the most part at least.

One week, perhaps even less.

Surely, he could survive one more week with the gremlin.

Give me strength.

V.

A week earlier, in an elegant study some five hundred miles from Oban, his Lordship the Right Honourable Percival Egerton, newly minted Earl of Brookton, had whispered a similar prayer to the flames he stared into, draped across the mantel, a generous portion of whiskey in his hand. So it had been for the previous fortnight, Percy wasting away the evening in the darkened study, praying for strength, praying for news beyond tiny notes from across the isle; and praying for Angelique. Turning over every scrap of information he possessed, every memory, every word, every shred of evidence Will and others had shared over the past year; about her, and about the villain he could not pursue yet who shadowed the bright horizon of his future.

And that of those he loved and cared for.

Right now, he should be with the woman he held most dear, and their unborn child as it grew within her. He should be at Briar Hill, lavishing love and affection on her, living the life he'd fought for even as he'd been disbelieving such a life could be for him. He'd thought this trip to London would be quick; long enough to fetch his grandmama, attend to some business, and to make the arrangements regarding his father's death. Society dictated he should be in mourning, but the man who had been earl before him did not deserve to be mourned; though Meg would surely disagree with that. She'd urged him to reconcile with the old man before it was too late, to speak with him at least, but now, it truly was *too late*.

How I miss you Meg my love.

Only he couldn't be with her now, because apparently some dark shadow from his past refused him that, and though he believed Will was right to say Angelique had run, he knew that now, more than ever, she was in danger from that looming reckoning.

But why did she run?

That was the question which tormented him most, which kept him awake until the pale purple light of dawn streamed through the cracks in the curtains of his grandmother's study where he apparently now dwelled. In truth, there was no use for a bed if his wife was not beside him to share it.

For the life of him, he could not understand the *why* of it all, even as he knew he had to, for it was the key to unlocking... So very many things. Over and over again, remorselessly, he turned Angelique's every word, every glance, and every report he'd ever gotten from his little bird over in his mind.

But there was nothing. A sadness in her eyes on occasion. A drive to learn and experience things a proper young lady never should, but that he lay at the indomitable Effy Fortescue's doorstep. All that, and a moment perhaps a year ago, when she'd come to the wharf.

'*You cannot live in fear Percy. Take it from someone who knows.*'

He had pressed her for more, of course he had. He'd never seen nor heard anything like it from her before. Angelique... Angelique didn't share. At least not with him; not that he could fault her for that. Who truly shared with others who they were? And despite their friendship, despite feeling that they understood each other in a way others couldn't, these past days, he had realized, he hadn't really ever *known* her. He knew the general facts of her and her life, knew her personality, or so he'd thought, but her, her dreams, her hopes, any of it, remained unknown to him.

'*Old shadows*', she had told him that day. '*Let be.*'

And he had, and hadn't. Will had been tasked with searching for more, but nothing could be found. And in the whirlwind of all that had happened, the attacks on the Sinclair & Egerton Shipping Co., his pursuit and marriage of Meg, the progress of the company, his father's death and his own ascension to the earldom, well. He was ashamed to admit that Angelique had become less of a priority. He'd not even seen her since he'd arrived in town.

Yes, he had worried about her. Yes, he had tried to involve her more in his own life, and Meg had taken her under her wing, given her things to involve herself with at the foundlings home, but he had sensed something wasn't right, and all in all, he had done nothing.

Clenching the crystal in his hand, he fought himself hard, fought the urge to fling it into the fire before him. Instead, he simply sucked in a breath, and downed the drink, before turning to fill his glass again. He blinked for a moment as he did, his eyes adjusting to the thick darkness after the welcome burn of the flames.

It is for Angelique that you should have fought harder.

He'd fought his entire life. For himself, for the business, for his friends, for Meg. But when he looked back on the past years' events, he couldn't truly say that he had fought for Angelique. He had an army, and what had he done with it, even now?

Nothing. Nothing for her.

Angelique, who was perhaps the best friend he had. The only one he had left in England really. She'd stood by him as he weathered the storm Harcourt Sinclair had wrought upon society four years ago, she'd cared for him in his darkest days, stood by him as he weathered the scandal of his marriage, and likely would have helped him through the death of his father. She understood him, he knew she did, as not many had, and he cared for her; for the essence of her that shone through all the gaps in his knowledge of her. As if she were his own sister.

And, he had abandoned her, under guise of sending another to protect her; of discharging his duty of care to another. If he'd been closer, if he'd pushed harder, he might've known what had sent her running from London, from her mother, and from all she knew.

From me.

Percy poured and downed another measure of whiskey, and shook his head.

Enough.

No more waiting. Tomorrow, he would go speak to Lady Fitzsimmons again, see if he could get something other than nonsense out of her this time, and then, he would go after Angelique himself. Perhaps he'd take trusty old Harrow or Lionel and follow the trail Will had left him. But no more -

A loud, ominous knock echoed through the house, stopping Percy in his tracks.

Angelique.

Percy dropped the crystal on the drinks cart and rushed out of the study, then down the stairs towards the dimly lit foyer. Thomas, magician that he was, was already at the door, the slightly untucked stocking on his left leg the only proof he'd fallen asleep on duty. Not that Percy could blame him; he didn't know quite what time it was, but it was likely well past three.

Hushed voices met his ears as he bounded down the final steps, convinced that if it wasn't Will returning triumphant, perhaps at least it was more news of Angelique.

Good news.

Half sliding, half running across the marble foyer, Percy skidded to a halt, nearly toppling back onto his arse as Thomas moved aside, and gave him a glimpse of his late night cum early morning visitors.

It cannot be...

'Hello Percy,' Harcourt Sinclair drawled from the comfort of the doorstep, his face half-masked in shadow, giving him even more the appearance of the devil he was. 'It's been a long time.'

'Your last letter was rather a call for help,' his better half, the indomitable Effy Fortescue herself smiled as she entered without preamble, passing her gloves and hat to Thomas. 'So here we are.'

'Oh thank God,' Percy cried, unable to hide his relief and joy at the reappearance of his old friends. He launched himself at Effy, embracing her tightly, before Harcourt joined them, and he pulled him into the embrace despite Sinclair's obvious surprise and distaste for such shows of emotion. 'You have no idea how happy I am to see you.'

'I think we have a pretty good idea,' Sinclair grumbled.

'Now, Percy,' Effy said gently, as she extracted herself and her companion from his arms. 'Tell us what has you so distressed.'

'Angelique is missing,' he said gravely.

Sinclair and Effy exchanged a look, before turning back to him.

'Well, it seems we arrived just in time.'

'Tell us everything,' Sinclair said.

And so, Percy did.

Thank you God, for hearing my prayer, and sending help.

I will not rest until I find her.

And then, I will never abandon her again.

VI.

Will awoke with a start, the sensation he was being watched pricking at the back of his neck. He blinked, trying to adjust his eyes to his current surroundings, the remnants of the past day's memories rushing forth. He groaned slightly as he felt the stiffness in his body, and the thickness of his mind. It felt as if he'd been asleep for a century. He hadn't woken once during the night, not once after he'd returned to the room to find it already dark save for the light of the fire, Angelique neatly tucked away beneath the covers, the privacy screen moved so that it obscured his view of the bed.

The little gremlin...

'You snore,' Angelique said flatly, pulling him back to the room.

He lifted his gaze, his eyes now mostly clear, and spotted her sitting across from him, munching merrily on some breakfast.

Will rubbed his eyes and sighed, hoping that the gesture would chase the final languid sleepiness he was somehow caught in, that made her look like an angel of light, glowing in the morning rays that streamed in through the windows behind him.

It had to be his fatigue, because though the creature might be pretty enough, attractive enough, well, he had never seen a woman that glowed, or thought of one as an angel. Generally, he didn't think much of women at all, unless he had to choose one to satisfy a need. And no matter their fine features, pretty full lips, or dimpled round cheeks, or chartreuse green eyes, or delicately curved bodies, none of them had nor ever would be angels to him.

Certainly never *her*.

Though, somehow, he did have to admit that she seemed much prettier, much more attractive than usual, not that he'd noticed it before except to note that she was pretty, and everything a girl could wish to be in her position for it made snaring a husband much easier.

And yet, today he noticed that he did notice, and that was odd because she was sporting another worsted brown gown that looked like something a country school teacher might don. It was about as grim as the widow's weeds she'd worn last night had been, and yet, he found as he reluctantly had when she'd sported her men's garments for her little escapades, that when she was bared of her satin gowns and starched ribbons and lace gloves, she was more...

Herself.

Which was nonsense, because he knew well who she was.

A spoiled brat. Yes.

One who was perfectly themselves in silk and velvet and...

Christ, enough.

'I do not snore,' he grumbled, straightening himself and rubbing his hands over his face. 'What time is it,' he asked, glancing over his shoulder at the near blinding light.

Wasn't resting meant to invigorate you?

'Nearly nine,' Angelique said, popping a bite of what looked like delicious ham into her equally delicious looking mouth. *Wait, what? No.* 'Now eat, and then, hurry up and get ready,' she continued, unaware of his current internal struggle.

'For what,' he asked stupidly, as he dove into the plate she pushed towards him.

'I haven't quite decided yet,' she grinned like the mischievous little monster she was under all the treacherously innocent and soft looks. 'But I'm sure I'll find something. What,' she asked, staring at him with that typical nonplussed, wry look of hers that was sure to mean trouble. 'You didn't honestly think I would remain holed up here for a week, and not make the most of my time, did you?' She chuckled lightly, and if it hadn't been mocking him, he might've appreciated the lightness of it. 'No. I am going to amuse myself whilst we are here. I've already written to Percy, and arranged for another room for you.' *Damn.* That wasn't good, none of it really. Luckily his own note had been sent last night before he retired, when he'd gone to fetch his bag and horse. 'The innkeeper was more than understanding when I explained my reluctance to share a room with you before you had made an honest woman of me,' she smiled wickedly, buttering a piece of toast with all too much enjoyment.

'I told you, I'm not -'

'It's the adjoining room,' she said, tossing him a key which he managed to catch, though some of the eggs on his spoon went flying to the floor. 'And there is a door there, which mind you I will keep locked at all times. I'm sure if the need arises you can break it down easily enough.'

The stroke to his ego was not quite enough to dispel his anger at being forced to let her out of his sight, but then, there wasn't much he could do to force her hand.

'I sent my own letter last night, you didn't need to send one,' he said mutinously instead, her self-satisfied little smile truly irking him to the core. 'And I made sure my own went with a runner that will give Egerton enough time to be here before the week is over.'

'As did I,' she replied, haughtily raising her eyebrow.

Whoever had taught her that move, had truly done well.

Likely the Lady Fitzsimmons, flighty witch that she is.

Stifling down his frustration at having been outmaneuvered, he stuffed more eggs into his mouth, and resolved to go along with whatever the gremlin wanted, for now. In truth, he hadn't really thought through what he would do for a week, or however long it took for the man to arrive. He supposed, it wouldn't really hurt to let the little monster enjoy her freedom whilst it lasted.

Not that he cared, for truly, he didn't; only perhaps it would make her less annoying if he let her have her way, which she was sure to have anyways, as she always did.

Spoiled -

'I'll wait for you downstairs,' the aforementioned declared as she rose. 'Get yourself cleaned up. I've already moved your bag to your own room,' she said, eyeing him meaningfully, and though he cared little what she thought of him, it was true he needed to change his clothes and wash off the scent of travel. 'Don't be too long or I might be tempted to go on an adventure without you,' she warned, smiling as she grabbed her coat, gloves, hat and reticule, and strode out the door.

This is going to be a long week.

∞

Angelique filled her lungs with yet another deep breath before she sipped down more coffee, not that it, or the deep breaths she'd taken since she'd left the room were doing any good calming her nerves. Not that steady, controlled breathing had done her any good last night either; it had taken her half the night to actually fall into a dreamless sleep, which in itself was a blessing. The last thing she needed was for Will to be witness to one of her nightmares. The big loaf however, had had no such dilemma, and had started snoring not ten minutes after he'd returned to the room.

How am I supposed to endure a week of this?

Not the snoring; that had been remedied, and besides, she was ashamed to admit that she'd actually found it quite adorable, and not annoying in the least really. No, it was his presence. It was the threat not only of that faceless shadow, but of Percy. Of having her short-lived freedom torn yet again from her. Of being forced back to her old life; if it could be called that, after everything, because it was what she was supposed to do. Because it was her duty.

But it is not, and you will not.

She wasn't entirely sure why she had promised to give Will a week, but she had. And no matter that she'd have been a lot smarter if she'd packed her things and crept off into the night, she wouldn't do it. She trusted him, for some inexplicable reason, always had, and so she would not break her promise.

Truth be told, he was right. If she faced Percy now, if she explained it all to him, he might just understand. And if he didn't, well... He would have to live with her decision, regardless. For it was hers. Her life, not his. No matter his good intentions, no matter all he'd tried to do for her, he had no right to command her. Only her parents might presume to have that right, but then again, not anymore.

The fact of the matter however was that she also believed Will with every fibre of her being when he said he would follow her to the ends of the earth, just as she'd thought he might; though she found that when he said it, it sounded reassuring rather than daunting. Which was not good. Just as her reaction to him in general, was not good.

In the weeks since she'd last seen him, she'd truly forgotten just how his presence both reassured and discountenanced her all at once, sending waves of electrifying life through her veins, whilst calming the fluttering of her ever-panicked and fretful heart. His presence was that which had won her over from the first. It was what had made her relent, made her accept the latest of Percy's security measures, and not chase him away as she had all the others.

And yes, with all the time they'd spent together over the past year she'd been drawn in even more, curious as to who precisely lay beneath the silent, still, and dangerous mask. Mysteries always made a person curious.

Yes, she'd had one too many inappropriate dreams which involved him and thoroughly compromising situations. It was natural. He was handsome, she was young, and alone, and lonely, and he was everything she could never have. Everything the men of the *ton*, young and old, were not.

That was why really, she thought about him more than she ever should.

Why she was so unsettled now. He was a curious little mystery, that silent statue with secrets he could never tell, and that was all. And this was all just a very unusual, highly inappropriate, turn of events, and that is what had her all in a flurry, not, *absolutely not*, how breathtakingly enticing he looked when he slept.

Not the feeling that something between them had changed since last night, despite her assurances to herself that it neither could, nor did. And it was not comforting at all that he was here. To protect her from the faceless man who was forever chasing her yet never came.

So this week they were forced to spend together, it meant absolutely nothing, and she would do well to remember that lest she lose sight of the brilliant future that awaited her far away from here.

Only a week. You can -

'Whatever have you found for us to do then, *dearest*,' Will said, making her start slightly, coffee sploshing over the side of her cup.

She found him looking *entirely normal, not dashing at all in normal, unbearably plain clothes rather than his footman's livery*, a sarcastic grin on his face that told her he was about as pleased with their current situation as she was.

Good. Reassuring. As it should be.

'We are going to visit the distillery,' Angelique managed to grind out with what was a sarcastically loving smile.

Will rolled his eyes as she took another fortifying sip of coffee before rising.

Perhaps, this might be fun after all.

She did enjoy riling him up generally, hoping to elicit *some* reaction, and now that he actually spoke words to her, it might make it evermore entertaining. Either way, she was not going to let him dampen her enjoyment of these few days reprieve before life, in some way or another, pulled her back into its cold embrace.

No sir, I shall not.

VII.

*T*here is no fathomable way both she and I will survive this week, Will thought as he tromped up the hill towards Dunollie Castle keep, ready to tear his eyes and ears out so that he would neither have to see nor hear her again. If he had thought her trying and generally a nuisance back in London, he had been sorely mistaken. The girl was drunk on this new freedom, and relentlessly exuberant, and enthusiastic about the smallest thing. She was like a butterfly, flitting from flower to flower, with no idea how short and terrible life truly was.

And he hated her for that.

He hated her for all he'd endured the past four days.

He hated her for the distillery visit, during which she had watched with fascination all the workers, and machines, hanging on to every word the foreman who served as their guide spoke, sighing as she sampled the admittedly fine whiskey that put an enticing tint of pink in her cheeks.

He hated her for the hours they'd spent wandering through the market, and all the smiles she had shot to this stall-keeper and that as she sampled their wares with relish, and purchased more things than she could comprehensively eat or use simply because she wanted to support them all.

He hated her for the long walks they took around town, the port, and the beach; for looking so damned breathtaking as she gazed out longingly at the Firth of Lorn.

He hated her for all the day-trips she'd managed to force him on, to neighbouring villages and sights of interest, including this one, to the ruins of Castle Dunollie.

He hated her for how tempting she looked, dashing up the hill towards the old keep, shining brighter than the sun did today, laughing and unfettered. She had done away with gloves and coat and bonnet, and looked no more a London society miss. She looked like some lass who belonged here, in the wild.

He hated her for making him forget that she *was* that society miss. For making him forget who *he* was, and what his purpose was. Just as he had many times in town. When she shot pistols, or got herself into trouble at some seedy pub, or her eyes lit up during a Southbank play. When she spent hours chatting and playing with toddlers at the foundling home or whores in Shadwell. He hated her for how she made him feel, as if perhaps things were possible, things were within his grasp, things which never would, nor ever could be.

A joyful life. A life of love, and wonder, and simple peace. Cottages and cows.

'Come now, Will,' she said, breathless as he crested the hill and stopped beside her.

She stood there like some victorious shield-maiden of old looking out over her kingdom, her shining aurelian curls whipping from the confines of the ribbon holding them back.

Before her, the firth, the town, the Isle of Kerrera, all laid out in greens, blues and greys like some offering. He hated her for that too.

It was hard to remember the cruelty of life and the world when such wonder lay before your eyes, and someone refused to let you miss it.

'La! Even you, surely, cannot remain so steadfastly unhappy when presented with such a glorious view as this.'

Care to wager?

He grunted, and shrugged, and the joy in her face evaporated like a drop of water in the desert.

Will was annoyed to discover he hated that too; hated the

hurt that clouded her eyes.

'No matter,' she said with forced cheer, turning away from the view to wander the ruins, her eyes affixed on the ground rather than the high keep to their right. 'I shall enjoy it for the both of us, since you seem intent to spend this week wallowing in whatever gloom you hold so dear.'

'Whatever pleases you,' he muttered, trailing behind her.

She rounded on him, fierce anger lighting her eyes.

'Precisely,' she said, her cheeks reddening as she struggled, he could tell, to keep her temper down. 'Whatever pleases me, I shall do. For once in my *goddamned* life.' *Goddamned life indeed.* The girl didn't even know the meaning. 'Unlike you, I choose not to clutch bitterness, and envy, and resentment close to my heart.'

'You know nothing of me,' Will snarled as she made to turn away.

Angelique rounded on him again, taking a step forward as she stared up at him, a well of unleashed anger and emotion rising up within her.

'And you know nothing of me,' she seethed. She stopped, breathing hard as she searched his eyes. 'Why do you hate me,' she asked quietly.

The starkness of her question, the hurt and confusion in her eyes and voice, struck through him like the sharpest steel and he found the truth shining out of himself utterly insane and altogether unbelievable.

'I don't hate you,' he said flatly, and it was one of the truest things he had ever said.

'Yes you do,' Angelique pressed, coming even closer, stepping into the shadow his body cast over her. 'I didn't see it before, disdain a little sometimes, but now... What is it about me that inspires such revulsion?'

Revulsion was not precisely the correct word for what he felt.

In fact, it was the absolute opposite of what he felt most of the time when he was around her, which was precisely the underlying problem. It was why he reminded himself that yes, he hated many things about her. Hated her position, her spoiled little girl's ways, her perfection, the ease of her life, the cleanliness of it, the untainted, untouched nature of her existence. He hated her for all she represented.

But her, for herself, in truth, he didn't hate her.

And God knew he'd tried.

'You are spoiled,' he said, voicing one of his thoughts at least, trying for some reason to be careful in how he chose to admit his feelings.

For years he hadn't even really thought he could have feelings other than anger, hurt, and loyalty. Even if those weren't quite *feelings* as others meant when they said the word, but that was all he'd ever felt. Those were the states of his being.

Until last year. He'd begun to feel other things. Protectiveness, wonder, concern, amusement, interest, guilt, fear. Though the latter he'd known well, once upon a time, even if it had been a different species of it. And this new species... He didn't like it at all. It itched him; itched his soul. Made him...

Restless. Stupid.

Will wasn't entirely sure why he was indulging her now, not doing what he should for himself, and simply saying *yes I hate you now go away until we are both free of each other*, but then, in the end, what did any of it matter either way.

'I come from nothing,' he admitted, surprising himself, and her, with that tiny mention of who he was beneath the mask of unnoticeable plainness he wore through life. 'And you... Everything was given to you. Yet you see fit to disregard it all, to behave as if it were all too much to bear, in search of vain charity, and cheap thrills and pleasure. Just like the rest of your kind.'

'I see,' she nodded, tears glistening in her eyes for the briefest moment before she shook off the emotions, and took a breath. 'Thank you for your honesty,' she said graciously, turning and walking away towards the keep, the light that shone so brightly moments before dimmed by the shadow he'd cast over her, literally and figuratively.

Damn it all to Hell.

In the grand scheme of things, it really shouldn't matter what *Will-whatever-his-family-name-oh-yes-Hardy-that's-it* thought of her, or how he felt about her. He had served as her bodyguard for over a year, he had kept her safe, as was his duty. He'd kept her secrets, and helped her get out of some rather uncomfortable situations.

As was his duty.

He was not her friend, her confidant; before this little escapade she couldn't remember him speaking more than a few single syllable words during their first meeting, and *Miss Fitzsimmons* on perhaps three occasions. It shouldn't matter because she was leaving, and he was nothing at all to her.

Only, the problem was, it did matter.

Apparently more than ever.

Angelique wandered the pittoresque ruins, which on any other day might've filled her head with dreams of past battles and land lost and won. But right now, all she could think of were Will's words, his feelings, and how awful, and sick it made *her* feel that he thought those things of her.

Of course they didn't know each other, she didn't think she truly knew anyone, perhaps Percy and Meg, and their family a little better than most people, but she'd been awoken from the fantasy of childhood where people were what they seemed a very long time ago. And somehow, amidst the little chaos that was her life, she'd thought that Will's piercing gaze which seemed to see so much, had seen at the very least a part of the truth of who she was.

Enough, to know she wasn't like the rest of them.

Manifestly not.

Which hurt more than it should. She'd never felt his obvious dislike, his obvious hate, until this week. A little disdain, on occasion. Or more aptly, disapproval. But this hatred...

Perhaps it had always been there, and she had been too blind to see it, masked as it was beneath the veneer of quiet servitude as it had been, and perhaps he no longer felt he had to try so hard to dissimulate it. Yet even though it shouldn't matter to her in the least, *let him think what he will, let him fester in his own resentment*, well, the truth was, it did.

If only because his attitude was spoiling her own enjoyment of these precious days of freedom. Every delectable bite of this local delicacy or that, every instant in the gorgeous sun or under the stormy grey skies was marred by his palpable revulsion.

Time to set the record straight.

Even if it meant putting into words that which she had never been able to before.

'My pursuits,' she began slowly, stopping to gaze up at the mighty keep.

Why she suddenly thought he might understand, or wish to hear what she had to say, God only knew.

But she knew that if she didn't say it all now, she would regret it forever. She felt him stop behind her, and she turned to find him standing there, hands in his pockets, looking more like a surly boy than a hate-filled man.

The image bolstered her courage, and so she continued.

'The sword fighting, the combat and pistol lessons, the horse-riding, trips to the Southbank theatres, to the brothel, the work on Meg's foundling home, all of it. It isn't about vain charity or cheap thrills.'

Will quirked his head, obviously open to her words, so she took a breath and looked to the horizon for inspiration.

'All my life, for as long as I can remember, I've been scared. It's like... A pit of snakes crawling over each other, here,' she said, placing her hand on her belly, and urging him silently to understand. 'I don't understand it, but it is there. And all my life, I've been told what my life would be. What it should be. Am I spoiled? Yes,' she admitted, shrugging. 'Do I disregard it? No. Do I behave as if it is too much to bear? Perhaps. Because it is. My life is a cage, Will,' she ground out, her throat closing around the words. 'I am a pretty bird in a pretty cage, to be passed on from one man to the next. I accepted that once, like a good little girl. Let myself be swept along the current of what my life should be. I thought I had no choice. And then, I met this woman…'

Angelique smiled, remembering those first days after meeting the bravest woman, the fiercest, the most incredible creature she'd ever encountered.

Effy Fortescue.

Remembering the courage she'd shown, to face down the men who wished to cage her; what she'd done to secure the life she wanted.

How she had lived for herself.

'I met a woman whose destiny was not dictated by society, or by fear,' she said softly. 'And perhaps it is selfish, and perhaps I am spoiled, but I wanted that. I wanted freedom, to choose my life. The same freedom you have. Freedom, from fear. When…'

She stopped herself, taking another deep breath, and gathering her thoughts.

She found she couldn't quite speak of *all that* quite yet.

'*Should* a time ever come when I must fight for myself, I wish to have the tools, and knowledge, to do so. Everything I have done, it hasn't been for thrills, but to better myself. To make myself strong, unafraid of every little thing; of every person. To make myself whole, and part of the larger world rather than simply frilled drawing rooms, and meaningless chatter.' The ferocity in her own voice surprised her, but at the same time, she felt free, sharing her innermost thoughts, and dreams, out loud with another being for the first time in her life. 'Think of me what you will, hate me if it pleases you,' she sighed. 'But at least hate me for the right reasons. Do not hate me because of my kind. For if I do have a kind, *they* are not it.'

Will just stood there, staring at her with an intensity that she'd never seen before.

After a long moment of silence, she nodded, and continued walking. She wasn't entirely sure what she'd been waiting for, definitely not for him to suddenly smile broadly and declare them friends, and for them to hop along merrily arm in arm through the rest of their time together, but she had expected *something*.

At least you said your peace -

'Why does it matter to you what I think,' Will asked, stopping her.

'I don't know,' she admitted, unable to look at him. 'But it does.'

She felt, more than heard his progress, felt him come in so close she could feel the heat of him across her back, across her entire body if she was honest, even though they weren't even touching.

'What are you so afraid of,' he whispered.

A faceless man who will come for me; for my soul.

A ghost that haunts my dreams.

'Everything,' she said instead.

It wasn't a lie, not really.

Only *that* fear, had come later, with her awakening.

Or perhaps, it was all tied into one.

'A life without purpose. A life without meaning. A life not of my own making. A life of living death.'

'The chief's wife, during the Jacobite rising,' Will said, his voice surrounding her in that strange haze again, comforting, and enchanting. 'She held the keep with twelve men. Fear, it does not stop us. It drives us.'

'Does it drive you,' Angelique asked, turning sharply, wishing she hadn't as soon as her breath flew out of her lungs.

They were too close again, both literally and figuratively, and the worst thing was, she felt far too safe just there.

Our own little world. My own little haven.

'No,' he said quietly.

'What does?'

'Loyalty,' he said, after a thousand other emotions crossed his face.

She believed him; but she also believed that under it all, something else, something darker, rage perhaps, or a wild hunger for something, truly made him who he was. Made those grey eyes darken until she could almost see the shadows of his past dancing in them, acting out the events which had made him. It should've scared her; only it didn't.

Simply made her even more curious.

'How did her tale end,' Angelique asked. 'The chieftain's wife?'

'She went to Kerrera,' he said with a small smile, nodding towards the island, a distant look about him now, as if he had just flown across the firth himself. 'Lived in a bothy until 1719. She returned here, to him, and lived until 1776. Outlived her husband.'

'A simple life then.'

'A good life,' he added, before taking one last look at her, and stepping aside.

Angelique followed him as they continued their exploration of the ruins, in silence.

But it was a comfortable silence this time, and she might've sworn that as they sat down later that morning to enjoy the small picnic she had packed, looking out onto the firth, that she saw what looked like contentment on his face.

And she smiled, knowing that she felt it too, at least for a moment.

VIII.

Something had changed between them beneath the shelter of the castle keep's walls, and though some might argue that such developments were for the better, Will knew it was not so. He wasn't entirely sure what had come over him earlier, why he had allowed himself to set down his protective shield of displeasure and disinterest, but he had. A power beyond his own had compelled him to. And no matter how hard he tried now, he couldn't seem to pick it back up again. The weight of it, the feel of it, was all wrong.

Actually, he did know why he'd put it down. That was precisely the problem.

She asked.

She was the greater power.

Miss Angelique Fitzsimmons had asked, and just like any other boy she had ever asked anything of, he had done it. Only this was not about fetching champagne or letting her win a hand at cards. This was something entirely more dangerous. Entirely more...

Life-changing.

He wasn't being dramatic. That wasn't something he could be even if he wanted to. He had felt it. There, on that hill, when she'd bared her soul to him, all vestiges of her own masks and shields crumpled and tossed to the wind, he had felt something shift. Something break, and tumble and crumble into a thousand pieces, and he had known, that he could never go back to the way things had been before. They had been tenuous enough to begin with, he'd had to cling harder and harder to his supposed hatred of her, cling on to it until his fingers ached and bled.

A few more days. That's all you need.

No, he couldn't go back to the way things had been. He wasn't foolish enough to believe that, not after that bloody picnic they'd shared, and... *Feeling*, all he had. What he needed to do now was remember. Remember all that had led him here, all he had sacrificed; all it had been for. He needed to remind himself of the priorities of his life.

Of his loyalty.

Of all that depended on him keeping his head, and the gremlin out of trouble for a little longer. These new feelings, well, not quite new, but recently fully acknowledged, of protectiveness, of concern for her well-being, after all, were not at odds with his purpose. So he did not have to dismiss them as much as he wished he could dispense with the annoying things as he would discarded bits of paper. As always, he just needed to remind himself of why he truly felt them.

Yes. Remember.

'How did you know all that,' Angelique asked, drawing him from his introspection, back to the noisy, crowded and smoky room of the pub she had dragged him into after they had slowly made their way back to town as the sun had set.

Will blinked at the untouched ale before him, reminding himself of where and when he was, then glanced across the tiny table that seemed just the right size for her.

'About the castle, and the chieftain's wife,' she clarified, tilting her head slightly so that the shadows cast by the candle between them sharpened her features and darkened the green of her eyes to that of an emerald. 'Have you been here before?'

'No, never,' he said after a moment, taking a sip of his ale as he glanced around.

He could leave it there, keep silent as he had all afternoon, indeed all evening, all through their meal until now.

If he did, she might stop asking questions.

But then, the light might go out of her eyes again, disappointment might creep in as it had this morning, and he realized, he didn't want to see it there again. Not for as long as he could help it at least. And besides, she only wanted some conversation. That wasn't so dangerous. These were not dangerous questions.

Fostering an amicable connection is.

'I read about her,' he added, and he saw the curious, encouraging smile that had been fading brighten again. 'In a book about local history.'

'You found, and read, a book on local history,' she said, a teasing, disbelieving smile replacing the other.

Will felt a twinge of his old self peek through at her surprise.

'My occupation does require me to know how to read,' he said bitterly.

Crossing his arms, he leaned back, and focused on the other patrons of the pub.

For no other reason than to avoid looking at her, all frowning, and hurt, and sad, and yet still somehow glowing; a shining light in brown worsted. He looked around at all the ruddy, red-faced sailors, and farmers, and the serving maids. He looked around at them all, cramped into the low-beamed room that seemed more a den than anything else. He looked, and he saw them all, in their simplicity, and the bitterness he felt towards *her*, extended to them.

For all they had, that he didn't.

Will never.

'That's not what I meant, and I think you know that Will,' she said softly, her voice drawing him back despite himself. She was leaning towards him, cradling her drink, her eyes urging him, begging him, *entreating* him, not to be who he was. 'I suppose I simply didn't picture you taking an interest, that is all.'

'I like history,' he grumbled, though she took the offering for what it was despite his tone, and nodded. 'I like knowing about where I am.'

It brings me comfort.

Makes me believe I am not alone.

'History lessons were some of my favourites,' she said, leaning back, though it felt less like she was making distance between them, and more like she was relaxing.

Which was...

The opposite of good.

The opposite of what it felt like.

'And not solely because my tutor was himself passionate about the subject matter. He was French,' she specified with a complicit grin. 'He never shied away from telling me the terrible truths of history,' she added wistfully, lost to her memories for a moment. 'He was one of the only ones in my life who never tried to shield me from the truth of the world. The blood that paid for all the great deeds. And he never discouraged me from having opinions.'

He saw her then, saw who she'd shown him this afternoon.

Saw who she had shown him since he'd known her, even though he had been so desperate to look away.

A girl who was lost, and trying to find herself, just as he had once.

Just as he still was.

'Let me guess,' he said chidingly. 'Napoleon was not so bad as we made him out?'

'Rather that Wellington was no better,' she laughed heartily, and yet again he was struck by the beauty of that sound. The purity, the wonder of it; the song of angels in the midst of Hell. 'Or that Charlemagne was not as much the heroic, benevolent king as everyone makes him out to be.'

'How controversial.'

Angelique shrugged, and sipped her ale, and it was fine, really, that he was smiling.

Because he could do what he had to, and enjoy himself in the meantime.

Even if enjoying himself wasn't something he did.

Things changed. Plans changed. He could change, a little.

So long as in the end, all was as it should be.

'Will you tell me something of yourself,' she asked after a moment, eyeing him over her tankard with a hesitancy, a shyness in her eyes he'd never seen before.

But then, he hadn't looked in her eyes as often as he did now, so perhaps that was it.

'What would you know,' he asked, delaying.

He couldn't…

The other question, it hadn't been dangerous. But what she asked now… It was.

Only one other person in the world knew him. For who, and what, he truly was. That was how he liked it. That was how it had to be. People may pretend to be interested, the few women who had shared his bed might've actually been somewhat interested, but if they knew, if they heard his truths, they would wish they never had.

And besides, he had never had the desire to share his secrets.

Unburden his soul, or whatever other nonsense people purported this sort of talk to be. He didn't need it. Need to be known, or seen, or understood. Quite the opposite.

Until now.

Now, he found he did wish to. Need to. He wanted to speak of things he had long buried, of what made him who he was. He could lie; he could not answer. But that greater power stronger than his own freedom of choice, *Miss Angelique Fitzsimmons*, urged him to show her something of himself, as she had shown him.

Not as reciprocity, not as a warning, but as sharing.

'You said…' Angelique stopped herself, biting her lip as if trying to find a better way to say something before deciding there wasn't. 'You said you came from nothing.'

Will nodded, and she looked at him expectantly.

Christ.

'I grew up in an orphanage,' he said, using the word people understood, but which in no way told them of the reality of that place.

Of its inhumanity.

Of all the terrible things that had passed there, that had forged him into who he was. And no matter that he had never wanted so badly to speak of it before now, he couldn't find the words. He couldn't bring himself to say anything more, because then, there would be pity in her eyes, and that he could not bear.

Besides, she could never understand.

'You never knew your parents at all?'

'I was left on the church steps,' he said, a bitter smile twisting his lips. He looked away, back into the crowd around them, unable to bear looking at her any longer. Looking at her, it made him forget things. Made him forget himself. *Perhaps she is a witch, not a gremlin after all.* 'Or so I was told. Even my name is not my own, the one my mother gave me, if she ever did.'

Which was doubtful.

Whoever had birthed him had most likely not even taken the time to give him that. Not that he could lay blame at his mother's doorstep, whoever she be. Her tale was likely that of so many others; girls, women in trouble, whose circumstances demanded they relinquish their own flesh and blood.

I am one of millions.

'I like William,' she said softly, her voice yet again tearing him from his thoughts. *Definitely a witch.* And damn her, for when he met her eyes again, in them, there was no pity. Only kindness, and understanding. 'It is the name of conquerors.'

Will laughed at the insanity of that statement, and her utter conviction of it.

She startled, and stared at him as if his laughter was the most extraordinary thing she'd ever witnessed. Which, granted, perhaps it was. He hadn't laughed, truly, well, ever.

Until he'd met her.

'I am no conqueror,' he said once he could speak again.

Were that I was.

'You conquered life, did you not,' she asked, shrugging slightly as she glanced around the room now, sipping her ale. He froze, her words touching on an open, festering wound he hadn't known existed. 'Made a life for yourself, however simple.'

Will stared at her, shaken, and stunned as he'd not been before.

While she just carried on, glancing around, smiling at all those around them, as if she hadn't just shattered everything he'd been so sure of, everything he'd known, everything that had kept him alive, and safe, and focused.

Damn the little gremlin.

'I'm sorry,' she said, reddening as she felt the full force of his stare and silence.

'Don't be,' he breathed. 'You're right.'

Angelique studied him for a moment, then smiled a tiny smile, nodded, and went back to her enjoyment of the room's antics which now included shanty singing.

They finished their drinks in silence, much to his great relief.

For he'd had quite enough with that one little remark, for one night, and for a lifetime. Any more and she might manage to strike him dead and make him question all that he was.

And that is the very last thing I need.

∞

'So it is to America you plan to go,' Will said, in a desperate attempt to break the companionable silence which had come over them after leaving the pub. They were taking a long, meandering way back, along the moonlit waterfront, and it was so hard to *not* enjoy the moment. It was so hard to not notice the splendor of their surroundings, the way the inky grey sea sparkled and danced, the perfect coolness of the air, the *peace* of it all.

It was so hard not to notice the enchanting woman by his side, his little gremlin not even a witch, but more of a *dame blanche*, some manner of ancient fae born of the heavens' light.

No.

It didn't help that the creature in question kept flicking her gaze over at him either.

'To begin your new life,' he clarified.

'Yes,' she smiled, surprised at his first true attempt at conversation.

Less evil.

'What will you do there,' he asked, watching his feet move across the cobbles. It was oddly reassuring, oddly stabilising, not that he needed to be stabilised, only it was reassuring, that no matter what, he could still move one foot before the other. It was all he'd ever done, and all he would ever do. 'It is a hard place, and you will be alone.'

'I have always been alone,' she breathed, and the starkness of that statement caught his attention. 'Even in rooms crowded with people, I have never been but alone.'

She looked surprised, and embarrassed at her own admission when he met her gaze, and quickly turned to the horizon-less night beside them.

You do not know what it means to be truly alone, little gremlin.

'I have… Friends, people in my life,' she said flatly, as if reading his thoughts. 'But they do not truly know me. And through no fault of theirs. Only, I wonder sometimes if one can truly know another…'

Shaking her head, she turned back and offered him a reassuring smile, which reassured him not one bit.

Not that he needed reassurance. At all.

It wasn't as if he'd shared those same thoughts, that same feeling a million times. As if he'd had similar thoughts not an hour ago. As if he'd been desperate for her to know, if not all, then at least, a piece of him.

It wasn't as if he felt a strange sort of kinship to this creature, so different from he, and yet, seemingly cut from the same cloth.

'But you asked of America,' she sighed, chasing all loneliness from her tone. 'In truth, I don't know what I shall do. Perhaps I shall become a teacher. I have the education for it. Either way, I shall make something of myself, because I have the will to. I have the strength to weather whatever comes,' she declared, more to herself than to him. 'And I do have means,' she chuckled after a moment.

'That does help matters,' he agreed with a smile.

A true smile.

Which he didn't do, just as he didn't laugh -

'What of you,' she asked, her usual lightness returned. As if she had been revived, restored by the moon's rays on her skin which reflected them so perfectly. 'What will you do once I am no longer in your charge?'

That inevitable conclusion hit him squarely in the gut, as if he hadn't fully realized that was their destined future.

Which, it irrevocably was. If there was one sure thing in all the uncertainty he'd felt in the past, well, year or so, well, it was that. That one day, it would all be over. There had never been a question of *if*, but rather, of *when*.

Yet somehow, in that moment, it was as if he understood, *felt*, the truth of that conclusion. He had grown accustomed to her. Despite all he didn't know of her, he knew many little things. The way she liked her tea, *with lemon*; the way she nibbled the skin by her fingernails when she was nervous and thought no one was looking. The way that one lock of hair at the back of her neck refused to be tamed into any coiffure, and the sound of her footsteps, the colour of her eyes when she won a fight or game of chess; and all the other little details that made her so... Particular.

And the loss of all those things, the loss of her presence... Well, he would feel something really rather unpleasant when they were separated. Something that he instinctively knew would irreparably change him again; shaping him even more into the monster *he* was.

But you shall be parted nonetheless.

'I shall find another to guard,' he said, and to his own ears it sounded strained.

'And another, and another, and another,' she asked, raising a brow, looking as if she knew something he did not.

'Yes.'

'There is nothing more you wish for from life?'

'I...'

Yes. No.

Once, perhaps, when he'd been a child, dreaming of impossible things as he curled into himself in the damp corner of a dark room, but even then, he'd known those were flights of fancy. Dreams, meant to help one survive. Only hope too, had eventually been driven from him, by reality, and by purpose. Which was good enough; it was enough to survive on.

Wishing, dreaming, is not for men like me.

'Is it not a good life,' he countered, ignoring the question altogether. 'I make a good living, I sleep in comfort, I do not want for food. I serve a purpose.'

'And when you are old and grey,' she pressed, gently. 'When your bones creak and ache, what then? Will you sit by the fireside in some little house somewhere, whiling away the hours alone? Should you not like a wife perhaps, or children, even a dog? And what of this house? Shall it be in the country -'

'You don't understand, little gremlin,' he exclaimed, exasperated, and tempted by her dangling dreams.

No more cottages and cows.

'Then help me understand,' she pressed, stopping before him.

He shook his head, and raked his fingers through his hair.

Christ, she was impossible, she -

'I live life by the day,' he blurted before he could stop himself. His need to make her understand overcoming his knowledge that none of this was wise, or useful, or even remotely acceptable. 'When you have lived as I, that is all you can do. You make it one morsel of bread to the next, one beating to the next, and you do not look past that. For with hope comes despair. I do not have plans for the future, Angelique, for I do not know if tomorrow will even come. I have neither want nor need of a wife, or children, or even a dog. I do not have it in me to offer them anything. I came from nothing. And I am nothing.'

Breathing hard, he stared down at her, willing her to see the truth of it.

The truth of him, even if he could not put it all into words.

And it seemed she did, eyes shining bright, with…

Pain. For me.

And wells of unshed tears.

That was worse than pity.

Stepping around her, he strode on, and heard her footsteps following a moment later.

'What did you call me,' she asked tentatively, a smile in her voice.

He opened his mouth, but was saved from answering by strident notes, laughter, and clapping on the air.

They both turned towards the square across the road, where a group of drunken sailors and hangers-on had gathered by moon and lamplight, apparently to dance a ceilidh in the middle of the night. And before he could say anything, Angelique was off.

Goddamnit.

Muttering curses under his breath, relieved that at least the heart to heart was over, he followed her, though not even his long strides could catch up with her before she made it to the group. She was already clapping along with the others as a burly old man with a beard that looked tangled in the strings, fiddled, and the rest of the merry group danced a reel in the centre of the square.

'*A dashing white sergeant I'd march away,*' they sang, and as Will turned to tell Angelique off, he stopped.

She was truly luminous, as if something inside her shined brightly enough to light the night for millenia.

She was smiling, and laughing, and did not have it in himself to ruin it. Who was here to see her, anyways? Who was here to reprimand her, or him, for allowing such? Who would be witness to this small impropriety, so insignificant, paling in comparison to some of the rest she'd done. What would it truly matter anyways?

It doesn't.

When one of the merry young ladies he recognised as a

serving wench from the pub they'd left took her arm and pulled her into the dance, he let it be. Soon, there would be no joy for her, he knew that. Her dreams, as surely as his own had been, would be dashed.

Destroyed.

So the very least he could do, was let her enjoy these moments. Let her make memories to last a lifetime; give her new things to dream on when she found herself alone in a dark room, all hope of another life, another future, extinguished. She deserved more than what would be her lot in life, and though he could not give her that, he could give her this, at least.

And so he resolved, not only to let her enjoy these moments, but to give her more to remember. To fill these final days with more joy than she could bear. It would be the one good thing he did in his life.

They remained in the square for what seemed the night through, but was likely no more than half an hour. Angelique danced, twirling and hopping and laughing around until she was surely dizzy, and Will watched her, entranced. He even found himself clapping along eventually, though he did not join in the dance.

Some things, would never, ever be for him.

IX.

C ome in,' Angelique called when she heard the knock on the interconnecting door. Setting down her book, *Lessons in American Farming*, she smiled as Will ducked through the door and came in. It was getting slightly ridiculous really, all the smiling she was doing. Today, she was entirely sure she hadn't stopped as they'd taken a boat onto the firth, and fished. It had all been Will's idea, and he had made the arrangements. They had caught two salmon, and made a bonfire on the beach, and eaten them.

Then watched the tide go out, and the sun lower in the sky.

She wasn't sure when, how, or why he had changed his mind, about her, or at least about the time they had together, but she didn't care. She couldn't. It was too good. Too priceless. A taste of what life could be.

Could have been.

And so, she enjoyed it, and smiled ceaselessly.

Sure, she had smiled a lot before, but she couldn't remember it ever being so natural a gesture. So, free, and true. Before, she smiled consciously, when she was supposed to. Occasionally with Percy and Meg, Meg's sisters or his grandmother the Dowager, it had been true, but then, there had always been that little pang of envy that sadly never left her heart. The one which had nearly struck her down the day Percy had proposed to Meg - no matter how fondly she looked on that day now - then, it had taken all she had not to burst out in tears.

For she had known, that such love, would not be for her.

Better enjoy the company, you've less than three days left.

'Get ready,' he said, his usually commanding tone softened by what sounded like playfulness. She might've even said *he* had a spring to his step. 'We are not spending the evening in here.'

Definitely playful.

Angelique decided she quite liked Will's playful side. In fact, the more she got to know all his different sides, the more she grew to like the whole that he was. And seeing that playfulness now... She couldn't help but feel privileged somehow. She knew it was not a part of himself he showed often, if ever, and to know that he did so with her....

Is neither here nor there.

'Where are we going,' she asked, grinning like a small child on their birthday.

Spending the evening in her room, reading, alone, had been precisely what she'd thought she would be doing; but doing anything with him sounded eminently better.

'To the theatre,' he winked, tossing her an orange.

Angelique laughed, and raised the fruit to her nose to inhale its crisp scent.

'La. There are no theatres in Oban. Whatever are you on about?'

'Ah, there is however a travelling troupe of Italians,' he countered, actually smiling now too, that crooked smile she'd seen more and more the past few days. It was a smile that promised many things. *Many things you cannot have.* 'What, you do not care to go,' he asked, the playfulness and smile both gone as he misread her expression.

He crouched down before her, seeking her eyes, and she shook off the sudden coldness that had enveloped her.

For a split second she wanted to fall into him, to curl up with him there on the floor, his entire being surrounding her, so that nothing cold nor harsh could ever touch them again.

Ninny.

Just, enjoy whatever this truly is while it lasts.

'I'm surprised, that's all,' she lied. 'Not two days ago you seemed intent on being the proverbial stick in the mud. And now you are whisking me off to watch a play after a wonderful day of fishing.'

'Several plays, actually, I think,' he said thoughtfully, quirking his head, his eyes still studying her. She could tell he knew she was lying, but for the sake of them both, that he knew better than to ask. *Or perhaps he does not care. There.* 'And I believe there will be puppets too.'

'Well then, if there are to be puppets, how can I refuse?'

Angelique smiled softly, and he rose, offering out his hand.

She took it, and he pulled her to her feet with such alacrity she would've toppled forward right into him, had he not steadied her with another hand to her waist. The gesture surprised them both, and they stood there, eyes locked for much longer than was necessary, or proper.

It wasn't the first time he had touched her, Hell, he had manhandled her into the dark street when he'd found her here, he'd pushed her out of harm's way, and helped her down from countless carriages, but this felt different. It felt... Inviting. Promising.

Right.

Yet again, a thousand unwanted desires and images passed through her head, and for the briefest second it seemed he could see them too.

'Five minutes,' he said, his voice a little unsteady and lower than usual. 'Then, I will leave, with or without you.'

With a quick wry smile, he turned, and left her again.

Oh dear, Angelique thought as she stared at the closed door before her.

Less than three days. Less than three days.

∞

There was already a large crowd gathered in the same square where Angelique had joined a bunch of drunken sailors in a ceilidh the night before. She wondered why suddenly he was not a stick in the mud? Well, that was why. That moment, which had changed his mind. This, this was part of the resolve he had made, not that she would know that until it was too late.

Then she will be the one to hate me.

Not that he wouldn't deserve it.

Not that he wouldn't bear it.

Shaking off the unwelcome thoughts threatening to spoil his mood, and hers again, he took her hand and guided her before him. It was strange, really, how profoundly he could feel her touch. When he did on occasion make contact with another human, by necessity, not choice, he never, felt it, truly. The warmth, the pleasure. Didn't feel it in his bones. Not even when he had been with women did he feel it thus.

Bringing himself back to the task at hand, he deftly negotiated the packed throngs of local children, curious onlookers, including some of the still drunken seamen from last night, and eager fellow travellers, to a spot where she could see the miniature stage at the side of the wooden cart. She moved so easily with him, as if she could read his mind through his touch. Just as she could read the rest of him.

Let go.

Will released his hold when they arrived at the edge of the standing crowd, overlooking a sea of children sat on the ground this way and that, then made to step back so his height would marr no one else's view, and so that he wouldn't be tempted to just stand there with her in his arms, as if that were something he did, but Angelique glanced back at him and took hold of his hand again.

Yes. Much better.

No.

Angelique smiled a shy smile that he'd never seen before; devoid of artifice and signifying an unease he'd never known she could possess. Without a word she settled herself on the ground like the children, to the amused, and sometimes judgemental stares of those around her. She tugged on his hand, and what choice did he have but to join her there? So he did, making a tremendous spectacle of himself as he twisted his limbs this way and that to settle behind her without harming any of those around them. Unfortunately his legs would cramp up within minutes if he sat cross-legged like this behind her, unable to move because of the now tightening bodies around him.

Just as he was trying to find another solution, some way to extend perhaps even one leg, one of the players popped up on the cart behind the stage, dressed like one of those old Harlequins, and the crowd cheered loudly.

'*Amici*, welcome,' he cried, waving his hands suitably theatrically. 'To Salvatore's *Mondo Meraviglioso*! We will amaze you! We will make you laugh,' he promised, and just as he did, Angelique shimmied back and slid into the circle of his legs. Will sat there stunned for a long moment unsure of what the Hell he was supposed to do. She wasn't leaning against him, touching him anywhere other than where her legs met his own, but still, this was... *Delightful. No, wrong. Uncomfortable. Very wrong.* 'We will make you cry, and we will make you dream,' the Harlequin continued, oblivious to Will's predicament. 'We only ask that if you enjoy the show, you make a little contribution at the end.'

The crowd roared with laughter and clapped as the player winked, and disappeared behind the stage again.

Will was about to stand up, and move far far away when the curtains were drawn back, and the crowd fell into attentive silence. He froze, and realized he would just have to deal with the current situation if he didn't want to make a scene.

Annoying little gremlin.

'You can extend your legs a little beside me this way,' Angelique whispered, leaning back so he could hear her.

She threw him a side glance and a smile, before turning back towards the show.

And just like that, he felt himself relax again. He'd thought for a moment... Well, what he thought didn't matter, as it wasn't the case at all, and that was all well and good.

Angelique was simply being kind, and thoughtful, and that was all.

Because, she was kind and thoughtful. He'd willed himself to forget that, willed himself for so long to see nothing but the pretty little spoiled thing he had to trail around and keep safe. But he'd seen it, even when he least wanted to. Seen the kindness she showed to strangers, to her friends, to the mothers and children in the foundling house, and even to the whores of the Shadwell brothel. Seen her sit in silence for days with the ailing earl, nursing him back to the world with merely her presence, and music. Seen her hold a crying child who had fallen into the mud and ruined their clothes. Seen her ask after every servant's health and family with *actual* interest. Seen it in every gesture, every word even when she sought to hide it most, among the *ton.* The lack of... pride. The selflessness.

Not that it changes anything.

Not that it could. What was done, was done. What would happen, would.

And whatever his feelings regarding her, not that he had any strong ones, to be sure; it *would* happen, for he had given his word it would be so, and that was all he had in this world.

Still, he found himself encircling her a little tighter, drawing himself around her a little closer than he should have, as he watched Dido abandoned by Aeneas, Hercules sneeze, and Pulcinella get up to all manner of mischief.

As they laughed and cried, and did all that had been promised, Will felt the world around them disappear, until only the little circle he and Angelique were enveloped in, existed.

And he vowed to remember it always, that feeling of comfort and contentment, scented with violets, the sea, and oranges, for it would never come again.

X.

*T*he balmy breeze of summer sweeps through the nursery.
Anna has forgotten to close the window, but even beneath
the heavy comfort of the down blanket, Angelique shivers,
as cold as ice. Nearly a week she's been ill, and she had been feeling
better today, even gone out and played with Anna in the park, but
now, the fever has returned. She should call out, perhaps Anna will
fetch her some warm milk, but something stops her.

What was stopping her?

Bare feet touch the chilled hardwood which somehow feels warm.
The echo of distant laughter surrounds her, and there is smoke on the
air. Her stomach clenches as she steadies herself, wrapping the small
wool quilt from the end of her bed around her shoulders. She does not
want Anna. She wants her mother. Mama was warm and kind then,
mama let her sneak into her chambers at night if she promised never
to tell father. Mama loved her and let her do things father would get
angry about, like dipping her toes in the waters of the lake.

Quietly, she goes to the door, the moon giving her just enough light
to see the way. She turns the cold brass handle slowly so that it will
make no noise, and creeps out into the corridor, the plush carpet
runner a welcome treat beneath her feet.

The laughter is louder here, but it does not sound fun. It sounds...
Harsh.

It makes her shiver as she shuffles along the passage, and carefully
makes her way down the steps, one little hand on the smooth oak

banister she can just reach, and the other holding the quilt tightly around her.

By the time she makes it to the second floor landing, there is sweat on her brow, and her nightdress is soaked, but still she is cold. The air is stifling, thick with smoke and a thousand scents she does not know. And the laughter, it is all around her, nipping at her skin like a thousand little pinpricks. It sounds like a party, but not like any of the parties she has heard before. She desperately wants her mother, but something is tingling at the back of her neck. She wants to see this party, she wants to know.

Why did she want to know? Why did she want to see?

Barely breathing, her head fuzzy and foggy and thick as the air, she continues her way, down further, every step taking an age. There are more noises now, voices, and screams?

Shutting her eyes tight, she holds the quilt until it is all she can feel, scratchy wool beneath clammy fingers curled so tight they hurt. She is afraid, so afraid, her little heart beating like a bird's. Someone is hurt. Someone is screaming. But no one is moving. No one is helping. No one is running to help them. She needs to help them.

Why?

Don't go...

Swallowing hard, swallowing nothing but dry scratchiness, she continues down further, down until she sees demon-like shadows dancing on the walls and floor of the foyer. The voices, the laughter, the screams, they are loud, deafening, and she wants to cover her eyes and her ears and run away to her mother, but she is being drawn, the shadows, the demons they are calling her forth.

Sweaty little cold feet slip as they touch the slick, cool, marble, and she blinks hard, forcing her mind to clear because something is wrong, and someone is hurt, and she has to see, has to know.

Where is papa? Where are the servants?

Following the demons, she goes to the wide-open doors of the red drawing room. That is for father's guests, mama never uses that one, she is not to go in there, but still she does, she has to find father now, and those screams, they hurt her. Tear through her little heart, tear through her mind, and they twist her insides and -

Fire, shadows, metal, blood, and bodies.

Laughter, cruel, yes, cruel, and cold, and scratching at her like claws.

And there are rotten teeth behind smiling lips, and the smoke of candles and cheroots, and wine, and brandy, it turns her stomach.

Clawing sweaty hands are on her, and there is more shouting, and screaming, and everything blurs, just a swirled mist of horror between sets of golden candelabra.

The faceless man, he is different, he is not sweaty, he is cold, as cold as the lake in the Pit, his eyes are burning coals, and his voice, it echoes in her mind and in her ears like the rustling of silk, never to be forgotten.

'One day you'll be mine little one. One day, she'll be mine.'

And then there is nothing but darkness.

∞

'Angelique,' Will shouted, his hands on her shoulders, half trying to wake her, half trying to keep her steady on the bed. He'd never seen anyone so taken by nightmares; whatever demons Angelique fought had to be vicious things indeed. She was writhing, and kicking and whimpering and whispering nonsense, though at least she wasn't screaming again. That sound, the one that had awoken him, and likely half the inn, though thankfully no one came running to investigate; it had torn through him like a hot blade.

He hadn't been able to stop himself from coming, from forcing open the door, only to find her twisted in the sheets, half on the bed, half on the floor, her face contorted in a mask of pain he wouldn't wish on his fiercest enemy.

'Angelique!'

'No,' she mumbled, tears streaming down her cheeks as she fought and clawed with every bit of strength she possessed. 'I am not yours. Let me go! Let me go,' she cried.

'Angelique,' he said, gentler now, straddling her to keep her safe, coming as close as he could to her ear. 'Angelique, please. Wake now, let go of the demons. Come back to me.'

'No...'

'Angelique, please... Come back to me.'

With a final cry torn from her chest, that tore something from his own, she stilled, and her eyes flew open.

God help her.

The fear he saw in those dark green eyes, the sorrow, all of it. It was like the night he'd found her, only a thousand times worse. He kept his hold on her, and willed her to see him, willed the fog and confusion to lift, which slowly, it did.

And he'd thought his own hauntings terrible things.

'Will,' she croaked, frowning slightly.

'Yes, I'm here,' he said soothingly, slowly removing his hold so he could sit beside her. Her breathing was still too erratic, and he was sure that if he lay his hand over her heart, he would feel it nearly jumping through her skin. 'It was only a nightmare.'

'No... I... I...'

Angelique sucked in a strangled cry, and her breathing, though he wouldn't have thought it possible, quickened even more.

She inhaled shallow breath after shallow breath, panicking as she tried to sit up and untangle herself, until she could barely breathe at all, and she clutched her chest as tears fell onto the sheets.

'Angelique,' he said harshly, readjusting so he could face her without caging her in, trying to force her out of the dark pit she was lost in again. He tore back the sheets, and took her hands in his. 'Angelique, look at me. Look at me,' he ordered, and she complied. 'Breathe with me.'

Taking deep, long breaths, he encouraged her to follow his lead, and shakily, she did.

Clasping his hands tight, she evened out her breathing, and slowly he saw her return to herself, though the sorrow lingered in her eyes.

'Thank you,' she managed after what could've been minutes,

or an hour.

'Here,' he said with a nod, releasing her hands to fetch the cup of water that lay on the table by her bed. She drank it down greedily, and handed it back. 'Are you alright?'

'I'm fine,' she whispered, annoyance in her voice. She wanted him to leave now, and never speak of this again, he could tell. But that was not going to happen, not in a million years. 'It was only a nightmare. You didn't have to -'

'Like Hell it was,' he sneered, surprising her enough to render her speechless. 'That was not a nightmare. What is it that terrifies you so?'

'Nothing,' she mumbled, grabbing up the sheets, and huddling into them as she shuffled to lean back against the headboard.

'Liar.'

Angry eyes flicked up at him, then down again when they presumably saw the same emotion reflected in his.

He wasn't sure *why* he was so angry, only that he needed to know what haunted her so that he could...

Do absolutely nothing about it because it does not concern you.

'I've heard you before. This isn't the first time. Though I had no idea it was so bad.'

'It isn't -'

'Yes, it is,' he said with quiet ferocity. 'I should know.'

Angelique shrugged, and looked away again.

'It hasn't been so bad before,' she mumbled. 'Mother, the doctor, they say it is night terrors, that is all,' she said firmly, meeting his gaze if only to convince herself as much as him. 'It's perfectly normal.'

'What I witnessed was far from perfectly normal.'

'Why are you even here, Will,' she exclaimed. 'Go back to bed.'

'Not until you tell me what you saw,' he retorted, in the same reprimanding tone.

Christ, all he wanted was to help, and that is what he would do whether the little gremlin liked it or not.

'Why do you even care,' she asked with a shrug, defeated.

As if she too was unused to people caring.

Or perhaps, he had been convincing enough to make her believe he cared for nothing, which in fact, had been the case until...

Very recently.

'Two more days, and we are through.'

'I care,' he said quietly, the truth sobering them both.

'It feels like a memory,' she breathed after a long moment, intently examining the edge of the sheets between her fingers. 'But I cannot remember, anything. In the dream, I am a girl, still in the nursery. We are in the old house, in Wiltshire. But I cannot remember much at all from that time of my life. Nothing at all really. In the dream...'

Angelique took a deep, steadying breath, and Will lay his hand on hers.

He didn't know where the impulse sprang from, but his body seemed to know what hers needed then.

'It's always the same,' she continued, her voice stronger, yet distant from the words. 'But it hasn't... I haven't seen so much, ever. I wake, feverish I think. It is summer. I get out of bed, to go to my mother. She was different then, or at least she is in the dream,' Angelique said when Will failed to conceal his surprise.

The Lady Fitzsimmons he knew would not be caught dead demonstrating any sort of comfort or affection to her own daughter; not that he could truly judge when those words were another language to him.

'And there are voices, and laughter, and screams,' she added, looking up at him, fear and confusion bright again in her eyes. He tightened his hold on her hand and she went on. 'I go downstairs, to my father's drawing room, and there are faces, and blood, and I feel sick, and the pain of others, I want to help them but I can't, and it's all just a mess, I cannot see anything clearly, and there is a man, and I cannot see his face, but he whispers in my ear, he says one day I'll be his, and then it all goes dark.' Will's gut churned, as Angelique wiped away some tears. 'He is who I fear. He has haunted me for as long as I can remember. He is who I run from. Even before the nightmares began, I felt him.'

'He will not have you,' Will promised, though how he could do such a thing, promise that, he did not know. But he knew, in that moment, it was a promise he must make. A promise he could make. And this one, it would define him too, God help him. 'Shadow or man, he will not.'

'I wish I could believe you,' she said with a sad smile.

Rather than try to convince her with words, he allowed a part of himself he did not know take hold of his actions.

A part, that knew how to offer comfort. A part, that wished to, for another creature.

Gently, he wiped more tears from her cheek, then rose, and settled beside her. When she did not protest, when his own body did not, he tucked her into his side, and pulled the covers up around her, and he held her tight, and stroked her hair for hours, well past when she finally fell back asleep, this time into a dreamless slumber. He stayed awake until the first rays of dawn pierced through, repeating his promise to whatever powers that be; an endless prayer, or plea, he knew not.

He will not have her.

XI.

After twenty minutes of wringing her hands, Angelique rapped softly on the door to Will's room. He had slipped away sometime before she'd woken; though not long as she'd still felt his heat on the sheets. As she'd washed and dressed, she'd considered not doing this, but she knew that what had happened last night needed to be addressed, not that she cared to; not at all. It was mortifying, and embarrassing, and above all, it terrified her, to face him after that. Not the same fear as the one she felt every hour of every day, but an intense fear that he would look at her differently now.

That he would see her differently now.

Broken. Pitiful. Silly.

With all the strides they'd taken these past days, with all they had somehow shared and with the rapport they'd built, she felt stronger. More herself than she'd ever been. But now, if he were to look at her like some mad, helpless little chit...

It wouldn't matter because come Monday you'll never see him again.

Quite right.

Still. It would sting.

And she needed to thank him. Without him pulling her back from the edge last night, staying with her, comforting her, showing her a tenderness she'd not known in a long time... Well. She wasn't entirely sure she would have made it out of the darkness with her sanity restored. Last night had been the worst it had ever been.

It hadn't felt a dream, or a memory. It had felt... Real. And his eyes, locked on hers, his touch, had been the only things to tether her to reality. To the present. His eyes, as they always had, anchored her. Broke through the haze, washed away the memory of another's eyes, and...

Perhaps that is what she feared most of all.

Not that he wouldn't see her, but that he would.

The door swung open, startling her, and she stood there for a moment, unable to find her voice. There were shadows under his eyes, and his hair was tousled to within an inch of its life. He wore the same shirt and breeches he had when he'd come to her last night.

He looked as if *he* hadn't slept a wink.

'Good morning,' she managed, in what she thought sounded a light, pleasant, airy, and unconcerned tone. Though the narrowing of Will's eyes told a different tale. 'I'm sorry I didn't mean to disturb you...'

'Good afternoon,' Will said in a gravelly voice, his eyes studying her acutely. 'And you didn't disturb me. I'm glad you managed to find some sleep.'

'Did you,' she asked gently.

'Apparently so.'

'I...' Her eyes fell to the floor as her voice faltered. She sucked in a breath and forced out the words. 'I wanted to thank you, for last night.'

'Unnecessary.'

Well, that was her told then.

And him, back to himself. The old self.

Angelique nodded.

'I'm going for a walk,' she said, heading to grab her things. 'Just to the beach, I shall not be long, no reason for you to come, I'll be perfectly fine.'

Please for the love of all things Holy do not come.

She needed some time alone, to think, to -

'The man in your dreams,' Will said, stopping her before she could escape. 'He is the other reason you ran. The reason you did so... As you did.'

'Yes,' she breathed after a moment.

It appeared when he asked, she was unable to keep anything at all from him.

In that moment, she knew, beyond any more doubt, that what she'd always suspected was true. Will saw her. Understood her in a way no one else ever could.

And more so now than ever, that thought, was reassuring. It soothed her, and bolstered her courage all at once. Whatever she said, or did, he would understand. He would know, the *why*. He would be there for her. Until then, she'd never thought it truly possible, to have that, but now that she knew it was, she saw it for the immensely incredible gift it was.

I am not alone.

'But you don't know him.'

'I feel him,' she admitted. 'Like a storm, brewing on the horizon. The air charging, and changing, and smothering me. I've felt it for years, but for the past couple, it's gotten worse. Do you remember that tea party, last spring, at Lady Rowan's,' she asked, turning, and Will nodded.

How could he not?

She'd fainted, right there in the middle of Lady's Rowan's immaculate gardens, sending two dozen women shrieking and fanning. Will had had to carry her inside to be revived, and she'd not come out of her rooms for three days after, barely able to move or eat. Even then, when they'd seemed to co-exist in different, parallel worlds, he'd been so...

Attentive. Concerned.

'I saw something, a flash from my dream, clearer than ever before... It just got worse after that. I'd be in the middle of a ball, and my mind would call forth these images, these feelings...'

Angelique looked at him, begging him to understand, and he did.

'Perhaps... Perhaps your shadow was there,' he offered.

So he did believe her.

Understanding was one thing, truly believing, another entirely.

But he believed it *was* a memory, long buried, which haunted her. A *real* shadow, not simply the conjurings of a young, terrified mind. She'd suspected as much, but truly admitting that to herself, even as she knew her shadow was real, opened up so many other possibilities. So many other questions.

So many other truths she never wished to know, and yet craved.

'No,' she stated. *That* much at least, she knew. 'I would've... I know I would remember him. If I saw him. I would,' she repeated, because that was all she had, that confidence that she would know the demon, and therefore be safe.

Yet, there was *someone.*

Someone whose eyes made her gut clench as much as those in her dream.

'What is it,' Will asked, sensing somehow her mind had wandered to someone.

'It's nothing.'

'What happened the night of the ball? You've lived like this for years,' he said, reminding her of her own words. 'You reach your majority in a few months. What made you decide to run then?'

He looked at me.

He touched me.

How foolish that was.

How simple, and yet...

'Angelique, tell me.'

'Laramie,' she said before she could stop herself, and Will's eyes flashed with surprise. 'Richard Laramie. It isn't him I see, I know that. But his eyes... The way he looks at me... It makes my skin crawl, and that fear, it... Rises up until I cannot control it. I've tried to avoid him best I could, especially after that dinner at the Dowager's last year, but the night of the ball...' Angelique took a steadying breath, the mere memory of it enough to send her emotions into the same freefall as they had been that night.

'We danced. I could not refuse, my mother... Well, you know how she is.'

She huffed a tiny laugh, but Will was not amused.

Fire burned in his eyes, and his jaw clenched so tight she thought he might break a tooth. The demonstration of outrage on her behalf was oddly...

Comforting.

'After that. I couldn't take it anymore. It was all too much. I couldn't breathe. I couldn't... I ran because I refused to live like that any longer. Afraid, either destined to be some doll in a great house somewhere, or some demon's possession. I wanted more. I deserve more. That is why I ran.'

Will nodded again, and if his initial judgement of her stood, she did not know.

A veil had passed over his eyes, and she couldn't read him anymore.

If she ever truly had been able to before. She liked to think so, liked to think that she too, could see *him*, his soul, that that was the reason why she'd felt so close to him from the first, because she'd somehow gotten a glimpse of a familiar spirit, but now...

There was a guardedness she'd not seen before, even in those moments he tried to shut her out when she asked of him, and of his past.

After a deep, steadying breath, she smiled, and turned again to go.

'You do deserve more,' he said, barely above a whisper, and yet to her it sounded as if he had shouted it from a mountaintop for all the world to hear. 'You deserve so much more.'

With a grateful nod, unable to look at him, she left.

For if she didn't, she might be tempted to go after something she could never have.

Two more days.

∞

Letting her go probably wasn't the best idea he'd had in his life, but he had seen that she needed some time alone. And if he was honest, so did he. To clean himself up, and to think. The more time he spent with her, the more he felt a stranded sailor at sea. At the mercy of the water, of the sun, of the waves, of the currents, of everything around him. Not a man anymore, but something other. Something foreign, and unknown, without ties, without moorings, with only an empty horizon.

In his life, he'd only been close to one person. One person who had seen him through the worst of times, and the rest. One person who knew him, who saw him for what he was, and who stood by him. His life was a barren wasteland, with only one pillar of strength that kept him rooted, and centered, and focused.

But these past days, this past year at Angelique's side, he'd been flung further and further away from that one centre. As if he'd found another, a true north, that guided him somewhere... He'd never dreamt existed. Or rather, that he had, but long forsaken.

Even through the dislike he'd had of her, through his prejudice, he'd seen something in her, *recognized* something. A part of himself, and of her, that not even his own brother knew of. That not even he had known existed until that very first moment his gaze had locked with hers. And damn him if he knew what that was.

It felt like closeness. Like what he felt when they talked. Like what he'd felt last night as she'd fallen asleep in his arms. Like the whisper of a tale he'd heard as a babe and long forgotten. And he craved to hear it again, to feel it again, even more than...

Everything else.

More than the one promise that kept him going, that made him who he was. That had defined him, always. That he'd always believed would define him, and yet that now was beginning to feel like an ill-fitting garment. It itched, and scratched, and felt...

Wrong.

And now he was going around making more promises?

Vowing to do more things he feared he never could? All for what? The sake of some pretty little chit...

Will splashed some of the frigid water from the basin onto his face, leaned on the dressing table, and closed his eyes as it dripped down, cleansing his mind and body drip by drip.

You need to remember who you are.

He needed to -

'Will, are you hungry, I -'

Will whipped around, belatedly realizing he hadn't shut the door after she'd left for her walk.

Not that he really could, having ripped out the lock the night before.

The faltering of her voice and steps would have told him she'd seen what only few others ever had, and what he wished she never would. Anger gripped him, anger that now everything would change, even as it had to. That she would see it all, and that she would know, and then she would look at him, see him differently; they always did.

It was always there, in their eyes when they did, *pity and disgust.*

No matter that it hadn't been so for her before, it would be now.

Grinding his teeth, fists clenched, he raised his eyes to hers, and prepared himself.

Only again, there was neither pity nor disgust in her eyes. There wasn't even any surprise, or horror. There was only a profound, heart wrenching sadness in them as they travelled across his marked body. The marks of his childhood, searing, torn, and beaten in flesh. The marks of his life after that, of knives and bullets and nails too. When she looked at him, it was as if she could feel it, his pain. As if she was making it her own.

But it was his, and his alone.

Instead of diminishing his anger, it propelled it forward, kindled it, made it rage and rise brighter and hotter. He rushed towards her, until he was towering over her, but she did not move, did not cower, did not flee, simply looked up at him, tears welling in her eyes. He wanted to scream, to push her away, to throw her out, to break everything that could be broken inside his tiny little room, but he couldn't move, he could barely breathe.

And yet he was, he was panting, he could see it, his own breath fanning the loose curls on her forehead. He was shaking too, vibrating, he knew that because he felt himself still when she lay one of her delicate little hands that had never touched anything but beautiful things on his cheek.

There was so much in that touch that he'd never known, and yet he felt it, recognised it. It was different from any touch he'd ever felt before. It was the story he'd forgotten, and it was full of something called tenderness. And something called care, and gentleness.

No one touched him like that, no one showed him those things, yet his body had craved them for so long. But even as it did, it revolted at the touch, at all those foreign things touching him, infusing him with something other than purpose and rage, and terror. It revolted against sweetness, and weakness.

In a flash, he had Angelique's wrist in his grip, not enough to injure her, for even the worst part of himself could never do such a thing, and he had caged her up against the wall. Still, she did not flinch, did not cower, or whimper, and he let go of her hand as if it had branded him.

He wanted...

'Don't look at me like that,' he growled, wanting to put the fear of God, and the Devil, but most of all of himself in her. If she kept looking at him like that, touching him like that... 'If you do -'

'What, Will,' she breathed, searching his eyes. 'What will you do? Not hurt me. I know that you never could.'

'You know nothing,' he seethed, slamming his fist into the wall beside her head.

'*You* know that's not true,' she cried, not with fear, but with a desperation that tore through him. That tugged at something, something that felt like hope, and light. 'I see you, as surely as you see me. I wish it wasn't so, as much as you do. But it is. And I hurt for you, as much as you do for me.'

'What do you want from me, Angelique,' he hissed, coming even closer, so that he could feel every inch of her body pressed against his.

Every heartbeat, every breath, as surely as if they were his own.

And he wanted to lose himself in that feeling, to seep into it, into her, until all the rest of it was gone; long forgotten noise drowned out in smooth, soft, silence.

Her eyes changed then, darkened, and he knew *that* look. That heat.

He smiled wolfishly, happy to distract himself with other thoughts entirely. Happy to scare her off with another reality entirely.

Safer thoughts; a safer reality.

'Is this what you want,' he asked, pressing his hips into hers, so that she could feel what his body now demanded. 'A tumble with the help? A seedy encounter against a wall with a low born like myself,' he taunted, his voice as cold as he forced his heart to be, even as it demanded he accept the warmth she promised. 'Something to set fans fluttering and tongues wagging?' Angelique shook her head, tears dripping from her eyes onto her cheeks, and he grinned. *Thank God.* If she didn't stop this now... 'Then be careful what bears you prod, little girl.'

'I just want you,' she whispered as he made to move away.

No. Please, God no.

Angelique shrugged, a look of utter helplessness in her eyes.

A look of defeat, and surrender; an offering.

The last shred of humanity broke within him, and unleashed the animal. The broken, injured, beaten animal that had cowered in corners and darkness, and yearned for light and tenderness. He didn't even have to take a step, she was there, still in his reach, and so he did.

He reached out and took her face in his hands and pulled her to him. She rose up on her toes to meet him, their lips coming together with a sweet savagery that was unlike anything he'd ever felt before. But then, perhaps he'd never truly felt anything until now. Until this moment, with this woman in his hands, so tiny, and as ethereal as will o' the wisps, and yet stronger than the oldest mountains.

He wrapped his arms around her, hauling her tight to wrap himself in her and her in him as he tasted every inch of her mouth, as he sought, and found all that she was.

Not all. More.

He felt her hands come around his neck, caressing him, gently smoothing the hair at the base of his neck as he stepped forth, Angelique still cradled in his arms, right where she belonged. Her back yet again met the wall and his hands found their way to her skirts. He rucked them up and circled her waist with one arm, lifting her so that she could be where she needed to be for him to come home.

Home. That is what she tastes of.

Angelique let out a strangled cry when he finally took his mouth from hers, but he needed... To see. To know. To give her one last chance to flee, to retreat, to leave him, as all but one had. He looked down at her, at her flushed face circled by hazy wisps of hair, looked down into the deepest ocean that lay in her eyes no longer filled with tears, but filled with something else. Something that felt like bright and shining truth, and impossible clarity. Something that felt like what being with her felt like.

Comfort. Tenderness.

Or at least, what he imagined those things felt like.

He asked the silent question, their ragged breaths mingling between them, a primal rhythm as old as the Earth itself. And she answered, sliding her hands down to his shoulders and lifting her legs to encircle his waist.

Damn her.

Damn me.

He freed himself from his breeches and pushed aside her undergarments until he felt himself at the entrance to her self. Clasping her tightly to him, his forehead against hers, their eyes still locked, he braced one hand against the wall and entered her in one swift thrust.

Regret and guilt rushed over him as he felt the barrier within her give way, the final vestiges of his good nature telling him this was all badly done indeed, even as it felt so right. Angelique did not cry out, merely sucked in a breath, her eyes flashing with a flicker of pain.

He froze, stilling within her warmth, until she tilted up her head and kissed him. It was barely a kiss, barely the whisper of a kiss, and yet it seared him more surely than a kiss of passion and desire. He returned it, willing himself to show her all she showed him with every breath, and when she wound her arms around his neck again, pulling herself flush to his chest, burying her head into the crook at the base of his throat, he dragged himself from her and thrust again.

Her breath was hot against him, her fingers clasping tightly, digging into his flesh, and he could feel her heart, he was sure of it, beating in his own chest, in time with his own, that had never beat before. And he was lost again, entirely now, lost in her scent, in their scent as they moved together, in her heat, and her light which swept through him, through all the darkest corners like a blasting wind of light, chasing cobwebs and illuminating rooms that had rotten in the damp gloom of his life.

And then there was a sweet nothingness, a void of reason, where there was nothing but the harshness of her fingers in his flesh, and the sweetness of her surrounding him, and he was not himself anymore, he was something else entirely, and they were not two bodies, but one.

He was not alone anymore.

∞

A ray of moonlight shone through the window and fell across Will's sleeping face. A tendril of silver hair fell across his forehead, and she longed to brush it away, but she was afraid of waking him. They had collapsed onto the floor after their, *encounter*, and sometime during the sunset that had thrown rays of fiery sun across the room, making it seem a far away enchanted place, he had fallen asleep, right there, his limbs sprawled across the hardwood, and her. He looked more at peace than she'd ever imagined he could, whatever burdens and darkness he carried stowed away for the night as he roamed the land of dreams.

Or perhaps, stowed away for longer.

Not abandoned, for she knew some things could never be left behind, but she knew the weight of them could be lessened. She'd seen it before, with Percy. It had been as if Meg, in taking his hand, had agreed to a covenant, where the burdens, as with the joys, could be carried between two souls, rather than one alone.

A covenant which lessened the power of the darkness; made it less a vital part of a person. Gave them the ability to open themselves to more.

She had longed for that, as she longed for it for Will now. She had felt like that with him sometimes, well, always, but more so these past days. Not so alone in the cold night. Not so afraid, not so heavy. And her demons were surely nothing compared to his. When she'd seen the marks on his body…

Somewhere, deep down, she'd always known, suspected he had been molded by something terrible, and then when he'd spoken of that place… Sparing her the details, perhaps unable to speak of it all himself. And today when she'd seen the remnants of his childhood, of his life, on his skin, if one could call it a childhood or a life at all, her heart had hurt for him.

She had felt his suffering twisting her own heart, wringing it so tight, as if it were hers. Pain, for all he had endured, all he had lost, and never known. She wished…

For many things that could never be.

She wished she could regret what they had done. Everything she had ever been told and taught, pronounced her unclean now.

A sinner. Dirty. Impure.

But when Will touched her, when he kissed her, and held her, and entered her body, it felt like she was anything but those things. It had even felt different from what the girls at Lily's had said. Yes, she had felt the sticky heat, the fiery passion, the twinge of pain and some of the pleasure they promised one could feel, but she also felt light, and pure, and part of something for which there were no words.

There wasn't even a twinge of regret within her for the manner in which she had lost her innocence; some regret that it was not proper, in a bed, *romantic*, gentle, sweet and slow, with her husband. Because what she had been given was some great, heavenly gift, bestowed on mortals to give them hope. She had felt desire before; there had been stolen kisses in gardens at parties and charming young men of the *ton* that had made her stomach flutter. But nothing, nothing compared to what she felt with Will. There was a connection, a bond forged long before they'd even met.

Or at least that is how it felt.

She looked over him, at the strength and power of him, even in repose. How tightly coiled he kept it, even tighter than Percy did, and that man was tightly sprung no matter how relaxed he pretended to be. But Will... He was something else entirely.

When she had touched him, simply laid her hand on his cheek, unable to not do so, unable to not offer some comfort, and gentleness to soothe him, he had reacted as if she'd struck him. Like a dog that had been beaten for too long. And she might've fled right then, but even as his anger grew, she had known he needed her. Known it with a certainty she hadn't ever really felt before. He needed her; perhaps as much as she needed him. As she needed his strength, and *his* comfort. Not simply to feel safe, to will away the fear, but because she needed it to breathe. To live. To be complete.

And even when he had seemed to lose his reason, his tightly even manner, she had not feared him. That same thing she'd seen in his eyes that first time whispered to her that he would never harm her.

Leaving him now will not be so easy.

Angelique shivered slightly, and curled up tighter against him. No, it would not be so easy. But she had to. No matter how *right* it felt to be with him, she still had to go. Had to take control of her life, and her future, far away from this place. Even with him, the fear still lingered, returned even as he soothed it. The demons inside her would not quieten so long as she was here. With him to help her tame them, or not. Bound together though they may be, connected as they may be, for there was no denying they were now, some paths were meant to diverge.

What he had given her was precious, and priceless, and she would treasure it always.

But *he*, could not be hers.

Not in this life. Though perhaps, in another.

Unable to stop herself, Angelique reached out and smoothed away that lock of hair, letting her fingers trail gently across his features. He was so beautiful in the light of the moon. He was a statue of secrets no longer, but a beautiful fae, come from a faraway land to dance with her, and eat with her, and laugh with her, and make her forget the real world. And yet he was a man, one of the best she'd ever known, and she...

He, was precious to her. Would always be.

Will's eyes opened suddenly, and she drew back her hand as he studied her, at first with longing, and appreciation, and then, sadly, regret.

She'd not considered that. That *he* might regret what they'd done. Suddenly she felt so unsure, so vulnerable and exposed. Will's arm slid from where it had been draped across her, and he rose slowly onto his forearms, staring down at the floor.

Closing in on herself, Angelique sat up and drew in a deep breath, preparing for whatever was coming.

'I...'

But she was not prepared.

Not for anything he had to say.

Before Will could finish his thought, Angelique scrambled to her feet and fled to her room, shutting the door as tightly behind her as she could. She stripped quickly, washed herself, threw on her nightshirt, slipped under the covers, and curled herself back up tight, the cold sheets a brisk reminder of the warmth she'd lost.

For a few more hours at least, she would cling to the precious thing Will had given her.

For a few more hours, she would live in a world where he didn't regret it, didn't try to make it right by man's standards.

For a few more hours, she would cling to the memory of *them*.

XII.

Will was about to knock on the half open door between their rooms when he caught sight of Angelique, and stopped himself. Now dressed and cleaned, she stood at the window, brushing her damp hair slowly, every move full of intention and care. And the look on her face, it was what really stole his breath, and stopped his progress. Yet again, he was reminded of an angel. Luminous, in the pale light of a dusky, misty morn. So beautiful, and so at peace. For perhaps the first time since he'd first met her, she looked truly, and utterly unburdened, untethered to the world mere mortals such as he moved in.

The image she created was so simple, and yet, so moving, it once again stirred unwelcome hope in his breast. Hope, of a life, other than that which was his. A life not of lies, and secrets, and danger, and violence, but of simplicity, natural beauty, and peace. A life, where he had something to offer.

A life, that image of her seemed to offer him, like a siren's song.

Be wary or you shall drown in it.

Soon, the peaceful quietude would be broken; as soon as she saw him, laid eyes on him, and remembered what he'd done. What he'd taken from her; done to her. Just as he had been reminded when he'd woken with her in his arms last night. He'd gone too far. Let himself be carried away, let himself be lost to her, and he had crossed a line which meant that when this all ended, she would hate him even more.

Which reminded him of his purpose.

Straightening, he cleared his throat, and she turned, the brush still caught in her curls. And much to his dismay, she yet again surprised him. By looking at him not with shame, or disgust, or regret, but with excitement.

Smiling, she dropped the brush, and tied her hair loosely with a ribbon as she came around the bed and strode over to him.

'Good morning,' she said softly, searching his face.

He tried, God knew he tried.

To school his features, to resist that damn siren's song, to frown, to put her off, to put the wall between them back up, but instead, he smiled back.

'Good morning. I have breakfast,' he said, stepping back to grab the tray he'd brought up. 'Though it isn't as warm as it might've been, we overslept.'

'I'm famished,' Angelique said, a grin in his voice that certainly spoke to his male pride at least.

She settled herself in what he now thought of as her armchair as he brought the tray of food into her room, and settled in what had become his.

Silently, they tucked into the meal, the air between them thick with expectation, and a twinge of awkwardness. He knew what he had to say, but that did not make the saying of it any easier. Particularly not when she kept glancing up at him and smiling, as if what they had done was the most delightful, natural, and wonderful thing in the world.

Which it certainly…

Was not.

As if they were not themselves anymore, but two other people.

Which they were not.

Liar.

'Angelique,' he managed to get out finally, choking down a sip of cold coffee. 'About what happened…'

His voice faltered as he caught sight of the disappointment creeping into her eyes.

'Don't,' she said, straightening, a wan smile on her lips. 'Please, don't, Will. What happened... Happened. I have no expectations, you should know that. You don't have to say anything. We shared... Something.' *Something wonderful, and incredible, and I* - 'But we both know that our lives are at a crossroads. Tomorrow... We shall part ways, and that will be the end of it.'

The end of it.

It would be.

Perhaps not tomorrow as she thought, but everything else was the absolute truth. He could not deny it, though something deep inside him wished he could. That same something that was touched by the resolute sadness in Angelique's eyes now.

He nodded, and she rose, delicately folding her napkin and placing it on the tray.

'Thank you for breakfast.'

'Marry me,' he said, his mouth working faster than his mind. Angelique stopped, and slowly turned to face him, the expression of confused distaste on her face both terrifying and reassuring. It was entirely likely he'd lost his mind. 'Marry me.'

'What are you doing, Will,' she scoffed. *Hell if I know.* 'I can't, we can't... This isn't what this was,' she said finally, the statement however true, filling him with regret. 'You don't owe me...'

'I know,' he lied.

He didn't know.

He didn't seem to know anything anymore, not really. Not with the utmost conviction he had not... A week ago. A year ago. Since he'd met her. He told himself he was doing this to salvage the enormous mess he'd made of things, but deep down, he knew that wasn't the *whole* truth. If it had been, he might've thought of it as an actual plan, not simply let the words tumble forth from his mouth.

It has to be.

It couldn't, not for one moment, be about him clinging on like a drowning man to a liferaft. Clinging to the one good, precious, wondrous thing he'd ever known. The one person who had shown him tenderness, and care, and affection. Who had shown him possibilities, and light, and made him want more. Made him want to be more.

And it certainly, not for one moment, couldn't be about putting one promise above another.

'Even if I were to... If I got with child, which by my calculations shouldn't happen, but of course one never knows,' she said slowly, her eyes searching the walls around them for answers he knew for certain were not there. He'd searched them long enough himself to know. 'It wouldn't change anything, Will. You have to understand that,' she said, taking a step forward, pleading once again in her eyes, as if he didn't understand that very well indeed. 'I would love it, with all I am, but I would still leave, and make my life far away from here. Nothing,' she added, a crack in her voice that she quickly pushed away with a breath. 'Nothing will ever change that.'

'I know,' he said quietly, though he hated how true her words were. 'I wouldn't... I would never lay claim, as your husband, or if there were a child, as a father.' *Liar!* 'I offer you my hand, to give you freedom, not to shackle you.'

He rose slowly, as Angelique's frown deepened, and it seemed to him the same hint of disappointment that lay in his heart at the idea this could never be true, lay in her eyes.

Enough nonsense. Fix this. You are out of time.

'If you are wed,' he continued, his courage and conviction growing with every second. He stepped forward, and took her hands. 'Egerton, your parents, they cannot force you back. You going to America, you must know it will not be enough for him. As your husband, I could shield you, from their attempts.'

Dawning grew in her eyes at the realization that what he said made complete and utter sense.

Thankfully something about this does.

He pressed on, before either of them came to their senses.

'I can protect you.'

Perhaps it is the only way I can.

'And when the time comes,' she said quietly, coming in ever closer, until she was nearly in his arms. 'I am to believe that you will set me free?'

Will nodded.

For as he stood on the precipice, as she looked up at him with those big green eyes, so full of doubt and fear, and yet, so full of trust, and hope, he found he did not have it within himself to lie outright. He was a man of his word, and so if he did not say the word, it would not be breaking it, when in fact he did.

Though he knew either way, he would break her heart.

Better than the rest of her.

'Why would you do this for me,' she breathed. 'You will never be free to marry another. Never free to have a family -'

'I know,' he said, in a tone that reminded her precisely what he thought of those possibilities, even as hope taunted him with another truth. *Never. Not for me.* He'd told her as much. 'Though, I could always have our marriage annulled after you've deserted me,' he added with a wry smile, and Angelique chuckled, shaking her head. 'As can you, if you find another.'

'There will not be another.'

The certainty in her voice nearly felled him.

They stared at each other for a long moment, and he saw the question still lingering in the depths of her eyes. A question, which matched that in his own he knew, and to which, the answer was the same.

Why?

God only knows.

Certainly, for himself, he couldn't give her the answer any woman would want; not that she expected that of him. In fact, it seemed she never asked nor expected more than he could ever give, merely accepted who he was, and what he could. Which meant far more to him than she could ever know, or he could fully comprehend.

I do this for selfish reasons you will never fathom.

105

'I would do this, because I can,' he finally said, which yet again, seemed answer enough for her.

'Then I accept,' she smiled with a shrug of her shoulders.

'I will make arrangements,' he said, before making for the door. 'It will delay you, as the ceremony will have to be tomorrow, but I will also arrange for you to be on the first boat Tuesday.'

'Will,' she called, and he turned back.

The calm and peace he'd witnessed when he'd first seen her, there, brushing her hair at the window, had returned. Though now, it seemed even more complete, as if the last of the great weight she carried had been lifted from her shoulders.

And set unto mine.

Though he would carry it his whole life long, and longer even if he could, he knew that soon, she would take it back, and more, and it would be all his doing.

Guilt nearly made him cry out and order her to run, fast as she could, as far from him as she could, but instead he only stood there and quirked his head, waiting for whatever she had to say.

'Thank you.'

He nodded again, sealing his fate, and truly damning his soul.

If he'd thought he'd done that long ago, he'd been very sorely mistaken.

But now the Devil will surely have his due.

With that bitter thought, he strode out to make arrangements for his wedding.

XIII.

There was no reason to be nervous. Absolutely none whatsoever. This whole affair was simply business. A means to an end. And besides, he didn't get nervous. Nervous implied he was anxious about something, which he wasn't, because all the arrangements had been made, witnesses and a minister secured, even though here one wasn't necessary, but Angelique deserved for things to be done properly, as they might've if this whole thing were real.

Still, for someone who didn't get nervous, and absolutely, categorically, was not at this moment in time, he sure was behaving like he was. Shuffling his feet as he stood before the tiny chapel, fiddling with his hat as he waited for the only thing he was missing.

A bride.

A wife.

A wife.

No matter that it wasn't real, it felt real. Despite his contempt of the word, the impossibility with which he'd always viewed it, it carried weight. He had turned it around in his head, even going so far as to whisper it under his breath as he arranged for the minister, and the candles and greenery, just to make the chapel look a little brighter, and as he'd gone to borrow a more proper suit of exquisitely crafted grey wool, and gone to the barber's, and spoken to the inn-keeper about their wedding tea.

Wife, he had whispered to himself.

Whatever the reasons for this marriage, in the eyes of God and man, she would be his.

And he, would be her husband.

Though he may doubt the existence of God as general rule, he had never quite had it in him to repudiate the notion completely, and as for his fellow man, well, laws may not be upheld as they should, and yet, again, he could not disregard the notion outright. Men of power may wield the law, and God, for themselves, yet both concepts seemed to exist on another plane, beyond reach; untouchable. And the word wife, seemed to as well. It seemed to exist beyond his life, beyond all he'd ever believed, something foreign and precious, which demanded respect, and care.

The realest dream he'd ever known.

This may not be real, but Will took it all with dead seriousness. Which is perhaps why he'd paid so much attention to all the details rather than simply gathering some witnesses by a forge. Or perhaps, he'd simply wanted to keep good on his promise. To make these memories as good as they could be for her. To make these last days happy.

To make *her* happy.

'Will.'

Startled from his disquieting reverie, he shook his head and turned towards the voice.

Angelique stood before him, clad in a simple, but elegant cerulean silk gown that made her shine like the sea in the twilight. She had arranged her hair into an intricate knot of braided curls, laden with sprigs of heather, and in her hands she clasped a posy of dog violets and thistles. Her smile was bright, but her eyes were questioning as they studied him, and he found himself speechless.

He felt strange, as if his entire being had suddenly come alive, as if all the tension had left his chest, and he could breathe, properly, for the first time. She was the most beautiful, the most precious thing he'd ever laid eyes on, and in a few moments, she would be his.

My wife.

'You look… Good,' she said hesitantly.

'And you,' he breathed, stepping towards her slowly, terrified to find this might all be a dream after all. *It is. Of your own making.* 'You look, beautiful.'

She smiled bashfully, her eyes dropping to the ground, only not as he'd seen her do a thousand times with the gentlemen of the *ton*.

This time, her uncertainty was genuine, and it made him smile. This may not be real, but she was. She was the realest thing he'd ever known, and that thing that most would call a heart that had been twisted and constricted for so long within him seemed to relax, and open.

He gently brushed his finger alongside the bottom of her chin, lifting her gaze to his.

'Thank you,' she said softly. 'I thought…'

'As did I.'

She smiled again, and he drank her in for a moment before holding out his arm.

Once she had tucked her own into it, he led her into the chapel.

Wife.

Life.

∞

An anvil, a soot covered blacksmith, some drunken sailors, that is what she had expected. Because that was what marriages in Scotland were for English society runaway girls like her. There was nothing wrong with it, really, and she hadn't expected for Will to make any effort beyond that whilst making the arrangements, because after all he was simply doing her a favour. It was a deal they'd made, not a true wedding, or marriage, though in another life, she liked to think that having him his as her husband might've been quite an extraordinary adventure.

Nonetheless, she'd had this one nice dress from Lily, just in case, which worst case she could sell, and she'd decided that regardless of the circumstances, it was her wedding day, the only one she'd have, and she wanted it to be marked.

All her life, she had been told this day would come. All her life she'd been prepared for it, even as she had felt it was not for her. She had been to all manner of weddings, society weddings, and smaller affairs, like Meg and Percy's, which had celebrated matches of love. Where other girls spoke excitedly of the day which would be their day, of what dress, and what flowers they might have, she had simply hoped that if that was to be her fate, she might at least *like* the man she was about to marry.

At least, today, she found that she did. And so, she had let herself be swept up by the enthusiasm of those who had surrounded her her entire life. She had decided that she did want to make this day special, mark it, in some small manner at least. Hence the dress, and the hair, and the posy...

Only she'd underestimated Will, or perhaps, preferred to think he was not the man she knew him to be. For he had made every effort to make this as special a day for her as he could.

He had borrowed a suit obviously, and been to the barber's, and he looked so handsome, so different than when she'd first met him. Almost...

Happy.

When she'd seen him before the chapel, the simple, but lovely little chapel at the foot of the hill, in the grey light of the cloudy afternoon, she'd felt sure of something for the first time in her life. Sure, that though this may not be real, it was the realest thing she'd ever known.

Sure, that this was right.

That whatever time she had with him, would be good, even if it was days, or hours. That though they might not have a life together, to call him her husband, to think of herself as his wife, even from a distance; it would be the greatest privilege, bring her the greatest pride.

Gazing over at him now, she was lost in a sweet daze, the daze of those first precious seconds when slumber and waking mingled, when dreams crept into the world. She spoke the words she had to, but she was lost in the dream that it was true.

In the dim light of the candlelit church, sprinkled with flowers, ivy, and holly here and there, before the severe but congenial old minister, in the presence of the ruddy looking, but kind old couple who looked as in love as two young people ever might, Angelique allowed herself to believe her wedding would not be all she had to show of her marriage.

But that she might also have a shared life with this man, who saw her, and soothed her, and whom she...

'The rings,' the minister said gravely, drawing her attention back to the moment.

Will extracted something from his pocket, then gently took her hand, and slowly removed her glove.

So he had prepared for this too.

'Angelique Marie Claire Fitzsimmons,' Will said intently, sliding a small band of tin which was more precious than all the jewels of England on her finger. 'I give you this ring in God's name, as a symbol of all we have promised, and all that we share.'

He looked down at the ring for a long moment, then to her, and it stole her breath.

There was a resoluteness, a gravity, that enforced her wishes, that made her dreams more of a hope. That they would have time to keep their promises. That there would be something to share. That he meant his vows, as surely as she did hers.

She smiled, and he offered out his palm, in which sat another ring like hers, only to his size. She took his hand now, and slid it on, sealing the pact.

For all time.

'William Hardy,' she declared. 'I give you this ring in God's name, as a symbol of all we have promised, and all that we share.'

Clasping both her hands in his tightly, he nodded, and grinned, as if he were as giddy and light as she was now.

As if the weight of the words, of the rings, impacted his entire being as much as her.

Could it truly be?

The minister finished the ceremony, and Will kissed her softly on the cheek to the sound of their witnesses' cheers. They signed the register, as did the witnesses and the minister, and then Will led her out of the chapel.

They stood just outside the doorway for a moment, and Angelique took in every detail of that instant to commit it to memory. From the view of the town, and the sea beyond, to the cries of the gulls, and the warmth of her husband beside her. From the scent of him, mingled with that of her violets, to the crisp northern wind that seemed to sing and whisper in promise of something great coming from beyond the horizon.

Everything, which marked the first day of her new life, as Mrs. Hardy.

Perhaps, this would be her most precious memory of all.

XIV.

The dazing fog of something that felt eerily like what happiness might refused to lift, and Will was glad of it. For one day, it could all be simple. Husband, wife. No secrets, no demons, no shadows, no lies. For one day, he could be the man Angelique saw when she looked at him, the man he could never be but for this moment in time. He could be the man the couple who had served as witnesses saw; the man the innkeeper and indeed the entire room downstairs saw as they lifted their glasses to toast the newlyweds.

A simple man, embarking on the road to a simple life with his tender wife.

After the ceremony, they had strolled leisurely back to the inn where he had invited the couple, and the minister, though the latter declined, to share in the wedding tea he had arranged. You might've thought he had asked the innkeeper to cook for the king when he'd made the request, tittering on about *what an honour it was they should choose her*, and how she would make it *lovelier than anything they might've gotten elsewhere*.

Along the way they had been greeted and cheered by passersby, and when they had finally arrived back at the inn, he had found that the innkeeper had not been boastful in vain. She'd prepared a feast indeed, full of sweet and savoury dishes that made his mouth water, even a pudding decorated with flowers and sweetmeats. They had all supped, and laughed, the room had toasted them and sang songs of love, songs of long lives and great adventures. And then the couple had given them a gift, which had left both he and Angelique speechless. Not because of its grandeur, but because of the thought, the kindness behind the gesture.

A little tin box, in which was a quaich, enveloped in a piece of tartan.

To bring them as much luck, and joy, as it had brought them.

Will had seen Angelique fighting back tears when they'd said so, before calling for whiskey, filling it, and passing it around the table. The moment had not left him unaffected either, in fact he'd felt a tightening in his chest and throat that not even the whiskey had been able to dispel. It had felt as if he were part of something, larger, greater than himself, than the minuscule circle he had dwelled in his entire life.

It had felt as if he were part of an actual family. Of people, who cared for him, and wished him well, and were *happy* for him. That elusive dream that had once kept him warm, and alive, but which he had long had to forsake.

He'd been ready to run, to flee, to repudiate all he'd done the past days, all he'd said, but then Angelique had taken his hand, and smiled, beamed at him, really, and he'd felt his soul quieten. Everything quieten, until only the warmth and sense of peace remained.

So it had been all afternoon as they celebrated, so it was now as he stood with Angelique before her door in the dimly lit corridor, knowing he should bid her goodnight, yet unwilling to see that feeling go.

To let her go.

Every passing moment ticked like a clock counting down the hours until it would all be over, and he didn't want to hear it. He didn't want to hear anything but her, her voice, the sound of her breathing, her laugh. He didn't want to be alone, not anymore, not today. Not in these final hours when he didn't have to be.

He wanted -

'Stay with me tonight,' Angelique said softly, as if she were as afraid as he was of letting go. 'Husband,' she added, offering out her hand, and she looked up at him with such hope and resolve, he could not have refused if he had truly wished to.

And he did not wish to.

For today, tonight, he could, and would be her husband; that man he so longed to be.

∞

In her life, she hadn't been bold about a great many things. At least, not in the grand scheme of it all. It had only been in the past couple years that she had learned to grasp what she wanted. To do so, without fear for her reputation, or regret, or shame; without asking for permission. To be; to live. But even all those things, even running away, here, it had all been in pursuit of something. Of bettering herself, making herself stronger, giving herself something. She had never truly wanted something, simply for itself. She had never wanted *someone*, simply for himself.

As she did now.

She wanted Will, tonight, to be her husband, in every way possible. She didn't want the dream of a day to end, she didn't want to remember it was a deal, and that they had not wed for love. She wanted him, with her, until the very last moment. So perhaps she was being wanton, and perhaps it was unforgivable in another world for her to ask for just that, but she didn't care. For her, it was being bold, and brave.

Will took her hand, and any lingering doubt that she might have that he didn't want her, that he didn't want this, as much as her, faded away. She opened the door and led him in, his touch grounding her again to the time and place. He closed it again, locked it, shutting them into their own little world, and she turned to him.

They stood there, gazing at each other, hand in hand for a moment, firelight the only thing illuminating the room, that might've been a castle if she could stay there with him all her life. It seemed as if he was studying her as intently as she was him, memorizing each detail as she was, to lock it away in the morning into a chest of precious things.

Will took a deep breath, and smoothed a curl back behind her ear, his fingers trailing down the line of her jaw with a gentleness she'd not known he could demonstrate. For she knew, that even though he possessed it, something within him prevented him from willingly showing such delicacy and care to another.

Until now.

'We don't... You don't have to do this,' he whispered, taking her other hand in his. 'As you said, you don't owe me anything.'

'I know,' she said, a small reassuring smile on her lips.

She willed him to see the rest in her eyes, all the words she could not say.

I want to believe, feel that we are real.

I want to be with you.

I want to share a life with you, as our vows promised.

And perhaps he did see, for when he pulled her closer, and set her hands on his hips, and set his own on her waist, and cradling her neck; when he kissed her, it was not like before. It was not a kiss of simple passion, and heat, and desire, but a reverent thing of unimaginable beauty. Of that same tenderness she'd never thought he could show but was now pouring out of him, with every move, every caress, every brush of his lips against her, or slide of his fingers against her skin.

It caught her off guard and stole her breath; stole her heart, though she could not yet admit it to herself even as she felt it, spring from her chest into his hands, for him to keep. He swallowed the moan she hummed then, and his grip tightened, and where yesterday she had clung tight to him, to everything, tonight, she let herself melt away into him. She opened to him, and his tongue swept in, dancing with hers, offering all he had, all he was. She felt him, not taking, but giving, and how drugging, how grateful she was, how softly she welcomed it, all of it, and all of him.

Entranced, she didn't realize what his hands were doing, they seemed to be everywhere at once, warming her, every nerve, ever muscle, every inch, until she felt a puddle of wax, malleable, and yet alight still; that is until she felt a rush of cool air against her back. Her dress was unlaced and swept off with a light brush of his hands, and as he broke the kiss to lavish affection across her cheeks, and her jaw, and her neck, and then her collarbone, so went her stays and chemise.

Lower still he went, his mouth and hands discovering her, bringing her to life, slowly, with incandescent vibrance. He latched onto her nipple, and she felt herself arch back, one of his hands on her ribs, the other on her back, holding her, keeping her from tumbling away, though she was tumbling into him.

Her own hand rose to his hair and raked through it, tugging it gently, and she looked down at him as he travelled from one breast to the other, a ravenous glint in his eye along with intent. An intent to please, to take it slow, to give back all he'd taken without offering before. And by God she would let him, she thought, letting her head fall back as he kissed and licked, and teased and tempted every bit of her he could find, igniting a hunger, a thirst she'd not felt before.

Down he roved, further, trailing kisses across her belly and hips as she cradled his head, and then her petticoats and shoes and stockings were gone, a pool on the floor, and she was in his arms, and he was holding her as a husband would his wife, and taking her to bed.

He lay her down as if she were a precious thing made of glass, and then stood there and looked at her, his eyes drinking in everything she was. She did not feel exposed or vulnerable, but wanted, and free, and more beautiful than she ever had. She drank him in too, the sharp lines of him in the flickering firelight as he divested himself of his wedding suit, as unashamed of himself now, as open to her gaze as she was to his.

He stepped forward again, but instead of joining her, of coming to lay with her where he belonged, *always*, he knelt by the bed, and carefully took hold of her legs, turning her until she was spread before him, her innermost self there, glistening and ready for him, begging for him.

How can something so wondrous and beautiful be sin, she wondered, as he latched onto her core as he had to her breasts, his hands kneading and stroking her thighs, and her calves, and her hips, and belly. As his mouth explored her sex, his lips and tongue seeking and finding parts of herself she'd never known existed; parts she'd never known could bring such exquisite pleasure and torture. There had been stirrings, a heat she'd felt, but nothing like this. Nothing like the mindless wonder of his flesh against hers, teasing it, worrying it, lavishing it with exquisitely excruciating strokes until she was lost to a world of stars and bonelessness.

Still, there was more to be discovered, and he took her there, with a restrained need and hunger that matched her own, only hers was unrestrained, and there was something, beyond the stars and the moon, beyond the room, and she cried out when she found it. His strokes slowed, but continued, and she floated back down, only to find him waiting for her.

He smiled, a strangely grateful smile, before he finally came to lay with her, above her, a shield from all else but himself. She reached up and touched his cheek, and smiled back, before rising to kiss him. It was not only what she now knew as him she tasted, but what must be herself, and the heat, the need was back, stronger, only now the destination they reached together would be sweeter. For they would be together, and today there would not even be a hint of pain to break their journey, there would only be the tortuous pleasure they could bring each other.

Tortuous, for like all else good, it had an end.

Will took her face in his hands again, his weight mostly on his arms, but also against her, and she guided him to where he needed to be, where she needed him, *always*, and wound her legs around him. He looked down at her with such wonder and reverence, as if he neither, could believe what they had found, and thrust within her. Long, slow, delicious, careful strokes, that seemed to tell her something.

His entire body, every breath, every heartbeat, which she could feel against her skin, seemed to tell her something in a language all knew but none could speak with words. The heat, the slick, dizzying passion between them grew as he took her, body, mind, and soul, to that place beyond reality again.

As they went together, to the stars, and further yet.

As they came, together, crested that unholiest of peaks that was no sin; but a miracle.

As they returned to the world, together, no longer two souls, but one.

∞

When Will had been with women before, it had been to chase away anger, to dispel the haze of bloodlust, or just lust, to forget... Everything. Even yesterday, with Angelique, though that had been so different from anything he'd felt, or needed, or taken before, it had been nothing as inexplicable as the evening they had just shared. He had wanted her, and he had wanted to make up for what he'd taken yesterday without giving anything in return. He had wanted to give her pleasure, to give her an experience that might make the sordidness of her loss of innocence... Less.

Only, somewhere along the way, he had found something else entirely.

Hell, from that first kiss. He'd found something within himself to give, full stop. He had found a tenderness that she had shown him, and that had made him recoil, but that somehow today, he remembered. He had found a joint experience, of giving, and taking, of not just simple pleasure, but of something words could not explain.

A connection, the forging, melding of something more than bodies. It had terrified him, but looking into Angelique's eyes, feeling her beneath him, surrounding him, it had pushed away the terror, and the craving for more had grown.

Not only to see her come undone, in that pure, unfettered and delicate way she did, but to go with her. To enjoy it, all of it, whilst it lasted. He had never craved anything so much as that; so much as simply *being* with her. She was another man's opium to him; an addiction he feared he would never tire of. Never cease to crave.

Though you will need to find a way.

Tomorrow...

Right now, he would enjoy the feel of her, as she lay over him, their chests rising and falling in time, the unbearable softness of her yet again surrounding him, the silk of her golden hair shining in the firelight like a strange halo.

My angel of light.

'How did you get out of that place,' Angelique whispered, her fingers tracing the stars across his breast.

The question stole him from his daze, and yet, not entirely, as it once might've.

She was still here.

He was still here.

They were here, together, and she would remain even if he answered.

'Another boy,' he said, admitting truths he had sworn to bury, and yet, that he could not keep from her.

He needed her to understand it all.

Him, most of all. No matter the consequences, no matter what might shine in her eyes. In the end, when all went to the Devil, at the very least she would have two things.

Memories, and the truth.

'I was not quite... As strong as I am now,' he said with a faint smile, which grew as he spotted Angelique's own when she turned to look up at him, her chin resting on his chest. 'I was rather a runt of the litter you could say. I might've died one day, from a beating others bestowed on me,' he breathed, holding tighter onto Angelique, to remind himself, he was not there again. Just as her own demons haunted her, so did his. But it seemed, when they were close, like this, nothing could tear them away from the present entirely. 'He was a sly, spry thing. He saved my life, that day, and many after that. We made it through together.'

'Where is he now?'

'Living his life, as I do,' he said, and Angelique nodded.

'So after you left that place, what did you do?'

'When I was free, I wandered for a while,' he told her, those first days, the freedom, and hopelessness still fresh in his breast, though not overpowering as they'd once been. 'And then, a man found me. He saw what I could do, saw what talents I possessed, and put them to use.'

'Do you regret that path,' she asked quietly.

'No,' he said without hesitation. 'It gave me purpose. If that man had not found me, I might be long dead. Or worse.'

Angelique slid her hand around his waist and held him tight.

A man could certainly lose his wits, his reason, his soul, to moments like this.

'Can I tell you a secret,' she asked quietly after a long moment.

'You can tell me anything.'

'I am glad he found you,' she whispered. 'For you found me.'

'Angelique...'

'Will, I mean it,' she said, raising herself again so she could see him. 'Did you never wonder, why I did not rid myself of you, as I had all of Percy's little spies before you?'

He raised a brow; that, he certainly had.

Though he had been grateful too, that she hadn't tried. She'd made his life difficult enough as it was simply being herself, what would it have been had she tried to rid herself of him as she had the countless others the earl had sent to her before finally finding him?

Little gremlin.

'That first day, when I saw you in the foyer... The fear, it melted away. For the briefest moment, I wasn't afraid anymore.'

You should've been.

You should be.

121

But whatever protests he might've spoken to save his soul, died on his lips.

Instead, he pulled her up closer, and kissed her, with all he could finally feel.

XV.

P acking had never felt so... Solemn. So final, and heart wrenching. Granted, she'd never done any packing before, not even the night she'd left London. Lily had packed a bag for her, just as maids and servants had packed for her in all these years before then. But even then... The magnitude of the moment, of what she was doing, it hadn't seemed like an ending, rather a beginning.

Every time her bags had been packed for her over the years, it had been to make a journey, to this aunt or that, this acquaintance or that. It had been to go somewhere new, potentially exciting. It hadn't been about leaving something behind; and if it had, it was something she could live without.

This time it wasn't.

This time, she was leaving something she feared she would miss, regret, her whole life long, even though that hadn't been part of the deal. It wasn't supposed to be part of the deal. She had done away with romantic notions long ago, if she'd ever truly had them. So why did it feel as though this was true heartbreak?

Leaving her mother, and Percy, his grandmother, and Meg, her family, even Lily, it hurt, but her heart did not ache as it did now. Which made absolutely no sense, because they were her family, and her friends, not a man she'd grown close to, who had been *assigned* to her protection, whom she'd married to be free.

Whom you married because you wanted to.

No.

Yes.

Partly.

Still, her love for him shouldn't be worth any more than the love she felt for the others.

Because yes, try as she might, after last night, there was no denying that what she felt was in fact love. She might've suspected it before, might've felt it before, might've known that the bond between them would change everything, but she had pushed away those suspicions, because nothing could come of it. She'd pushed them away just as she had last night as she lay in his arms, and all this morning, since before dawn.

Because they had made a deal, and the time had come. She was leaving.

Percy had not come in time, so she would go, and be free, only not of Will.

'Drat,' she muttered, tossing a pair of kid gloves into the carpet bag angrily.

There really was no use trying to make sense of it.

She was leaving, and no matter that it hurt, that it felt as if the bright future she'd pictured for herself was now dim in comparison to what she might've had with Will as her husband in truth. No matter that it made her want to ask him to come with her. To run, and start anew.

No matter that it made her want to stay and face whatever chased her, and -

A knock on the main door of her room tore her from her useless meanderings of the mind, and she went over to open it, hoping it was one of the maids with the extra ink and paper she'd requested. She'd not leave Will alone to face Percy without at least a letter to calm him down. And she couldn't have him thinking they could come chasing after her again to all -

Angelique froze when she glimpsed the man in the corridor, her hand clenching the brass handle until it bruised her palm. She couldn't breathe, her chest was too tight, and refused to expand just as her feet refused to move. Her heart beat manically against her ribs, and fire and ice mingled in her veins. Faces, the echoes of distant screams, and the image of the eyes assailed her all at once, paralysing her.

No. No, no, no, no, it cannot be.

Laramie.

Yet there he stood, as Percy had once said, in all his surly glory, like a ruddy, angry Viking clad in dusty silk and wool, with those dark eyes, and that sickening, cruel grin.

Run.

Everything within her seemed to come alive again and she threw the door closed, throwing herself against it, but it was no use. His foot came up against it hard, knocking it open, and her back before she could latch and lock it.

What little breath she had was out of her as she went flying backwards, landing on the floor with a dull thud.

'Will,' she screamed, scrambling back across the floor towards his room, her feet catching in her skirts and impeding her progress. God, if only she could think, and move... 'Will!'

Laramie continued his advance, and shaking, she fumbled for the penknife at her ankle.

She managed to grasp it, and thrust it out towards him. The only effect it had however, was to widen the maniacal grin on his face, and kindle the flames in his eyes.

'Stay back or I'll -'

In a flash, her wrist was trapped in an iron grip, and her arm was twisted behind her back as she was lifted effortlessly to her feet.

The blade dropped to the floor with a shuddering thud, and she froze again at the realization of what had just happened. Not in panic, but in despair, as the truth burned through the impossibility of it. She felt ill, and confused, and angry, and above all, she did not understand.

For it had not been Laramie who had disarmed her.

Not Laramie who held her tight against him, but Will.

'I'm sorry,' he whispered in her ear.

And if one could die of a broken heart, she might've, right

then and there.

It's over. I am lost.

∞

'I don't understand,' Angelique said meekly. It hurt, he'd known it would, when the moment came. When he betrayed her, and she realized it, but now that it had, it was far worse than he ever could've imagined. It felt as if a demon had risen from the Pit to claw open his chest, to pull free the ribs and eviscerate him. He wanted to scream, wanted to renege every promise he'd ever made, or really, only one. He wanted to run, far far away, and never look back, but he couldn't. All he could do, was stand there and stare at his brother. 'Will, say something, please,' she cried, shaking now, the pain in her voice paramount to a blow. 'For the love of God say something!'

'You took your time,' he spat at Richard, who sneered, and went over to what had been her armchair, making himself cosy indeed.

His brother couldn't see, couldn't know what he'd become.

What he *felt*.

Or he wouldn't be able to protect her.

'I was stranded in Gloucestershire for three days after a carriage accident,' his brother drawled. 'But I'm fine, thank you for your concern.'

'All along,' Angelique said slowly, the pieces, the magnitude of what he'd done slowly sinking in. *And you haven't heard it all yet...* 'Percy isn't coming.'

'No,' Richard grinned, crossing his legs, and setting his interlocked hands on his knees. 'Egerton isn't coming. Now, sit,' he said, waving at the other chair. 'We have some matters to discuss.'

'I don't know what you think you're doing, but whatever it is -'

'I know you don't,' Richard sighed. 'That is precisely what we will discuss.'

'If you think -'

'Sit her down,' he exclaimed, and Will flinched, making no move to obey.

'Control yourself, Richard.'

Taken aback, his brother examined them both closely, his expression moving from shock, to rage.

Something, in Angelique's face or his own, betrayed them.

'Do not tell me you have ruined this,' he hissed.

'Richard -'

'What did you do,' he screamed, rising to his feet.

Instinctively, Angelique fell back against him, reminding him of her presence, of his vows, and his promise to her.

Protect her.

'Sit down, Richard,' Will growled. 'Angelique will do so as well, and we shall all have a civilised talk, and resolve this.'

Civilised indeed.

'Like Hell I will,' Angelique hissed, squirming against him again, her fire returned as his brother at least settled.

'Angelique,' Will said, turning her sharply in his arms. The look of utter disgust on her face stole his breath, but he forced himself to remain steadfast. Emotions it seemed, once so easily controlled, were becoming less and less so with every moment around her. But if he was to keep the silent promise he'd made to her, he had to manage this situation. 'You will sit, and you will listen, or I will be forced to make you do so. Scream, I will gag you. Run, and I will bind you. You have skills, but you are outmatched with both of us.'

She looked at him as though she didn't know him, or perhaps, as if only now she could see him for what he truly was.

Shaking her head, he saw her push back the pain, push back the tears, and nod.

Releasing her slowly, he remained ready for her if she tried anything, but she was too clever to do so. Instead, he saw the Miss Fitzsimmons of society return. Saw her back straighten, and her chin rise, as she turned and walked to the chair as Queen Bess herself might, though her eyes... Her eyes were glazed, and distant.

I am sorry.

'Say your peace then,' she ordered as she sat on the edge of the seat, her hands in her lap, the tin band on her finger a shining beacon of his failures. 'And let us be done with whatever this is.'

'Tally-ho, Miss Fitzsimmons,' Richard grinned, as if they were all just good friends about to have a party. 'Brother, I think we could all use a drink.'

Party indeed.

Will nodded, and went to fetch a bottle of gin from his bag, along with some cups.

By the time he returned, and served them all a good measure of it, settling himself on a stool between them both, and between Angelique and the door, any surprise she might've shown at the revelation of what he and Richard were to each other, was gone. Not that the simple word could ever explain what they were; what meant Richard forever had his loyalty above all else.

Above all others.

'So, shall we begin,' Richard asked.

Let's. So we may finally see the end of this sordid escapade.

XVI.

rother, Angelique thought desperately, her mind whirling with all that had happened in the past five minutes. How her entire world had been not only turned upside down, but torn apart, as if the hounds of Hell had bounded from the fiery depths and destroyed all in their wake. Everything had been a lie. Everything he'd ever said, and to think, she'd believed him the only one to see her, to understand her. She'd believed to have seen him; but the secrets this statue kept were beyond her imaginings. He'd been the only one she'd felt truly safe with, and in the end, he'd been the one to betray her. To *Laramie.*

And all for what? They were brothers, apparently, but why did Laramie even want her? This was all some scheme, but to what end? If she understood, at least she might stand a chance, be able to find a way out of this.

What's the point, a part of her screamed.

She was trapped. Perhaps not by *the* demon, but by a demon. The man she had fallen in love with, idiot that she was, had betrayed her. All her dreams vanished like morning mists. She had run away, fought for weeks to make her choice, and in the end, it was all being stripped away from her. What was the point really, of living? What was there to live for now?

Yourself. You are stronger than this.

Yes, she was. Stronger than heartbreak, stronger than these men so like any others she had met who sought to use her, or control her, or whatever it was they wanted. Breathing deeply, she forced herself to find reason, and logic, and meaning; forced herself to put together the pieces when all she wanted was to succumb to the nothingness that beckoned her.

She was drowsy, and her body felt heavy, and yet on fire, and shaky all at once. She felt nauseous, and as if she could cry for a lifetime, and terrified, but also, so angry. For being so easily fooled, and betrayed, and useless. For not having taken them both down, and run, and gotten herself out of this. But she would. She would not just *give up*. She couldn't.

Never a caged bird.

No matter that Laramie had power and money. She wasn't actually afraid of him, of what he would or could do to her. Strangely enough. She should be, he held her life in his hands, she knew that, but somehow, though she had been scared because of him, she wasn't afraid of him now. As if, with his appearance, some of his threat had diminished, even as its reality grew.

No matter that Will owned her as her husband. Owned, despite herself, her heart. She could do what she had to, just as he apparently had.

No matter that no one would help her.

She would fight. And be smart about it. Be as emotionless about this entire situation as Will apparently could, and hide herself away as she had for years behind the cold mask.

And then she would strike.

Those last vestiges of reason those were all she had to keep her sane, and safe, and to keep the panic from paralysing her again.

'Why are you here,' she asked with a frown, the burn of the gin Will had thrust in her hand somehow helping to clear the mire of her thoughts, not to mention calm the rush of terror and pain in her heart.

Though she knew, it would never, ever go away entirely now.

'Excellent question,' Laramie said, raising his glass with a sickening grin.

She met his eyes for a moment, then returned to looking at a freckle above his eyebrow.

Every time she looked in his eyes... Though she didn't fear him, the rest... It all became a little too much to handle right then.

The feelings his gaze had always made rise, were still there, and she needed to focus best she could.

'I'm here for you. You and I are to be wed.'

Angelique couldn't help but laugh.

Well, snort. Then, it transformed into a hearty, hysterical laugh, which helped expend some of the pain. Laramie eyed her curiously, and Will sat a little straighter, and the insanity of it, the irony of it all, along with that image, sent her into another minute-long fit.

Finally, wiping away tears of laughter and despair, evening out her breath, she shook her head, and smiled.

'You are a bit late for that,' she said flatly. Laramie's brows shot together, and he quirked his head questioningly. 'I'm already wed. Yesterday, as it happens. We neglected to invite you I'm afraid.'

Because she couldn't resist, she raised her hand, flashing her wedding band at him.

Even now this band of tin holds power. Not only for my husband, but for me.

Laramie's eyes shot to Will, who squirmed in his seat, and chuckling again, Angelique helped herself to some more gin. There were times to keep a clear head, and time for liquid courage.

At least it seems they are not so united a front after all.

'What did you do,' Laramie growled.

'I salvaged a desperate situation,' Will said with more assurance than she knew he felt. *And you are not so emotionless after all.* Despite it all, apparently she could still read him. Well, enough. 'She was going to run, and she was terrified of you. It never would've worked.'

'Then you stop her,' Laramie exclaimed, rising, and pacing, the ends of his travel-worn greatcoat whipping with each turn.

'You hold her until I arrive. The courting period was long over, we knew that already!'

Is that what he'd been trying to do with intent stares that made her stomach roil, and touches that made her want to tear her skin off? Courting her?

Who knew.

Regardless, she knew slightly more now. He'd been after her hand, and was willing to go to great lengths to get it. He had positioned Will to watch over her, presumably to ensure any other suitors were chased away, and that he knew everything of her movements and appointments, and...

Wait, did he go after Percy?

'This can still work,' Will was saying, his voice pleading. Laramie stopped, leaning against the mantel and heaving a sigh as he dropped his head into his hands. 'Perhaps it's better this way. Surely this is more effective revenge, having her marry a nobody like me -'

'My father wanted it to be me,' Laramie exclaimed, turning back on Will.

Revenge? His father? Reynold Fulton, Earl of Oster?

Had his father chosen her to raise his son's standing? Laramie was a bastard after all, at least in society's eyes, though he had technically been legitimised before this Season with some cock-and-bull story about youthful mistakes, and lost marriage certificates that magically reappeared. His father had done everything to ensure he could inherit, and was acceptable in the highest echelons of society, but still, everyone knew the truth. Laramie was a bastard; in every sense of the word. He remained Richard *Laramie* to everyone; not Richard *Fulton*.

As for her, her dowry was sizeable, and her lineage excellent, but why her? There were a couple duke and marquesses' daughters on the Marriage Mart, far better prospects than her. She knew nothing of the earl other than that he was a man of power, and fortune, and influence. She'd only ever really heard of him, and glimpsed him across crowded ballrooms perhaps once or twice. He ran in circles far above her, and her family's own, so what would he want to do with her? Even with the talk, and sneers, his bastard who was no longer a bastard would have good prospects, without needing to trap her.

Christ she was lost now.

'What the bloody Hell is going on,' Angelique finally shouted, rising to her feet. It was enough to bring the men back to the room, and remind them of her presence. They froze, and stared at her, and at that moment, she felt... *Less powerless.* 'What in the Devil's name does your *father* want with me? What is this really about?'

'Tell her,' Will said gravely after a long moment of silence, when she might've sworn she saw a flash of pain in Laramie's dark eyes. It softened him, ever so much, just enough to chase some of her discomfort of him away. 'She deserves to know.'

Laramie turned his fierce gaze on Will, and the two fought a silent battle before finally the former relented, shaking his head and falling into the armchair with the air of a defeated man.

I am not powerless.

By the time Will and Angelique had both settled back in their own seats, Laramie's weakness was gone however, and the cruel, cold mask had returned.

'Will is right,' Laramie said, death in his voice. 'You deserve to know who has brought this all upon you.'

∞

Letting out the breath he'd been holding for perhaps a year, Will leaned back, downing his drink, before going for another. The urge to lose himself in liquor had never been so strong as it was now; the sweet oblivion it offered so tempting he nearly downed the bottle rather than simply pour another measure. He didn't, his control somewhat returned. His heart, beating once again, though never again as it had....

Never again.

At least now, she would understand. She would understand

133

why it had to be this way, why it could be no other. Perhaps, it would make what was about to happen more palatable, less of the death sentence he knew it was. It would make his betrayal... Less. It was all he could offer, and he had tried to make Richard understand that. Make him understand that perhaps, it might just win them a little compliance. Though he knew, Angelique would never stop fighting.

She wouldn't be herself if she did; she was the most courageous person he knew.

'Your father, killed my mother,' Richard said, emotionless, as always. Though he knew his brother's pain was as fresh as the day it had been caused; as was his own. 'And left me to rot in what some would call an orphanage, but which Will and I both know to have been Gehenna. You don't believe me,' he sneered, spotting the same doubt and confusion on Angelique's face as Will did. 'But I assure you, it is the truth.'

'Even if it was,' Angelique said evenly, surprising him again with her strength. He knew how she felt about his brother, for whatever reason, and yet here she was, sitting across from him, demanding answers. 'I still don't understand. Why would you want to marry me? Why not just kill me, as you tried to kill Percy?'

'I didn't try to kill Egerton,' Richard said, almost offended. 'And as for killing you... Too easy. Your father does not deserve easy. He deserves to watch you suffer, all your life. To know what his own sins, wrought upon you, his perfect little daughter.'

'And your own father,' Angelique said after a moment. 'He told you to do this?'

'He told me what yours did to my mother,' Richard spat. 'How he used her, until my father saved her. And loved her. How your father took her again,' he seethed, his emotions coming forth in his voice for the first time in a very long while. 'And me. How he slit her throat and threw her in a ditch, and left me in that place!'

Angelique flinched, and Richard took a deep breath and sat back, as surprised by his own outburst as her.

'But why,' she asked feebly, shaking her head. 'Why would he do that?'

'Because to him she was property,' Will said before Richard could.

His brother needed a moment, and Angelique, well, she might be more receptive if this devastating truth came from him.

She turned to face him, her eyes like ice. All the warmth that had seeped from her every pore, into him, was gone. Denied to him, forever. But she had to understand.

It was all either of them had now.

'Your father, is in charge of a certain circle. A repugnant, despicable circle which provides men of wealth and such acquired tastes with the means to satisfy their twisted lusts. Amongst other things.' Will paused, giving her a moment to make sense of his words. For all he knew, all he could say of what Richard, Fulton, and he had uncovered, he couldn't find it in himself to paint a more vivid picture. 'You know it's true,' he said softly. 'Your dream,' he added, and he saw the terrible dawning in her eyes. The same dawning he'd had when she had told him of it. 'It was of a certain type of party. The things you must have seen...'

Angelique's eyes widened as her mind revived the images, and she looked to him pleadingly, begging him to make it not so.

And God, how he wished he could. That he could cry that it was a ruse, that yet again he'd betrayed her, only he couldn't. It was the truth, and now, she knew.

I am sorry.

∞

It couldn't be true, and yet, in her heart, she knew it had to be. However much she wanted to laugh at them, to mock their spurious and demented claims, she could not. She could not refute the charges, for they made far too much sense, even through the haze of despair, and incredulity. From what little she remembered, her father had always been... Cold. Distant.

Haunted. He had removed himself from her life, and her mother's, nearly fourteen years ago. Around the same time she must've stumbled upon that... *Party.*

She shuddered, knowing that Will and Laramie were right.

Whatever she'd seen that night... Had been far beyond what anyone could imagine, let alone a child. Terrible, terrible things, not enacted by demons, but by men with black hearts, in her own family home. A home, her mother and her had been exiled from, sent to London to live their own separate lives. Her father's absence had seemed odd, but wasn't unusual. How many husbands in society lived apart from their wives? Though typically the men took to town, and the women to the country.

But hearing this... It all made too much sense.

Still, there was something, that didn't quite fit.

Not that she could put her finger on it, she felt as if she had been thrown from a cliff into the churning sea, and spat back onto shore like a piece of driftwood. Memories, fears, the men's words, all she had felt for Will, all she felt now, her hopes and dreams, they were all jumbled together, knotted together in a giant knot she couldn't untangle.

One thread however, she could see, and pull free.

'I am sorry,' she said softly, addressing herself to Laramie, ignoring the urge to throw herself into Will's embrace and shut out the rest. 'For what happened to your mother, and to you. I understand how that would drive you to the lengths it has. But you are sorely mistaken if you believe this scheme of yours, will succeed.'

Laramie's eyes narrowed, and that sick smile reappeared.

'It already has,' he chuckled. 'Perhaps not as we may have wished, but you are wed to Will now. Bound to him, in matrimony. And no matter what you believe, if you think that he truly felt something for you, you're wrong. The ability to feel, was driven from us, in that place we forged our own bonds. He can still deliver a lifetime of suffering for you.'

He already has.

'No, he can't,' she said simply. *Brothers of bond. The boy who saved him...* Later. Later she would examine that. Now, now was the time for blind courage. For unbreakable strength. For what little fight she had left in her today. 'We are wed, yes, but that can be undone. In time. And you can bind me, force me to come with you, but the truth is, you cannot force me to stay. Do you truly think that Percy will let this happen?' Laramie's jaw twitched, and he knew it was the truth. 'No matter your power, or that of your family, he will always find me. He will find me, and even if what I have done cannot be undone, he will find a way to send me somewhere far out of your reach.'

I am not alone, nor shall I ever be.

Not until that moment, had she realized, or been willing to acknowledge, how lucky she was. In her friends, if not, apparently, in her family. Even if she lost, if she could no longer fight, others would fight for her. Others would protect her. Help her.

As I had thought you would, Will.

'We shall see,' Laramie sneered, though she knew she had struck a nerve. 'You forget, we have power, and leverage. On you, on him. You care for people. That is a mistake.'

'You underestimate him,' she smiled.

He may know Percy, but he did not know the Ghost of Shadwell.

And he did not know her. Years she had trained, years she had spent searching for herself, and her strength. And though she may feel lost at sea, weary of mind, and heart, and body, as if her soul was leaving her slowly, she would survive. Because she *did* know herself. She was strong, and smart, and she would not bow, or cower, and by God she had lived with fear her entire life. They were old friends, it and her.

Draw strength from the fear. It drives us.

'And you underestimate me.'

'Pack your bags,' Laramie instructed Will after a moment. 'And hers. The carriage should be ready now.'

There was doubt in his eyes, and that was all she needed.

Whatever came next, might be the most difficult part of her

life, but she would survive it. She would never give up, and one day soon, she would be free.

Nevermore a caged bird.

XVII.

They had been on the road for three days now, making
good time as they sped south towards Herefordshire,
where they would meet with Richard's father to discuss
the future. Whatever that was to be. Something grim, and
terrible, and bloody. Something that would destroy Angelique,
and him more so than he already was; which he never would
have thought possible.

They stopped only to change horses and gather provisions,
or to relieve themselves, but otherwise not even to sleep. He
and Renfeld, Richard's other trusted right-hand man and driver,
another rescue from their childhood *home*, took turns resting
in the carriage with Angelique and Richard, determined as they
were to ensure they made their plans before anyone could
intervene.

Though Will's updates had kept Egerton in London, it would
not be long before the man grew restless and decided to go on
the hunt himself, particularly once he stopped receiving news,
or received Angelique's letter. They would have to be prepared
for when he came, for Will knew that Angelique had been right.
The earl would never stop chasing her, and them, and he would
never let them win.

Unless we ensure it.

He didn't like the alternatives that presented themselves in
order to do that, but they had come so far, and were so close to

achieving all they had set out to. What was another life ruined, really, in the grand scheme of things? They had already broken so many others.

They had broken Angelique.

She had not spoken a word since they'd left Oban. She forced herself to drink, and eat, walked when they stopped, but that was all. Otherwise she sat in the carriage, staring out of the window bleakley, pale, and forlorn. She had not tried to run, get help, or leave messages. He knew a fire still raged inside her, that she would fight whatever future they prescribed her with everything she was and had. He saw it in the flaming emerald of her eyes when he glimpsed them.

But she was different; broken, defeated, and if he hadn't known better, he might've thought heartbroken. Only he knew better than to think that even as he had been with her, no one could ever love him to that extent. If she was heartbroken, it was because her dreams had been snatched from her. Because her entire life, everything she knew, had been torn from her.

It had all been his doing, and he wished that she would scream at him, that she would strike him, unleash her rage upon him fully; indeed he'd expected it once the initial shock of his betrayal had passed, only she hadn't. Everything she'd ever feared, he had brought upon her, and he had pushed her beyond the point of raging, into desperate sorrow, and grief.

It was the sin for which he would gladly serve his sentence in Hell.

He longed to make it right again, to comfort her, to relight the brilliant fire that had shone within the darkest places of his soul, but that could never happen again. All he could do from now on, was what he'd always done.

Watch, and protect.

'Whoa,' Renfeld cried outside, drawing his and Richard's attention.

The carriage reeled to a sharp stop, and they both glanced out of the windows.

Nothing.

They were in the middle of the road, in the middle of the country, and there was no reason to be stopping. It hadn't even been a couple hours since dawn, since they'd left the last posting inn with new horses.

'Stay here,' Will told Richard, who was already arming himself.

He glanced out of the window, saw only flat, grey horizon, then climbed out of the carriage, pistol in hand, and moved carefully and quietly to the front to see what had happened.

The ominously loud click of a pistol by his own ear was his answer.

∞

Be it an overturned cart, an insurmountable hole in the road, a gang of highwaymen, or even a pack of wolves, it mattered not. Everything within her had shut down completely. She couldn't find it within herself to care; about anything. Since Will's betrayal, and their departure, a numbness, a sense of disconnect from everything and everyone, had overcome her. Even the fear, her constant companion, was gone.

Whether it was shock, or exhaustion, it mattered not. In time, she would fight. Fight the currents sweeping her away into another life, sweeping away her freedom and sense of self, but for now, she would drift upon them, and let be.

For now, she would enjoy the strange sort of quietude and peace she'd found, from fear, from the heartbreak of Will's betrayal, from her own racing mind. A moment of silence in the midst of the coming storm, when she had to do no more than move and eat and sleep when told. Just as she had for all those years.

Perhaps this shall be my entire life - a waking dream of it.

Waking death; the fate she'd always feared and which she now welcomed with open arms for the respite it afforded her mind, and her heart.

At least, until she heard the gunshot.

She and Laramie both sat up straighter in the squabs; the same thought she suspected running through both their heads despite their differences.

Please God don't let it be Will who was hit.

Fear coursed through her again, though it was a different fear. It was pure fire; clawing at her veins like demons. It was not fear for herself, but fear for another. It was spurring, and reviving. No matter what Will had done to her, if he was killed...

No.

She turned to Laramie who put a finger to his lips and she nodded. They both strained to hear what was happening outside.

Voices, shouts, the sounds of men struggling and nervous horses.

'Stay here,' Laramie whispered, before quietly slipping out of the carriage.

More shouts.

Another two shots of gunfire.

Well, if this is how I die, so be it, Angelique thought as she set her jaw, and launched herself out of the carriage. It may not be *the* time to fight, but it was a time. She would not sit prettily in the carriage and wait again for fate to meet her.

She hit the ground with a quiet thud, and whirled around towards the front of the carriage, as ready as she would ever be to face a band of highwaymen or similar miscreants on her own, with no weapons but her hands and wits.

Only, the sight before her was the last she'd ever have expected.

Percy? Harcourt? Effy? It can't be...

XVIII.

And yet, it was. There was Percy, and Harcourt Sinclair, the dark devil of a rake who'd wreaked havoc on London four years before with Effy. Effy Fortescue, who was here too, dressed in men's clothing, her bright red hair shining even now in the grey light, looking as fierce and fearsome as ever. Her friends. They'd all come, for her. To save her, as she'd known they would.

Though no one, not them, not Laramie, nor Will noticed her, so caught up in the chaos of their own making they were. She stood there, stunned for a moment by the arrival of her friends, dazed by the sense of relief that washed over her; though it did not quash the fear now growing again inside, clawing at her veins. Someone, likely someone she cared about considering all but Laramie fit that bill, would be maimed, or worse, within moments. Already, they looked worse for wear.

The driver was unconscious at the edge of the road, worryingly close to the watery ditch. Laramie was currently fending off both Percy and Effy, the latter coming at him with a nasty looking blade, which by the looks of it had already taken a bit of his arm, and cheek. Will was busy with Harcourt, they were wrestling and punching themselves more than bloody in the dirt, far too close to the nervous and prancing horses.

She rushed towards the fray, and finally someone noticed her.

'Angelique,' Percy screamed, narrowly avoiding a right hook

from Laramie. 'Stay back! Get away! Effy, go to her!'

'Stop this,' Angelique screamed. 'Stop this madness, please, all of you!'

No more death, no more blood, please.

They all ignored her, though Effy did try to do as Percy had instructed, only to be waylaid by Laramie's arm around her neck, and a quick catch of her knife aimed at his head.

A brutal grunt and thud caught her attention, and she turned back to find Will and Harcourt both scrambling to their feet, Harcourt grasping a pistol from the ground, and raising it. Will backed away as Harcourt aimed it square at his chest, and before she could even think of what she was doing, Angelique threw herself in front of him.

Not that shielding his body with her own would do much good if Harcourt really wished to take a shot; there was plenty of Will's body left to aim at.

'No,' she screamed. 'Please, stop,' she begged, her voice cracking.

Harcourt cursed, straining with all the tension it took to avoid shooting her by accident.

She sucked in a ragged breath as he raised the pistol in the air, then dropped it back by his side. He deflated suddenly, his own breathing less than steady, and wiped a trickle of blood from his mouth.

Thank God.

'Christ, Angelique,' he hissed, his scarred left eyebrow raising judgingly. 'I might've shot you! What the Hell were you thinking?'

Well, for one, she hadn't been thinking.

All she knew, was that despite everything, she couldn't watch Will die.

She couldn't watch any of them die, not even Laramie.

The girl she had been years ago, the spiteful chit who had thrown her friend to the wolves for retribution and a better chance in the Marriage Mart would have gleefully cheered on her captors' demise. Would've cried for bloody vengeance. But she wasn't that girl anymore; if she ever truly had been.

And vengeance, only seemed to be begetting more.

'Call them off,' she told Harcourt, glancing to where Percy and Effy were still viciously engaged with Laramie. They wouldn't listen to her, fine. They would listen to Harcourt. The man could likely march into Whitehall and have his bidding be done. 'Call them off!'

'Percy,' he shouted. 'Effy, enough!'

The others froze, and stared at her, mouth agape as they kept their fists around each other's necks and blades high in the air, a grotesque and violent picture for a brief moment.

'Enough,' she said, exhaustion and sorrow making her voice shaky. But she needed to keep her head; considering somehow she was now the only one left with a modicum of level-headedness. *Why do I have to always keep my wits, even when I am the one being saved from a kidnapping?* 'There has been enough blood, and revenge, and hatred, and anger. No more.'

'Angelique -'

'No more, Percy,' she said harshly, turning her gaze on him. 'I thank you, all, for coming to my aid. But this cannot be resolved thus. We are all going to drive up the road, and find a private room in a pub, and discuss this like civilised men.'

The plan, which she made as she spoke the words, seemed as good as any.

Civilized talks were going to be the things that changed her life it seemed; not great battles fought with swords and fists, but words.

As much as she might've dreamt for them to swoop down and save her, to save her from Laramie and his father, and even Will's grasp once not so long ago, now, she knew she had to have answers. She had to see this tale through, to understand what had happened all those years ago, and who her father truly was. And she never would, if they kept coming after each other, intent on murder.

She shot a pleading look to Effy, who nodded, dropped her blade and raised her hands. Laramie in turn released her from the punishing hold he'd had her in.

Percy was last, still coiled and ready to strike, death in his glare.

'Trust me, Percy, please,' she said. 'Give me this.'

Against his better judgement, against all she knew his body demanded, he nodded, and backed away from Laramie, arms raised.

'Harcourt rides in the carriage with you,' he growled.

'You and I will take the reins,' Laramie continued, eyeing the group with a mixture of disgust and calculation. 'Renfeld,' he asked the man, who was now coming to. 'Are you able to take the rear?' The driver nodded. 'Will can take a horse, and lead along the other two.'

'Agreed,' Effy said, before any of the men could argue.

'Thank you,' Will said quietly, as everyone began slowly getting ready to move.

'I didn't do it for you,' Angelique replied, harsher than she meant to, turning to face him. She forced herself not to flinch as her eyes flitted across his face and body, noting the cuts and bruises; the blood dripping from his nose and split lip. 'I did it for myself. I want no one's death on my conscience. And I want to be free, of all of this. I want it over. Once and for all.'

Her husband swallowed hard, and nodded.

She could see the hurt, the disappointment in him, and though she hated herself for thinking that way, she was glad. She was glad that in some small measure, he was perhaps feeling the pain she felt. What she had said was the truth; if not precisely all of it.

And deep down, she was glad, most of all, because in that moment she knew, that despite all that had been done to him, all that he and Laramie said to the contrary, all her own doubts, that he could feel.

Not that it did, or rather *could*, mean anything for her.

He may be her husband in name, but she knew he could never be in truth.

'How did you find me,' Angelique asked when the rattling of the carriage and whirling of her thoughts threatened to drive her mad, breaking the silence Harcourt Sinclair seemed more than happy to loom in. Then again, he had always seemed born of the shadows, a right handsome devil who would give Lucifer himself a run for his money.

He hadn't changed, some silver now peppered his dark hair, and though there were more lines on his face from what she'd seen, they seemed like lines of laughter. She'd known from Effy's letters that she had been happy these past four years, but seeing him now, she truly felt the joy their love had brought them both.

A twinge of envy tightened her heart a little further, a feat considering how twisted and knotted it was already.

'Did my note to Percy reach you in time,' she continued, and was graced with a pensive look. Harcourt's gaze raked her, as if he were cataloguing every inch. They'd never been close, not as she had been to Effy, which even then had begun under disguised circumstances. But as he examined her now, she felt he might notice all that had changed, even if she hadn't truly felt he'd noticed her at all before. 'And how is that you are here? Not that I'm ungrateful,' she added.

'We received no note,' he said in that low, menacing tone which had made men squirm, and maids, well, squirm. He turned his gaze to the whirring, darkening landscape out the window. 'After what happened last year to Percy, he's been increasingly concerned. His last letter was a rather desperate plea for us to return and so we did. Right on time, as luck would have it,' he grinned, turning back to her. 'We left a fortnight after you and that turncoat bodyguard of yours did. Pacing about drawing rooms and waiting for news is not exactly what any of us were built to do.' Angelique nodded. 'We tracked you much as I suspect your... That man did, and arrived in Oban not hours after you'd left.'

'Well, thank you,' she said quietly. 'For coming. Though I might've regretted it days ago, today, I am immensely grateful.'

'He was out of his mind you know,' Harcourt told her, and Angelique shrugged and turned to look out her own window.

'I surmised as much.'

'Why did you run, Angelique,' he asked, a softness in his voice that few likely knew could exist. 'If something troubled you, if you were afraid of something, you could have spoken to him. Even with all that was happening, with his father's death, you could have. You could have spoken to us.'

'Could I,' she asked with a wan smile, and she heard him sigh, conceding. 'You know how he is. He cannot bear to lose control. He would have tried to fix it, to fix me, and I... Just wanted to be left to my own life. As for you and Effy, you were so far away.'

'A note to Percy explaining at least that much might've been wise,' he quipped, raising that scarred brow again.

'Perhaps,' she admitted. She'd thought she was being so clever, so brave with how she had run; planning and reasoning through the fear. But now, she truly saw how severely she had been mistaken; about the others, and herself. 'I know how I went about things was wrong, but I just... It doesn't matter anymore,' she finished bitterly.

It didn't.

Whatever she had thought, and felt before, none of it mattered now.

'He will not be pleased when he realizes what you've done,' Harcourt said, tearing her from the landscape. She frowned, and he nodded at her gloved hand, under which was just visible the imprint of her wedding band. Damn the man for his perceptiveness. 'I'd not like to be that bodyguard when he finds out.'

Sadly, Harcourt was right.

She'd have to speak to Percy, make sure he didn't do anything rash.

The last thing she needed was to let loose the Ghost of

Shadwell on Will; though it was a fair bet either way on which man might survive that encounter. The last time he had lost his control, he'd nearly taken a man's life, and she knew that crossing that line was one thing which would destroy him. And if Percy had been enraged about this situation before, that was likely nothing to what he would be if he learned of her marriage.

Wedding. Not marriage.

Angelique nodded, and returned to look out the window, realizing as she did that Harcourt had never asked whether she had been coerced into the match. *What you've done*, he had said, proving that the man did see everything.

Better even than I see myself apparently.

For even now she realized, she couldn't regret what she had done.

Her choices, however miscalculated, were her own.

And she would live with them.

After all, that is all she had ever really wanted.

XIX.

Some two hours later, they finally slowed, and pulled into the courtyard of a simple, weatherbeaten, but large, well-frequented and welcoming inn. Then again, anything other than the blasted, cramped carriage might've seemed welcoming, if only because it offered more distractions from her thoughts. The dazed numbness she'd been in for days had worn off with all the adventure of that damned fight on the road, and Angelique was sorry of it. For it meant that she'd spent the past few hours thinking incessantly again, of all she'd done, and all she felt despite herself.

Of all she faced ahead, and all she'd left behind.

Promises of lost futures, and a joy she'd likely never find again in her lifetime.

And thinking on it will not bring it back.

Right now, you must bring these intemperate bullheaded fools together.

Harcourt opened the carriage door, descended, and offered a hand, pulling her from her thoughts.

She stepped out, glancing around at the somewhat busy courtyard, where other travellers were coming and going, stable hands and grooms and patrons hopping about their business, carefree. Glancing towards the entrance to the inn, she spotted Percy, closely trailed by Laramie, Effy, and Will.

No better time than now...

'Percy,' she cried, stopping him before he could disappear inside. He turned, and raised a brow inquiringly. The look of pure rage in his eyes told her that no matter how much she wished to avoid him, some things needed to be said immediately. 'A word, please.'

'I'll make arrangements,' Effy said, gesturing for Harcourt to follow.

Angelique kept her eyes on Percy as he advanced, and Harcourt passed her by.

She saw Will hesitate out of the corner of her eye, before Laramie grabbed hold of his shoulder and ushered him in with the rest.

'Are you ready to tell me what the Hell you were thinking,' Percy exclaimed as soon as they were alone, well save for the curious stablehands and grooms milling about.

Aware she was stomping like a slightly spoiled child, Angelique moved away from the courtyard where they could have at least a semblance of privacy.

Percy followed her to the edge of a field by the side of the inn, and was about to open his mouth again when they stopped, and she whipped off her glove, holding her hand high enough for him to see the ring upon it.

'I'll kill him,' he said simply, past rage, now eerily and insanely calm.

Harcourt was certainly right.

Now to bring him back to reason.

Or at least, to her side.

'You will do no such thing,' she retorted, gloving her hand again, using a tone similar to the one that always seemed to work wonders for Meg. 'And that is precisely why I tell you this now, and here. So that I can be clear. What was done, was my choice. Regardless of what *he* has done, you will not touch a hair on his head.'

'Don't tell me you're in love with him,' Percy spat, as if that could be the most extraordinary thing he'd ever been witness to, he, the earl who played vigilante on the docks and married a lighterman's daughter. 'After everything he's done -'

'I am not in the mood to quarrel with you, Percy,' she hissed. 'When the truth of what occurred is laid bare, perhaps you will understand better, as I do -'

'Don't you dare defend -'

'Shut up, Percy,' she screamed, very near to the end of her tether, and with so much more to endure before she could finally rest. *God, I am so very tired.* Startled, Percy froze, and blinked at her like a frightened deer. 'You want to know why I ran, this, this is why,' she sighed, gesturing at everything he was. 'You are so intent on controlling everything, you never listen.' He flinched, as if she'd struck him, and if she hadn't been so concerned with ensuring peace, she might've felt a little sorrier for it. 'Swear to me, if you've ever cared for me, for our friendship, that you will not touch him.'

Percy shook his head, and gritted his teeth.

And then, with what must have been all the strength he possessed, he ground out two words.

'I swear.'

'You should also know, they are not the ones who came after you last year. And before you ask how I know, they told me so. And as extraordinary as it may be, I believe them.'

With that, she walked away.

He cried after her, but she kept moving, kept going, because that was all she had right now. That was all she could do. There was more to say, so very much more, but right now, she couldn't speak those things. Right now, she needed to force everyone to lay their cards on the table, so that they could find a way to resolve this utter catastrophe, and perhaps, find a way to the truth, and her own freedom.

No matter the cost.

∞

Having all seen to their wounds, and generally refreshed

themselves, everyone now sat around a worn old oak table in the best, *of two*, private dining room the inn offered. It was a warm, cosy place, though not even the fire that raged in the immense hearth could quite warm Angelique through. It felt as if the fiery fear had given way to an icy gloom; so like the damp Scottish mists, that seeped into your bones and refused to leave.

The ale before her gave her courage though, and steadied her nerves, as she looked at everyone's faces, shadowed and wary in the dim candle and firelight. They had all eaten, in sullen, tense, but peaceful silence, the dishes had been cleared, and now, they all waited.

For me.

'Well, we are all gathered, Angelique,' Effy said, setting down her tankard, taking charge of the peace-talks, or meeting, or whatever it was meant to be. 'As you requested. Now, perhaps you would care to begin by telling us what happened.'

'As you know,' she began, throwing Effy a grateful smile, before turning her attention to Percy and Harcourt. 'I ran away. I was afraid of... A great many things,' she said, throwing Will a glance. He clenched his jaw, but stared intently down at the dregs of his drink. 'Will found me,' she told them, looking to Percy, willing him, for once in his life, to listen. *Truly.* 'He convinced me to stay until you and I had spoken, and so I did. However, as it turned out, it wasn't you we were waiting for.' Angelique looked down at her own ale, drew a deep breath, and swallowed a healthy measure. 'We waited for Laramie, for the two of them had a plan to force me into marriage, and make my life a living Hell,' she said with bitter amusement, eyeing them both.

Laramie remained steadfast and steely-eyed, and Will...

Rustled with what looked like guilt, and shame.

'The reason for that,' she continued, more forcefully as she could see Percy's patience waning, his knuckles white as he nearly crushed the tankard he held. Thankfully, Effy also sensed his discomfort, and placed a hand on his, urging him to calm himself. 'Is revenge. Against my father.'

'You say that as if it excuses their behaviour,' Percy exclaimed. 'As if you agree that you should be sent to slaughter -'

'Of course I don't -'

'Then what the Hell are we all doing here, when I should be stringing them up -'

'Because I can't do this anymore,' Angelique shouted, silencing Percy. She hated yelling, yelling at him, but it seemed to be all that could reach him through the anger. 'I told you, no more blood. You all would wallow in it like pigs in the mud, but I cannot. We have to find a way to… Resolve this.'

'You say that as if it were a simple dispute,' Laramie spat, eyeing her as if she were newly escaped from a madhouse. 'A matter of cows and chickens, not -'

'What is your father supposed to have done to merit this,' Harcourt asked, the calmest among them all, his voice so measured it sobered the rest instantly, and they seethed on in silence.

It was no wonder, the man understood revenge probably better than anyone.

Not that she quite knew the details of what precisely had pushed Harcourt to lay waste to London society all those years ago; but she sensed it was immensely personal.

It had to be, to go after some of the most powerful lords in the land, and to annihilate them as he had.

'Lord Fitzsimmons deals in murder, and torture, and abuse,' Laramie said, a challenge in his eyes. As if he expected any of them to laugh in his face, or declare it none of their concern. 'He is the head of a clandestine circle that offers men of power women, men, children, whatever they want, to do with what they wish.'

'How do you know this,' Harcourt asked, shooting Percy a warning look as he began to open his mouth.

'My mother was one of his toys,' Laramie explained with a grim smile. 'My father told me all. Of Fitzsimmons, and his partners, who are now sadly all dead, or beyond my reach.'

'Partners,' Effy asked with a frown.

'Bolton, Campbell, Almsbury, Mowbray, and Russell,' Will recited.

Harcourt stiffened, and Effy took his hand, gaging him with concern.

Percy's eyes widened, and he glanced to Harcourt.

'You didn't know?'

'Of course not,' Harcourt gritted out.

'What,' Will asked, finally coming fully back to the room, looking between them all.

'Harcourt Sinclair, and Effy Fortescue took them down four years ago,' Angelique said, garnering everyone's attention. Percy, Harcourt, and Effy all looked at her questioningly and she huffed out a hollow laugh. 'What, you thought I hadn't worked that out? I'm not stupid. Percy did an admirable job keeping it all quiet, but you forget the role I played in Mowbray's demise.' Effy looked away, guilt in her eyes. 'Though I could never figure out why.'

'They took my own mother from me,' Harcourt said quietly, and she knew this was not a secret easily offered to others. Laramie nodded, and in that moment, a sort of recognition appeared in both men's eyes. 'So I took everything from them.'

'You missed one,' Laramie said with a sardonic smile, though it had the intended effect, and lightened the mood every so slightly.

'Where do we go from here,' Percy asked after a long moment, proving he could in fact be the reasonable lord he pretended so often to be. 'Though we may sympathise with your reasons, we could never let anything happen to Angelique.'

'We go see my father,' she said, the decision a long time coming, yet only made in that instant.

Some pieces still didn't fit, and she needed to know, needed to hear it from her own father's lips.

That he was the monster they purported.

'You still don't believe me,' Laramie sneered.

'I believe there is truth in what you say,' she corrected, and he froze, seemingly disbelievingly that she could. 'But I need to hear it from him. And regardless, if he is who you say, *what* you say, then there is more he could tell us.'

'Us,' Percy repeated. '*You* are going back to London with Effy, and *we* will go see your father.'

'No, I won't,' Angelique said simply. 'This is my life, Percy. *My* family. I will not be coddled and wrapped up in the back of a carriage to await news of my fate. If you don't like it, *you* can go back to London, or back to Briar Hill and Meg.'

Percy grimaced and shook his head, fighting yet again his instincts.

'It is her decision to make, Egerton,' Will said, and her heart twisted a little at the show of loyalty.

Not that it matters. For even more so than before; it cannot.

'You -'

'All of you, enough,' Effy exclaimed, rising, her dark brown eyes promising retribution to anyone who dared disagree. 'We will all go to Wiltshire, and that will be the end of this conversation. Now, I suggest we all retire, and leave at dawn. As for the rooms... Harcourt, you share with Will, Percy, you with Laramie. That way we will all be sure to behave ourselves.'

No one it seemed, had it in them to argue with her.

Satisfied, Effy extended her hand to Angelique, who rose, and took it, grateful for her friend's support. Grateful for all of them; though she dreaded the conversation she would have to have with Percy eventually.

Without even a glance behind them, the two women left.

XX.

I did not have the opportunity to say so before,' Effy said, closing the door behind them, and making herself busy with their bags as Angelique wandered over to the hearth, and settled on the rug before it. Even though she knew it would not work, she was willing to sit before a thousand fires if it meant someday she might chase the cold from her bones, which she was sure would never leave now. 'And I am sorry it is under such circumstances, but I am happy to see you again.'

Angelique turned, and offered her friend a wan smile, which was returned with a brighter one, though concern shone bright in Effy's eyes.

'As am I.'

Turning back to the fire, Angelique watched the flames dance, wishing she could see the future in them as the prophets of old could.

She heard Effy rummage around for a few moments, then her friend settled beside her, offering her a cup of what smelled like licorice.

'From a small town outside of Angoulême,' Effy said, sipping her own drink, leaning back on a hand as she too stared into the fire. 'There was a farm next door which also made excellent goat's cheese that sadly does not travel so well.'

'Thank you for your letters,' she said softly. 'And your friendship all these years. I enjoyed hearing of your adventures, though I suspect you left out much so as not to corrupt me further.'

'Indeed,' Effy laughed heartily. 'Though I left out things rather to spare your poor mother's heart should she ever chance upon them, rather than to avoid corrupting you. I do not believe the realities of life can do such a thing, so long as one is true to oneself.' Angelique glanced over at her, and she smiled. 'I am sure Percy would disagree however,' she added, raising a brow with a sly smile. 'He believes me to have been the devil to lead you down the path of sin you have been on these past years. Learning to fight, visiting seedy brothels -'

'Lily's establishment is not seedy!'

'I am sure it is not,' Effy laughed, gently patting her leg. 'But to hear Percy tell it, as he has in his letters, and all the way here, you would think you had been frolicking about town naked with Lucifer himself.'

'Percy has been good to me,' she shrugged. 'His entire family has. But he doesn't... He cannot... *They* cannot...'

'Understand you.' Angelique nodded, and took a sip of the liquor, which was odd, but also, delicious. 'As with anyone, he was brought up a certain way, to believe certain things, and he struggles to see the world with different eyes. And he is a man.'

Angelique found a giggle escaped her, and she was grateful for that too.

I can still laugh it seems, though my heart is so very sore.

'I thought Meg might help him to,' she admitted. 'But she too feared what I would become if I continued down the path I chose. And the Dowager, well, you remember her.'

'They only want the best for you. As do we all.'

'I know,' she nodded, taking another gulp of her drink before settling back as Effy had. Whether it was the heat of the alcohol, or the fire, or simply the company of one she thought might understand, she didn't know. All she knew, was that she felt she could finally speak of what ailed her heart, as she had only been able to with Will. 'And if I am truthful, I also feared what I might find down that path. But I remembered the courage you showed.

Perhaps you did corrupt me in that way,' Angelique mused. 'Though we did not know each other long, I felt a sort of kinship with you. What you did, and all you said in your letters... It made me want to explore life, rather than live in fear, in the shadows.'

'You saw something,' Effy whispered, and Angelique felt her eyes examining her closely. She nodded. 'That is why you believed Laramie and Will so readily. Why you wish to see your father.'

'Yes,' she breathed. 'I thought it a dream, a nightmare... But I believe it is a memory. I cannot remember it clearly, but I know my father will tell me the truth of it. I have to know.'

Angelique looked to Effy with pleading eyes, and the other woman nodded, then set down her drink, and offered out her hand.

Setting down her own, Angelique took it.

'We will discover the truth,' Effy said reassuringly. 'I promise.' Angelique nodded, and they both turned their attention back to the fire, its ferocity oddly hypnotising and soothing. 'Your marriage...'

'Was my choice,' she said, answering the unspoken question. 'Will... May have deceived me, but it was my choice. He never encouraged me, or tried to charm me into it. If anything he tried to push me away.'

'And you love him?'

Love, not loved.

'Yes,' she managed before her throat closed with the swelling of emotion the realization brought.

Despite it all, or perhaps even, in some measure, because of it all, she did still.

Hours she had spent reexamining it all. He had lied about many things, but he had never lied about himself. *That* was who she loved. Not what she had felt with him, *safe, fearless*, as she had tried to convince herself a few times without success, but him. And he had never pretended to be anything, anyone, other than who and what he was, and in his own way, she saw now how hard he'd tried to shield her, even as he knew he would betray her.

Though it cannot matter.

'I did not marry him with the deluded notion it was so for him,' she said after and a deep breath which helped keep the tears at bay. 'But neither did I believe it to be such an impossibility. Not that it matters now.'

'I never thought Harcourt capable of love,' Effy said pensively after a moment. 'What was done to him, what he became... Even myself. I did not think I could, after all I endured.'

Effy fell silent for a moment, shadows similar to Angelique's own in her eyes.

They had discussed Effy's past in their letters sometimes, not in detail, but enough for her to know just how much darkness there was in it. How much pain, and suffering; enough to make a strong man relinquish hope, and love, and the joys of life.

As much pain as there is in my own past.

'But even if he had never loved me back, I would never have regretted what I felt. Love, in whatever form it comes, is a gift. It is all we have,' Effy shrugged, leaning forward so she could wipe away a tear. 'I clung to revenge, and anger, for so long,' she continued, her voice thick with emotion that tugged at Angelique's own heart; her words giving her, if not hope, then some peace. 'Let it drive me, let it keep me warm at night, and fuel every action. In the end, it was nothing. Nothing compared to something so inexplicable, and wondrous, as love. Never let them take that from you, or take it from yourself.'

'I won't,' Angelique promised softly.

They sat there, hand in hand, watching the flames for a very long time.

I won't, she promised herself, over and over, until finally, she fell asleep, right there, before the hearth, her head in Effy's lap.

XXI.

*N*o one but the masters were allowed here. It would be beatings or a night in the yard if he was found, but it would be worth it. It would be worth it if he could have one moment, one tiny infinitesimal moment of solitude, of peace. A moment, to imagine something more than this life. Something more than the storeroom that was more blistering cold than the snow-laden, frozen outdoors. Something more than this place, than the boys like him who were more hungry dogs than humans because a hungry dog was easier to control, easier to wield, as a tool, and as a weapon.

Something more than the endless days of toil, and torment; of pain, and cruelty.

Sometimes he wished he could be like the rest of them. That he could quash the flame, the longing inside him that came from God only knew where. The flame that ignited his hope for an actual life when the others accepted their fates. They would die here, or somewhere just as rotten. Hope was the first thing they extinguished; hope of escape, hope of release, hope, sometimes, of death.

He had been here all his life. The walls of the orphanage as it was called had seen him grow into the tiny rat he was now. He knew nothing of the world, of what lay beyond, save for the fleeting visions visitors brought with them, or the glimpses of the surrounding village when they were brought to work someplace else. They were taught little of it, the only lessons they needed were those of the Lord, *and those of the trades they learned. Digging, building, cutting, boiling, tanning, whatever it was.*

So where his dreams had come from, he knew not.

Perhaps they were a gift from the Lord.

Perhaps they were a gift from the Devil.

Eternal torment was this, wasn't it? To dream of things that could never be.

To dream of being something when you did not even know your true name, or your people, or even how old you really were.

To dream of being someone when you were nothing and would never be anything but.

He clutched the heel of stale, mouldy bread close to his chest and carefully made his way through the piles of food not meant for them to the darkest corner of the cellar. He could eat it all, the salted meats, the dried fruits, even the wine. He could get drunk on it all, but then, he would never be able to return.

No.

He wanted to return.

He wanted to have a haven to escape to if he couldn't escape from these damp grey stone walls. So he'd made a plan.

It had taken months. Months of searching, for the perfect time, the perfect place, the perfect way to get in and get out undetected. He'd found the small hole in the wall leading here by accident; or perhaps it had been a miracle. He'd known then, he had found his place. The only way into the otherwise locked rooms, so far from everything else, he could go undetected.

Still, he had waited, until he knew he could do it. Until he was sure he knew perfectly every move, every timing, for every master and every boy, and every mouse. Until he found this mouldy, stale heel of bread that was a treasure to his empty belly.

They were all starving; it was winter, the masters said, and they had to be careful with their provisions. The boys all knew what lay down here, but they said nothing for there was nothing to be said. He was starving with them, more so, for the others took from him anything he had. It was the way of this place. He was not strong enough, big enough, scrappy enough to stake his claim. He was different, and they knew it. He blended, became invisible. He didn't puff out his chest and beat smaller ones to assert his place. He faded away, like mist.

But not tonight.

Tonight, he simply was.

And he was not here.

There were no boys. There was no orphanage. There was no cold.

Tucked into the corner of the room, he was tucked in tight, into warm down blankets, in a warm cottage. The bread was not bread, but the most delectable cake made by his mother. And his father, and his family, those dreams he couldn't quite imagine but which he could feel, they were there too. Sitting around a warm, blazing fire. There were cows, and chickens and sheep too. And a dog. All tucked into the cottage to keep away from the cold.

All together.

He bit into the bread, taking care, taking his time, savouring every bitter crumb.

He would not waste any of it.

He was so lost in the dream, in the illusion, in the embrace of the ephemeral, faceless ghosts, that he did not hear the others come in. He neither heard nor saw them until it was too late, until the bread was ripped from his numb, ice-cold fingers, and then still it took him seconds to see them, to blink away the dreams, and see the three boys standing before him like snarling wolves.

Those seconds cost him whatever chance he might've had of escape from his three usual tormentors, those three tall, skeletally thin monsters who gave him no quarter. Who now, from the glint in their eyes, wanted to finish what they had started years ago. They wanted him dead, for no other reason than that was how it worked, and there would be one less mouth to feed.

He curled into himself as the blows began, smaller and smaller with every kick, every punch, every scratch. He could feel himself slipping away, feel his life leaving as his blood coated the walls and the floor, and he clasped tight to the dream again, knowing that at least he could feel that warmth one last time.

He would get his moment; only it would be his last.

163

But then there were no more blows. The pain was still there, harsh, and throbbing, and his blood was still leaking from him, but there was no more new hurt. No more snarls, no more cuts.

He couldn't move, didn't even dare try to open an eye, if even he could, because maybe it had stopped because he was dead. Maybe if he opened his eyes the life he still felt inside him would rush out and then there would be no more dreams, there would only be nothing.

Just like him.

'You still alive,' a harsh voice whispered. 'Oi.'

Something poked his shoulder.

He was pretty sure angels wouldn't poke, and then devils would do it with something more than bony flesh.

He felt himself nod, and two hands took him by the shoulders and pushed him back so he was sitting against the cold wall.

'We gotta get out of 'ere,' the voice whispered again. 'Get you cleaned before the masters find us.'

So he wasn't dead.

Was this a cruel trick then? Something worse than the dreams God had given?

No one helped another here.

No one came to save you.

And yet...

'Oi!'

With difficulty, he managed to open one eye.

Through the haze, through the dizziness, through the blood dripping from his scalp he saw another boy before him. He'd seen him before, he'd seen all of them before. Only he had noted this boy because like him he was always alone. He'd grown up here too. He had blonde hair too, and dark eyebrows always in a scowl. He had eyes as dark as coal, and was taller, stronger than him. No one ever took his food, blankets, or hit him other than the masters.

'Richie,' he muttered weakly.

'Yeah, good,' the boy said. 'Haven't lost your wits then.'

The boy smiled, and Will blinked at him.

How did he know how to do that?

No one smiled, no one laughed, not even at Christmas when they sang hollowly joyous songs and received an extra serving of bread with their broth.

'What d'you want,' he ground out, everything hurting more now.

Everyone wanted something.

This boy wouldn't be here, helping him, if he didn't want something.

'Not be alone.'

The words stuck him in a place that was alive only in his dreams.

Richie offered out his hand, and it took a long while for Will to accept it.

But when he did, he knew, neither of them would ever be alone again.

'I'll be your brother, and you'll be mine,' Richie said as they hobbled off together slowly, stepping over the bloody, unconscious bodies of the other boys. Tomorrow, there would be a sound retribution, for all of them, even those who had slept through the night with as much tranquility as one could here. But it wouldn't matter. Because he wouldn't be alone anymore. 'Until my last breath,' Richie promised.

'Until my last breath,' he promised too, before they crawled through the hole.

Until my last breath.

∞

The memories faded into the air like dust motes, and Will dropped his head into his hands. Once, like Angelique, those terrible days had been all he could see. Every moment of every day after Richard had saved him had been filled with horrors, and pain. And then, slowly, as his brother's purpose had become his own, so had those days been locked away, just as he had. They were part of him, defined him, but it was another life. One, that some days he doubted he had lived.

Rather it felt as if it had been another, that small child he'd been, who was both himself, and not. At night, he'd revisited the horrors in his dreams, but when he awoke each morning, he had flung them back into the locked recesses of his soul where they belonged.

Now, it felt as if the doors had been flung wide open, and the boy had been set free.

He had been set free. He could look back on his life, his childhood, and not flinch at every blow as if it came today. Inside, it felt as if his entire being was rearranging itself; as if he was rebuilding himself into something new. Something better, stronger, he'd never dreamt he could be. And he knew who had flung open the doors. It was what made it all the more painful. Different parts of himself were warring with each other.

One loyal to Richard; stalwart and steadfast in his promise to do whatever was necessary to serve his brother and pay back the debt he owed.

One loyal to the little boy who dreamt of more, who wanted a life of joy and tenderness, and affection.

One loyal to the promise he'd made to Angelique; to the vows he'd made before God and man to be hers, always.

'She really has you tied in knots, doesn't she,' came his brother's voice, and Will lifted his head. Richard stood at the door, arms crossed, and a frown on his face. 'I thought we should have a word, before we embark on this journey. We haven't had a proper chance since we left Oban.'

Will nodded, and Richard strolled in, closing the door as he did.

Whatever his brother had to say, he'd welcome it. Perhaps it would help the warring factions inside him find a winner. Perhaps it would help him refocus his intent, and stop behaving like some lost puppy.

His brother's strength and drive had always fed him; so he wished they would now.

'No matter how I look at it,' Richard said wistfully, pondering the room as if it were a museum filled with treasures rather than the tiny barren thing it was. 'I cannot seem to make sense of what you did. Marrying her.'

'I told you -'

'I know what you said,' Richard snapped, pinning him with a glare as he jumped to his feet. 'But you and I both know you went soft. You could have subdued her in so many other ways, and yet you chose to make deals with her, and then marry her.'

'There were too many people around,' Will protested, the excuses sounding as weak to his own ears as they were. 'If she had raised a hue and cry -'

'You're smarter than that,' his brother scoffed. 'You and I both know you are lethal, and quiet, when you wish to be. Which suggests you did not wish to be.'

'I told you I would do what needed to be done.'

Richard nodded, and slowly came to stand before him, his gaze and stance as predatory as Will had ever seen.

'The girl believes her father will dispel what we've told her as lies,' Richard said, all confrontation gone in his voice. His brother, the one person who'd cared if he lived or died, was back. 'She clings to that hope as you clung to your dreams of cottages and cows,' he whispered, his hand coming around Will's neck and pulling him forward so their foreheads touched. The gesture had been theirs, always. It had centered them, bonded them, shut out the world around them, and so it did now. 'But you and I both know what becomes of hope.'

Yes.

Well, he had. Until Angelique. Until Scotland. And then everything, everything had changed, and he had hoped again. He hoped still.

But you cannot hope and be the man you must be.

'Yes, brother,' he breathed.

'I need you by side, always,' Richard pleaded fiercely. 'I cannot do this without you. I know she tempts you. I know she makes you believe in impossible things. But that is not for the likes of us. Please, do not say I have lost you.'

'Never,' Will promised, his own hand encircling the back of Richard's neck.

Their gazes met, and they silently renewed the promise made

all those years ago.

Until my last breath.

'Time to finish this,' Richard said.

Will nodded, and his brother released him and strode out of the room.

Loyalty. That is what drives me.

He'd told Angelique as much. It was woven into the fabric of his entire being, and he could no sooner deny it than cease to be. It was that simple.

It had to be.

∞

That resolve carried him through the painfully awkward and quiet breakfast he sat through. Somehow he and Richard had managed to arrive in the private room to dine just as Sinclair and Effy were leaving; just as Egerton and Angelique were arriving. It had been twenty minutes which had felt like hours as they'd all sat there in a tense, suffocating grimness, the only sounds those of their chewing and sipping. Egerton had glared at him, Richard at Egerton, Angelique at her meal, and he…

All the while he had been fixated on her, like a goddamned moth to the flame.

If only he could look at her, and not see everything he did. Not be so spellbound by her, not be so willing to deny all he was at the drop of a hat if only to see her smile one last time. If only he could lose himself in her one last time.

If only he could look at her and see the pawn she was, not the living, breathing creature he would protect with his dying breath. Not the being who had infused him with more than he thought possible; more than he was worth.

Loyalty to Richard, he kept repeating to himself every time he glanced at her.

Loyalty to your brother, that is the only thing you have.

And would ever have, because whatever promises held within

Angelique, whatever he might've hoped and dreamt for, were dead. No matter that she had saved his life, and his brother's, nearly giving him a heart attack in the process; she had, in her own words, done that for herself. As she should. He deserved nothing. She would never smile at him again; and there was nothing more he could have from her.

Not that he wanted to take; he wanted only to give.

But you have nothing to give. Nothing to offer her, even if you could.

It was all he'd ever wanted, he realized, as he rose, and left for his and Richard's rooms to collect their belongings.

'Laramie was the man who found you,' came Angelique's voice, and Will froze on the steps.

He didn't quite have it in him to turn and face her properly, but he turned just enough so that his back was no longer to her.

She made no move to come closer, and it seemed the space between them was a giant chasm, that he was watching her fall into it from a great height, and all he wished was to offer out his hand, and for her to take it, to trust him again, but he knew that would never happen. He didn't want it to. He wanted to be as free of her as she was of him so he could do what he had to.

What he had promised.

'And the boy who saved you, in the orphanage.'

'Yes,' he said quietly.

Will didn't know why she was asking, why she cared enough to, what she wanted from him, but this was his chance, perhaps the only one he'd have, to make her understand.

Fully.

She had guessed most of it, clever gremlin that she was, but he needed to say the words. To give her the final piece to the demented puzzle that was his life.

Hate me if you will. But do it for the right reasons.

'Richard saved me in that place,' he breathed. 'It was the two of us, against, everything. And then his father came for him, when he was eleven. I was sent away to work in a tannery not a year later. I tried to escape, many times, and only managed to do so properly after about four years. I wandered, found food and work where I could, until Richard found me again. I don't know how,' he shrugged, the relief he'd felt that day, the gratitude, thick in his voice. 'But he did. He took me on as his valet, taught me all he had learned himself, and together we made a plan.'

'You never lied to me,' Angelique whispered.

There was certainty, and wonder in her voice.

An earnestness, a question underlying, *why*, that he couldn't answer.

He finally found it in himself to look at her, and in a second her expression turned from questioning, hopeful even, to unyielding.

'Save for when you told me you'd written to Percy. And of course, when you promised me freedom you never intended to give.'

Yes.

No.

'It was the only way I could think of to protect you,' he pleaded.

'It was the only way you could think to make me stay,' she corrected.

And yes, that was true, to an extent, but...

It was so much more than that.

If it hadn't been, all of this would be so much easier.

Whether or not he could, or *would*, admit it; to himself or her.

'Would you have done it,' she asked, steel in her voice now. 'What he asked of you?'

'I don't know,' he admitted.

'Thank you for your honesty,' she nodded, her voice tight again.

God, please...

'Angelique,' he called as she made to turn away. She stopped, and he pressed on. 'What Richard said, about our ability to feel, it was true. *Was.* But with you... I would never have laid a hand on you, that much I do know.'

'You didn't have to.'

XXII.

T he days on the road to her father were the longest of her life. Angelique wished she could find that blissful, empty surrender she had when she had travelled from Oban with Laramie and Will. But try as she might, she couldn't. With every mile, her nerves tensed, her heartbeat quickened, and her mind plunged further into the darkest depths of questioning.

They travelled the same as when they had left Oban; people taking turns with her in the carriage, sleeping, others taking turns driving and riding. Everyone was as anxious as she was to arrive, to get the final answers to the questions which affected all their lives now.

They stopped only twice for provisions. During one such time Angelique stood in the field by the small market set up at an inn, and stared out at the flat, gray, horizon, which no longer whispered to her.

Effy and Harcourt were the only ones who tried to speak to her, Effy with more enthusiasm and verve, not that it mattered. She listened to every tale, every adventure her friend recounted, even though some she'd already heard about in Effy's letters, but she never said a word in return. She was grateful for the distractions they tried to provide, but she couldn't quite find it in herself to converse.

Percy, when he shared the coach, stared at her, as if willing her to open to him, or perhaps, himself to her. But in the end, he always returned to his horse having spoken not one word. Laramie was the same, though he was careful *not* to look at her, mirroring her and staring out instead at the changing landscape blurring past them. And as for Will...

It took two full days of riding to persuade him to set foot inside the carriage, and even when he finally made it inside, he stayed only for an hour even though he looked dead on his feet. She hated to see him that way, hated to see him killing himself for her, because she knew it was for her that he kept away, but neither could she bring herself to say anything about it.

She hated that his presence still soothed her even as it reminded her of all she should *truly* hate him for and couldn't. She was angry, and grateful, and sad, and he was part of the ongoing tormenting war happening in her head and heart. She wished he wasn't; that she could dismiss it all as easily as dust to the wind, but she couldn't. She couldn't seem to get anything she wished for.

Not for all of this to be a nightmare, and for her really to already be far away, on the deck of a great ship sailing for new horizons, with no past, only future.

Not for all of this to be a simple misunderstanding. For her father to laugh when they all arrived, and muse at this great lark, and perhaps tell them it was some other villain who had committed such monstrous deeds, but was now long dead and burning in hellfire.

Not for her life to be what others' was. A happy family. A man who loved her and whom she loved. A life full of simple joy and quietude.

If she had grandiose wishes, she might understand God or whatever power bestowed miracles, denying them. If she dreamed of great riches and power and conquests, she might understand. But she asked so little.

As do so many others, even more destitute than you. Be thankful for what you have.

And somewhere, she was. She was grateful to not face

this journey alone. She was grateful that even in her darkest moment, she had known someone would come for her, fight for her. She was grateful for the love she had felt; Effy's lesson well learnt. She was grateful for so much, even that she was still alive, and breathing, and rational. She was grateful for the anger, growing inside her. Grateful for the drive, that would keep her strong, keep her fighting, until it was all over.

And then you can rest.

Where, how, with whom, for how long... Perhaps not even God knew at this point.

The clear picture she had formed of her future was gone, snuffed out, so that only the present existed. Only the questions swirling in her head existed.

What did you do father? If you did what they say - how could you?
And you, mama, did you know? How could you live like that?
How could I trust you?
How could I trust Will? How could I not see... So much.
How could I love him? How can he be the only thing tethering me to myself now?
How can I move on and live after what is to come?
How?
How...

∞

All too soon, and yet, not nearly soon enough, the carriage stopped. She knew without looking, without hearing anything, that they had arrived. A strange sense of calm, of having arrived, of meeting fate on the road, came over her. The other emotions and thoughts faded into the background, until all that remained was a stark certainty.

Renfeld, who had been the latest inside the carriage with her, quietly stepped out, and she heard the voices' of the others on the cold wind that smelled of rain. *Debating.* Wondering how to proceed, who should go first...

Angelique drew in a deep breath, and stepped out of the carriage.

'I will go. Alone,' she decreed before any of them could make a move.

The others all froze in a strange tableau before the securely chained and locked gates of her family's oldest estate, their hushed dispute about *the plan of action*, silenced.

And they all asked why she'd run, why'd not trusted them with the truth. Why she hadn't trusted them not to order her about like a weak and useless child, when they stood here deciding matters and making choices that were hers and hers alone to make.

Before anyone could find words to protest, she stepped towards them, and the pedestrian gate that had been tested she presumed, and now stood open, inviting her in.

'I shall send someone along to open the gates for you.'

'You have no idea what awaits you in there,' Percy protested.

She shot him a glare, and the others looked to each other, hesitant, but unwilling to go against her in this at least it seemed.

'My father awaits me in there,' she said coldly, wrapping her coat tighter around herself against the nipping wind. 'If something truly sinister did take me, well, at least it shall not take you too and you can come save me again later.'

Percy opened his mouth to say something, but Harcourt laid a hand on his arm.

She nodded to him gratefully, and without sparing any of the others a glance, she took a deep breath, and stepped through the open gate.

It was as if she'd passed through a veil into another world. The air felt different, even though it was the same air she'd breathed seconds ago. There was a heaviness to it, even as the biting, damp wind swirled around her, shaking the limbs of dying trees and shrubs and grasses. The grey light was the same, and yet, it wasn't. The ground seemed to crackle beneath her feet, everything else around her still and quiet in their endless movements.

Straightening her back, she forced herself to walk on into the oppressiveness assuredly, without looking back, without hesitation.

Time stopped as she approached the house, as its looming form grew before her, the ancient elms lining the drive shrinking away as if turning their eyes from the grim sight. And grim it was, the once awesome mixed splendour of Tudor and early Georgian splendour now decrepit.

Rotten, and gnawed at by the elements. The house was no longer white, but grey, grey as the skies above, grey as the smoke pouring from one of the chimneys, and it was not only a trick of the light. It looked as if it had been battered by a thousand storms, as if lightning had struck and blackened the thing, even as dead ivy and bindweed clung to it, their browning leaves shrieking and shivering in the wind.

As she drew closer, she noticed paper-covered windows, and missing panes. Broken moulding and cracked columns. Even the weeds that tried to grow through the gravel and along the facade where once impeccable flower beds had bloomed, were dying. The fountain which had once lulled her to sleep with its delicate tinkling, and in which lily pads had bloomed in the summer, was now full of nothing but brown grime and green slime.

This place was dying; a slow, terrible death.

She wasn't sure what she'd expected, perhaps to find her father living a life of luxury or even quiet and comfortable contemplation, but either way, it hadn't been this. Whatever doubts remained of her father's culpability vanished as she stood before the once white and gleaming, now dusty and black steps leading up to the entrance.

But she had to know.

Up she went, steady as she could, in a daze as she was. She stood before the great black doors, as ominous and imposing as they'd been when she was a child. Only when she'd been small, they had been open, always. Ready for her. She'd run straight up those steps and through them, onto the chessboard marble tiles of the foyer, her mother in tow. She'd -

Angelique closed her eyes and forced herself to take in generous gulps of air to even her breathing again. This was not the time for remembering. So many times she'd tried to conjure up memories of this place, of her childhood, unsuccessfully, and now it was as if that veil she'd passed through had been laid over her entire childhood. She'd remembered bits, flashes, a flower, her mother's scent, the sun shining through the leaves, but never something as vivid...

And now is not the time. Finish this.

She lifted her hand, and grabbed the end of the cobweb laden bell. She pulled hard, and waited, for what seemed an eternity. But nothing. No sound, no movement, nothing. And yet she knew he was here. She knew someone was here, she had seen that puff of smoke escaping from one of the chimneys, and it had to be him. There was nowhere else he would be.

Trying her luck, she reached for the great brass ring which served as a doorknob, as rusted and cold as those of a church. She turned it slowly, it creaked and caught, but it finally gave way. Pushing all her weight against it, she opened the door. It cracked and groaned, as if it fought her, begged her not to enter, but in the end, she prevailed.

Without hesitation, she stepped in, and was nearly sent reeling back. She had traversed another veil, a thicker one, and come into a kingdom of cold, and lingering death. Not crisp, tidy death, like that of plants, but the sickly sweet death of an animal. It lingered in the cold, humid air, and stuck to her lungs.

A hundred slivers of memories, of sounds, and smells, and colours assailed her, and she shivered, gooseflesh forming on her skin; not from the cold, but from the fear. It sprung to life within her again, familiar, and tormenting.

Breathe. Just breathe, and get this done.

'Hello,' she called, stepping forth further into the dim foyer, all dust and cobwebs and limp white sheets covering the furnishings, her voice shaky, but as strong as her determination. 'Hello! Is anyone there? Mr. Warton?'

She halted, waiting, sure she could see her breath misting before her.

Nothing.

Not even the rattling of a mouse, or the wings of a bird.

But he is here. I know he is here.

Grasping what remained of her courage, swallowing hard, she stepped forth towards the stairs again, her heels clicking on the floor and echoing throughout the house as if a mighty roar.

And then she couldn't move forward, not anymore. Her feet clung to the marble as if they'd been stuck there, trapped in molasses or quicksand. Her body started shaking and trembling, and that fear gnawed at her insides, and she felt tears in her eyes as her heart beat faster and faster until it was but one beat.

Turning to her right, she saw the door that haunted her nightmares, closed now, not open and shadowed by candlelight, but then it was. And someone was screaming again, it rang in her ears so loudly she wanted to scream too, ask why no one else could hear it.

And there was blood, and footsteps on the marble, not her own, and the smell of brandy in her nostrils, and smoke choking her, and fingers on her arm, and blood on her tongue, and that voice -

'Angelique!'

No.

That wasn't the same voice. That was another voice. She knew that voice.

It was a good voice.

'Angelique, breathe,' the good voice said, and she did, her body listening even when her mind could not force it to.

'Keep breathing, that's it, listen to my voice, come back to me.'

So she kept breathing.

Her stomach roiled, and she kept shaking, her body ready to run but unable to, but the other sounds, the screaming, and the bad voice, they were gone, and the door wasn't open any longer, there was no light, it was slowly itself again, as it was now, closed, and foreboding, but not alive. And though she could still taste the blood, the rest she couldn't smell, and instead she smelled damp, and death, yes, but another scent, warmer, and it belonged to the voice.

Will.

Finally she saw him, standing there before her, looking about as terrified as she felt, close, not close enough and yet too close. He raised his hand then stopped himself and she shook her head, coming back to the present, *yes the present, not the past,* and she felt sick, and dizzy, and her feet could finally move but only to stumble a step.

Will made to catch her but she didn't want him to, and instead she fell to the floor and cast out whatever little had been in her stomach, the cold hard floor hurting her knees, but keeping her here, now.

'Angelique, please say something,' he said, his voice closer now, full of concern.

'I'm fine,' she ground out, just as a handkerchief was put before her eyes.

She took it, and wiped her mouth before stowing it back into her pocket.

'Oh dear God,' cried another voice making them both jump. 'Miss Fitzsimmons is that you?'

XXIII.

Though loath to take his eyes off Angelique who looked like death, Will focused his attention on the new arrival, who he guessed must be the butler, or some manner of upper servant given the man's airs, though he looked nothing like the servant of a grand home like this. Or rather, once grand home. The man, somewhere in his late sixties, looked as run down as the house itself, and wore plain brown breeches, waistcoat, and shirt that looked as if they too had seen better days.

'Miss Fitzsimmons is that you,' the man asked again, coming closer.

Will shot him a fearsome glare and he froze in his tracks.

'Yes it is Miss Fitzsimmons,' he answered, offering out his hand to Angelique, though she refused to take it, preferring to push herself up off the floor back onto her still shaky legs.

He didn't blame her, he had a feeling she would bear being touched by no one just now.

Which is why he hadn't when he found her, even though that's all he'd wanted to do, pull her into his arms and protect her from the ghosts which had taken her again; with a vengeance.

'Who might you be then? Where is everyone? Where is his lordship?'

The man stared at him for a moment, startled, and trying to make sense of who he was, then recovered, and adopted his most proper air, complete with hands clasped behind his back, and a spine of steel.

Definitely a butler.

'And *who* might you be,' the man asked, and Will made to go for him, but Angelique stepped forth instead.

'Where is my father, Mr. Warton,' she demanded, the icy society miss returned.

The butler eyed her for a moment, then dropped his head, all bluster gone.

'Upstairs, Miss Fitzsimmons,' he told her. 'In the library.'

'There are people waiting outside the gates,' she drawled haughtily, though he could still feel her upset. As if, she were trying to dissimulate that with false disdain. Just as she'd once tried to keep him at a distance with such methods. 'See to them, and their horses, and send them to meet me in the library. We will also be requiring a meal this evening, and at least four rooms, five if you can manage with whatever staff remain in this place. And get this cleaned up, I'm afraid the journey didn't agree with me.'

'Only me and Mrs. Warton,' the butler said weakly, stopping Angelique as she made to launch herself up the stairs.

'What?'

'For five years now, Miss Fitzsimmons,' he said, some of his pride returned.

'I will see Miss Fitzsimmons to her father,' Will said before she could say anything more. 'And then I will return to help you.'

Warton nodded, and Angelique marched up the stairs, Will on her heels.

No wonder the place was a mess. Two servants to take care of a house such as this, which usually employed fifty times that if not more? What had happened here, and to Lord Fitzsimmons? Whatever it was, didn't bode well for them. Likely he was mad by now, or on his deathbed, or something equally grim that meant they would never get the answers they sought.

That *she* sought.

'Thank you,' Angelique said quietly, bringing him back to the present.

They had arrived at the top of the stairs, and were now heading down a nearly pitch-black corridor, the only light coming from the shuttered windows to their left. Everywhere he looked, there was dust, and grime, threadbare carpets and dusky sheets covering the furniture, paintings, and few *objets d'art*. It was as if the house had been closed up, and forgotten, those within it entombed.

Nothing more than he at least deserves.

'We would still be waiting for a bed tomorrow had I not,' he replied, harsher than he meant to.

This place, it felt, wrong.

He felt like it wanted him gone, wanted to return to its quiet rotting. Which he would happily do, soon enough. He would happily burn it to the ground when they left too, if it meant Angelique would suffer no more.

She likely only wouldn't so long as you were in it when you set it alight.

'Warton looks as if he'd barely make it to the gate.'

'I meant... Oh, nevermind.'

Angelique heaved a great sigh, and shook her head.

Oh no you don't.

Before he could think better of it, he launched himself around her, and forced her to stop her progress. She refused to meet his eyes, and instead studied the floor.

Will forced himself to calm down, if only for her.

'Was it the same again,' he asked gently.

'Yes,' she breathed. 'Worse than ever. I couldn't... Find my way out.'

'That door...'

He didn't need to finish his question.

Angelique nodded, and he clenched his jaw.

That would be the first place he would set a match to.

'Is there anything I can -'

'No,' she said quickly, meeting his eyes, but yet again, she'd shielded herself from him. Pushed back her demons, and returned to herself. 'You've done enough. Go help Warton, and then you and the others join me in the library. It's just at the end of the corridor, on the right.'

'Angelique, I know you hate me -'

'I don't hate you, Will,' she snapped, and the words slammed into him, nearly sending him sliding back across the floor.

The whole journey here, her words, *you didn't have to*, had haunted him.

Repeated themselves remorselessly in his mind. He had sworn to protect her, to never hurt her, no matter what his brother demanded, and yet he had done just that. Worse, than Richard might've done had he had his way. He hated himself for that. And she, should too.

The alternative...

'I don't hate you,' she repeated, meeting his eyes, a challenge in her own he refused to accept. He couldn't accept. 'If I did, it would make everything so much easier.'

Without waiting for a response which they both knew would never come, she slipped past him, and strode down the corridor.

He watched her go, watched her silhouette grow smaller and smaller, until it disappeared in the shadows, as much a ghost of this place than any other who dwelled here. He wished she would have let him go with her, face whatever her father was now, stand by her side, but yet again, he was reminded that by her side was never his place. It had felt like it, but never would it be.

And if he wanted to stand by the side of the one man who had never abandoned him, he would do well to remember that, and to keep a clear head for what lay ahead.

For whatever it was, somehow he knew it would change everything.

∞

'Is it time for supper already,' her father said in a weak,

tired voice that sounded nothing like the one she remembered. His voice had always been firm, and clear, nigh-on tyrannical sometimes. But now... It was diminished, just like everything else. 'I have not seen the time pass today...'

Angelique remained where she stood just inside the doorway, shadowed in darkness like the rest of the library, which seemed to be the only place not entirely forsaken.

The curtains were all drawn, and she suspected the windows shuttered as they had been in the corridor. Still, she could see him clearly from here, as he sat in a hulking wingback chair by the fire, facing her.

He was so small now. For a man of not even sixty, he looked as if he were nearly a hundred. Bone-thin, his skin sallow, and thin, translucent almost. Dark circles beneath his hollowed green eyes once so like her own, now cloudy, his limbs contorted as they clutched a book, and a blanket. His thinning hair was swept back into a queue, and he sat there in what appeared to be his nightclothes, remnants of a tea tray beside him.

Her hand flew up to her mouth, and she stifled a sob. Tears stung at her eyes again, and she forced herself to focus on the taste of bile that remained in her mouth to root her here. More lost memories assailed her, of her great, towering father, so imposing he filled every room. Now, he was swallowed by it, a husk as much as this house.

Sadness threatened to overcome her as badly as the other memories had, and for a moment she mourned the loss of Will, of his own towering presence, his warmth, and reassurance which she could not deny still comforted her though it should be the last thing to do so. But that was why she'd sent him away; every moment she spent with him threatened to make her forget what he'd done, threatened to tempt her to lower her guard yet again, to allow him in.

He doesn't even want in, he simply wants what he can take for his brother.

A lie, she knew, but a steadying one just now.

'Warton?'

'Not Warton,' Angelique said, going towards him. She watched the expression of his face change from confusion, to fear, to shock, when finally he saw her as she stepped into the circle of light drawn by the fire. 'It's me, father.'

'Angelique,' he croaked, tears misting in his own eyes, piercing at her heart. Her father never showed emotion. It wasn't something lords like him did. 'Is it really you? My girl, you are grown now... What are you doing here, where is your mother?'

'Mother is in London,' she managed, swallowing the pain as she so often seemed to now. 'She does not know I am here.'

'Angelique,' he said, his voice stronger as he made to sit up, and fluttered nervously. 'What has happened, dear God...'

'Much has happened, father,' she replied gravely, and he stilled. 'That is why I am here. In a while, some friends will be joining us. It seems we are long overdue for a talk.'

Fourteen years overdue.

XXIV.

How have you been,' her father asked, after they'd sat in tense silence across from each other for God only knew how long. They'd been staring at each other, seemingly each trying to reconcile what the other was now. Trying to prepare themselves for all that was to come. 'How is your mother?'

'Don't,' Angelique said sharply. 'We both know why I am here, and pretending you care about either of our well-being is hypocritical.'

'I always cared,' her father breathed, and she shook her head, turning away.

She was saved from answering by a sharp rap on the door followed by the sounds of a little scuffle.

Angelique turned to find Warton leading a train of people, a candle in his hand. Effy was behind him, holding a tea tray, whilst Percy, Laramie, Harcourt, and Will brought up the rear, seemingly shoulder to shoulder, and she suspected they had all tried to enter at once before being reminded to behave as gentlemen; or at least the best they could.

Effy smiled graciously as she set down the tray, laden with meagre, but sufficient bread and cheese for them all, on the small table before the fire.

'Anything else, Miss,' Warton asked, his eyes glued to her rather than his master.

'No, thank you,' she managed.

He bowed, and left, and Angelique turned back to her father, who was now intently contemplating his hands.

'Are you well, Angelique,' Effy asked kindly, rubbing a hand down her arm. She nodded, and Effy smiled gently. 'Let's get this coat off you then, and those gloves. It's stifling in here.'

Had she not taken off her things?

Lord, no. So close to the fire, and yet she hadn't felt its heat. But neither did she feel cold, not even inside, as she had before. Instead, she felt nothing. As if the air did not touch her skin, as if her entire sense of touch had been stripped from her. She sat there and let Effy take her things, as the men scrounged for chairs that would hold them and settled in a half circle between her and her father. They all settled quietly, no one helping themselves to food or drink, though a cup of tea was placed in her hands by someone, presumably Effy.

Only Will remained standing, posted between her and the hearth.

'I should've known this day would come,' her father said quietly, shaking his head. 'My sins are plenty, so you will know. But you should also know that I did everything in my power, to keep you safe,' he insisted, lifting his head to meet her gaze. 'To give you a life. To keep you, untainted by it all.'

Angelique said nothing, even if her voice had worked, what was there to say?

After a moment, the baron nodded sadly, and began his tale.

'I inherited the title in 1790, after my own father swallowed a bullet,' he said, his voice cold, distant, and emotionless now. 'We were drowning in debt, having lost everything after America gained its independence. I was young, and desperate. I had the people on the estates, my mother, my sisters to care for. I was approached by another young lord, who offered me a way out. A way, to ensure a good life, for everyone involved. To my greatest shame, I accepted his proposal.'

'Which was,' Laramie asked in the silence that followed, snaring her father's attention back from the past as he leaned forward, hands clasped before him, his knuckles white.

'You look just as he did then,' the baron said wistfully, with an infinite measure of disgust.

'What?'

'Fulton,' he said on a hollow chuckle. 'There truly could be no doubt you are his son.'

Angelique's heart stopped beating and her chest tightened.

Why hadn't she seen it before?

Fulton. The Earl of Oster...

The whisper of a memory, cogs ticking into place.

Laramie's eyes. A promise unfulfilled.

'You would know,' Laramie bit back. 'You took me from him.'

'Is that what he told you,' her father laughed, shaking his head. 'I see.'

'It is what happened.'

'No boy,' the baron exclaimed harshly. 'Whatever he told you, was a lie. To preserve himself, to clean up his own mess, to achieve his own aims. For *he* was the young lord who approached me.'

'Liar!'

'Richard, please,' Will said, staring down his brother intently. 'You promised to hear him out.'

Laramie looked as if he were about to protest but Will silently urged him to relent and so he did, falling back into his chair with an air of sullen resentment, which did seem to be his natural state.

Not that anyone could blame him with all that had happened to him.

'Continue, my lord,' Effy said conciliatorily.

'Fulton's proposal was thus,' he said, eyeing Laramie, but turning the full force of his gaze back on Angelique. 'Procure him women, men, children, whatever he asked for. He was starting a club, he told me. One where men of fortune could come and indulge their pleasures. At first, I admit, I did not see the harm in it,' he explained, and Angelique grasped the arms of her chair as if they alone could keep her rooted, present, sane.

Her heart still would not beat, her ability to breathe had disappeared, and if she lost her hold on this world for one second, she would crumble, tossed into the black churning void of emotions rising within her.

Disgust, fear, anger, resentment, incomprehension, pity, guilt; all mingling together in a black ooze that crept through her veins, and her flesh, killing all in its wake.

'So many such places existed already, what was one more,' the man who was her flesh, her blood, said, as if that answered the unspoken question of *why*. 'I found what he asked for, recruited prostitutes for the most part, and I was paid a good fee. It continued thus for years, only as my debts decreased, so my doubts grew.' Her father took a fortifying gulp of the tea that had been set beside him, and shook his head again. 'Shipments became more regular, too regular, too frequent. There were whispers about town, about what sort of club this truly was. I did not stop and question any of it, not until after I met your mother. Not until after you were born. Something... Changed. I discovered the truth then. Saw the reality of what I'd helped to create with my own eyes.'

The baron took a deep breath, and choked on a sob.

Suddenly, Angelique felt an urge, both to reach out and hold his hand, and to strangle him. He was both her father in that instant, a man she could rationally see *had* cared for her, *did*, care for her, and also, something even more foreign, more distant than a stranger.

He wasn't a monster, simply a coward, whom she did not know.

A man, only God could judge; yet a man she judged with every fibre of her being.

'I thought to try and stop it,' he cried, looking at her, begging for forgiveness. 'But by then it was too late. Fulton had created an empire. He was well-protected, and so was his creation, grown far beyond a simple club. There were dozens, across the country. And other pursuits, gambling, smuggling, whatever he could make a price off of.'

'I remember a party here,' Angelique managed, though her voice sounded as if it came not from her own body. This, this was why she'd come. To piece together every twisted piece of the puzzle covered in blood. 'I remember...'

The words failed her.

She choked on the rest of them, and tears streamed down the baron's face.

'Fulton was trying to keep me in line,' he said. 'But in the end, it was what finally broke me. You were so young... I had hoped you might forget the horrors you saw.'

Again, Angelique said nothing, merely waited, her heart beating again now, a million times in an instant.

She longed to bury herself in Will's arms, to cover her ears and never hear the rest, but she knew she had to. This truth, was at the heart of her.

It was what she had come for, God help her.

'You had been ill,' her father continued, and she felt Will's presence, closer, and she was grateful beyond measure for that. 'You went down to my drawing room... Fulton saw you, and I... I had never seen such a look in his eye before. He swore... He swore -'

'That I would be his,' Angelique finished.

The memory sharpened, the faceless man, faceless no more.

The rest of what she'd seen, etched as clearly as the lines on her father's face.

Her nails dug into the upholstery, and her skin burned and broke. She saw it all now. The men who had come to torture and take lives. The remnants of the broken lives splashed across floorboards and walls and idyllic pastoral paintings that hung and mocked those whose souls had departed the world. Her father, among them.

And Fulton.

She sucked in a breath, her body wanting to run, as it had that night; yet frozen now as she had been then. Everything in her being screamed, and it was shutting down again, she was losing the battle with her own mind, until she felt Will's hand on her shoulder.

Before, the touch would have broken her, but as his voice had brought her back, so now did his weight, his heat, which she could finally feel, seeping through her; a light chasing away the black poison, chasing it back to the depths from whence it came.

Focusing hard on that touch, on that light, she brought herself back to the present.

'Yes,' the baron said after a moment. 'I could not let that happen. I broke ties with him,' he sighed. 'By then, I had gathered enough leverage to ensure our safety, but I knew, one day, he would come for you nonetheless.'

'As did mother,' Angelique breathed, realizing the desperation behind all her mother's actions.

'She never forgave me,' he shrugged. 'Nor should she. Nor do I expect you to,' he said, and there was no denying that. 'She tried to marry you off before he could take you, tried to keep you far from his reach, and his gaze. But if you are here now, not even marriage has succeeded in keeping you safe.'

So he'd seen her ring then.

For a moment she pondered telling him the whole ironic tale behind her *marriage*, but instead Angelique nodded, and the room fell into a thick, heavy silence.

'What of my own mother,' Laramie asked finally, as if he were afraid to hear what they all had already guessed.

'She was a favourite of his, exclusive to him,' her father told him as gently as he could. 'He would've killed her before, had he not discovered she was with child. No one survived those clubs. By the patron's hands, or the owner's, that was the way. But when he learned she carried you... He took her away, set her up in some cottage until you were born. Then he killed her and sent you to be raised in an orphanage. When his first wife passed leaving him no heirs, and the children of his second union succumbed to smallpox, he took you back. And told you what he needed to make you his own.'

'I... I don't believe you,' Laramie said shakily, all his bluster gone.

'Yes, you do,' Fitzsimmons said simply. 'And were I to wager, I would say he sent you after Angelique, didn't he?'

Gaping, Laramie looked between Angelique and her father, then, the horror of understanding plain on his pale face, he rose, and went to pace before the fire.

'The leverage you spoke of,' Harcourt said, his voice clear and emotionless. 'You still have it I presume?'

'Of course.'

'We will be needing that,' Percy said.

'It will do you no good if you are thinking of going after him,' the baron said dismissively, as if they were all consummate fools. 'He has too many friends, associates. That leverage serves only to keep Angelique and her mother safe.'

'You will tell us where the leverage is, *father*,' she ground out, in a tone as commanding and proper as her mother had once taught her. 'And you will tell us who these friends and associates are, and you will not stand in our way!'

Everyone stilled, and Laramie looked at her with both surprise, and gratitude, but she sat tall, Will's grip tighter now, keeping her strong as she pushed past the limits of her endurance to ensure this *would* be the end of it all.

'There is a lock box in Cobretts,' her father nodded sadly after a long moment. 'Warton will get you the key, it is in my name. I will write the necessary permissions. As for his associates, I know only two of the three who serve at the head of the organisation with him. There is another, whom I do not know, and those who work under them... The web is too intricate. I have not unmasked them all.'

'Tell us,' Harcourt instructed, taking a pencil and notebook from his coat pocket.

'Captain Dunderville,' Fitzsimmons said. 'Fourth Sea Lord of the Admiralty.' The others all stared at him now, their eyes widening at the implications, and he shrugged. 'I warned you,' he continued. 'The other is Mr. Gresham. A plantation owner and merchant, shipping magnate from Bristol.'

'What of Bolton, Campbell, Almsbury, Mowbray, and Russell,'

Laramie asked, recovering his voice.

'Bolton and Campbell aided in shipping,' her father explained. 'The others, smugglers during the wars, but then only clients. Some of the first, as far as I know.' A crack sounded in the room as Harcourt's pencil broke, and out of the corner of her eye, Angelique saw Effy place a steadying hand on his own. 'But they are all dead now, as far as I know. Some years ago.' Laramie sighed, and raked his fingers through his hair. 'Why do you ask?'

'No reason,' Percy said shakily.

'So long as you are alive, Angelique,' her father told her warningly, a sudden fire of terror in his eyes. 'He will never stop coming.'

'I know.'

And she did, now.

Perhaps, she'd always known. That even with the truth of the faceless man's name, the truth of her fear, she would never be free. That even after all this, it still wasn't over. A tidal wave of emotions crashed over her, and she rose, unable to bear this room, to bear him, to bear the weight of any of it any longer.

Always a caged bird.

'Angelique, please,' her father cried as she turned away. 'Forgive me.'

'I forgive you for what was done to me,' she croaked without looking back at him, taking her strength from Will who remained at her side. From her friends, all around her. 'But as for the rest, only God may do that.'

With that, she strode out of the room, straight through the house, until she reached a set of doors that led out to the gardens.

It was locked, covered in paper and disuse, but she was beyond searching for another way. She tugged at it, wrenching it, kicking it, expending all her anger and frustration upon it until finally it released, cracking from the doorframe with a mighty bang. She ran, tripping on vines and leaves, and piles of dirt, across the terrace and down the stairs, through the maze of brambles and weeds which tore at her and her dress, into the now pouring rain. She ran further and further until she was in the grand park, once manicured lawn, now burnt and tall grasses.

The rain had soaked her in an instant, but she didn't care. She felt too much, and nothing, all at once. When she was far enough from the house, she screamed, out into the park, out into the world. She screamed away her pain until her throat was hoarse, and her voice was gone.

And then, she crumpled to the ground, wishing she could be swallowed into it whole.

A figure came some time later, and picked up her frozen, seemingly lifeless form.

XXV.

I s she alright,' Will asked, scrambling to his feet as Effy closed the door behind her, the light of her candle tearing him from the gloom. He'd been sat by the door to the room they'd put Angelique in for close to an hour now, going madder with every minute that passed. As she had once seemed to feel his pain, so he'd felt hers as she sat there, facing her father and the truth of the secrets at the heart of her, with such strength he'd never witnessed before.

As she'd scrambled out of the house, and screamed...

He'd felt it then, all that had been done to her, by her father, by him, by life. It had torn through him, and made him understand with dizzying clarity that no matter how he wished it wasn't so, no matter how much he wished he could deny it, she was part of him. When he'd seen her crumple into the grass, soaked, and pale, he'd been so scared. Terrified *for* her. As he always had been, but could only now recognize.

He'd gotten her back to the house, and to Effy, but if he lost her...

'Any longer out there, and she might not have been,' the woman said, eyeing him.

She had closed the door, and he longed to push past her, through it, to see for himself that Angelique was alive, and as well as she could be, but something in the woman's eyes warned him she'd have him on the floor with a blade to his neck before he managed to take one step.

And to top it off, he felt naked before her, her gaze as piercing as Angelique's had always seemed; though deadlier.

'I didn't... I didn't know what else to do,' he said, raking his fingers through his still damp hair. 'She needed it.'

He'd felt that too, her need for release, for freedom.

Her need to run.

'Walk with me,' Effy said.

Will hesitated for a moment, until she started off without him, turning to look at him beckoningly over her shoulder.

He strode after her, and together they walked the deserted corridors of the ghastly house, both careful it seemed, to remain in the small circle of light cast by Effy's candle.

'Angelique told me your story,' she said after a moment, gazing up at the covered paintings and portraits lining the walls. 'At least, I presume it is your story, and that you did not lie to her about it, though you did not tell her everything.'

Will nodded.

That was one thing he'd been unable to do, lie outright. At least, in all that mattered. All he told her of himself.

A small sin in comparison to the rest.

And yet, he felt, that which would have been the most egregious of all.

'It is understandable, to choose the path you did. Despite their bluster, Percy and Harcourt understand too. I think, Laramie and yourself managed to somehow find the few people in this world who could. Life is interesting in that way.'

Life, fate, or God.

Whoever had had a hand to play in this tale.

Whoever brought you to her; the one creature who could... Stop.

'Understanding is one thing,' Will said gravely, knowing she was right. Whoever's plan, this story could have ended very differently indeed if not only for Angelique's choice in friends, but also, and chiefly, because of her courage. 'Forgiveness is another.'

'Angelique, for all she has lived,' Effy said, turning into the portrait gallery. 'Was not born and shaped as the rest of us were. She did not live with revenge, and anger, held tight to her breast. And yet, without her, we might all be dead. We might've all killed each other on the road, had she not forced a truce. We were mere moments from it as I recall.'

'She wanted the truth,' Will pointed out. 'To be free.'

'Yes. But she might've gotten it without you and Laramie,' the woman countered. Will stopped, and Effy smiled back at him. 'Understanding is the first step to forgiveness.'

'Why are you telling me this,' Will asked softly.

'Whatever is decided tomorrow,' she said. 'Angelique has a long path ahead of her. Of healing, and rebuilding. Of freedom. Whatever must be done, we shall see to it, so that she, at least, may have some peace.' Beckoning him along, Effy began walking again, her eyes on the invisible Fitzsimmons all around them, neatly shielded from the world. 'What we think is our purpose, what we think is our duty, often blinds us to the simple truth.'

'Whatever is decided tomorrow,' he said, understanding and not liking where she was going with this talk. 'I made a vow. I will be a part of how this finishes.'

'Will, I am not asking you to make a decision now,' she sighed, almost exasperated, but with a softness that spoke of care. If not for him, then for Angelique, though for the first time, he liked to think for him too. If there were ever people he might count as friends, it would be such people as her, and her partner, and perhaps even Egerton. 'I only think, that before you make *any* decisions, you should consider that perhaps, there is another path for you. I know you love her.'

'I don't,' he said, the bare truth of it wrenching at him in a way he'd never thought possible. God, how he wished he could, only... 'I can't. It is not something... The ability to love was driven out of me long ago.'

'The love of my life used to think as you do,' Effy smiled, stopping them again. 'I do believe some are incapable of love. But you, you are not one such,' she whispered, searching his eyes, his soul, and finding something there that made him believe her. 'Harcourt's past, my own, Percy's… We thought it made us unable to love, properly. But love, pierces through darkness like the first snowdrop in spring. It is not the same for everyone,' she continued, earnestly, as if she could see how desperately he clung to her words, to the hope they brought. 'Love is not the same for all of us,' she said. 'For Harcourt and I… It is raw, and blistering, and unshakeable. Fortifying. For Percy, it was an awakening I think. Liberating. If love were the same for us all… Life would be so much simpler, and a lot less interesting. Just, think on that,' Effy said, touching his cheek gently, wiping away a tear, *a tear?*, he'd not even felt fall.

'I…'

'Goodnight, Will,' she said, glancing to the wall one last time before leaving, her candle in his hand, her footsteps echoing in the darkness of the evening and the house.

Will turned to the wall of portraits, all covered in dusty white linen.

Save for one.

One, that even had it not been the sole uncovered, would have shone brighter than all the others, so luminous, and enchanting was its subject.

Angelique.

It did her as much justice as such a painting could, showing all the facets of her, her kindness, her gentility and gentleness, her beauty, but most of all, her light. The light, he'd seen dim, until now, it was barely an ember at all.

And he knew, in that moment, that there was only one thing he could do.

Set her free.

XXVI.

Angelique woke enveloped in warmth, and in a scent she never thought she would smell again. Her mother's. Not the scent of Lady Fitzsimmons on parade, all sweet lilacs and powder and sweat, but the scent of her *mama*. The one she'd smelt when she had been a child, and had climbed into her mama's bed before the sun rose. It was rose water, and lavender, fresh linen and the essence of her. It surrounded her like a thick down blanket, and for a moment she refused to open her eyes, curled up tight on her side; refused to think on anything but that scent that made her feel at once so comforted and yet so alone.

For despite it all, she knew her mother was not here.

She was not a girl anymore.

And she was all alone now.

Slowly, painfully, Angelique's eyes blinked open, quiet tears dropping from them onto the soft pillows beneath her head. The window before her had not been covered like the others, and through the gap in the curtains shone the bright yellow light of a glorious sun-soaked morning. Dust motes swirled hypnotically in the rays, and she watched them for a long while, wishing she were one of them.

God, she was tired. Bone weary, and exhausted. Though at least, she was not so cold anymore. And her chest was not quite as tight as it had been... Her entire life through.

The previous day's, *days'*, events rushed back in a blur, and she held the comforter tighter around herself, inhaling deeply of her mother's scent. It had all just proven to be too much. She shouldn't have run out like that, been so weak; she'd thought she could face her father's tale, the truths of her life, but in the end, she hadn't. Not after... Everything else. She had needed to be alone, to be... Free. To scream, to lose herself, to forget all the hurt.

So she had.

And Will... He had brought her back.

Not only *here*, to this room, she'd felt him, felt his warmth, and *his* scent surrounding her as he'd lifted her into his arms, drenched and nigh-on unconscious as she'd been, her mind caught somewhere between this world and the world of memory.

Not only had he carried her, whispering gentle words that had pierced through the pain as his touch had, but he'd brought her back from the edge of oblivion she had courted. When she had run out yesterday, when she'd screamed, and fallen to the ground, she had wished it would swallow her whole. That it would all go away, that she would disappear. But Will had somehow, yet again, managed to bring her back. To make her want something more than to disappear.

That hurt too.

The fact that no matter what he'd done, he still held that kind of power over her.

The fact that try as she might, she could not hate him.

The fact that soon, whatever came next, he wouldn't be by her side for it.

The fact that she would have to do it alone; even if that's all she'd ever wished.

Sniffing loudly, Angelique wiped her tears away and turned to lie on her back and gaze up at the moth-eaten lace canopy above her.

And what does come next?

More blood, more revenge, likely.

They would go after Fulton and his associates somehow, she

knew that much. She would be swept up into whatever plan they would make, to be used as a pawn, or perhaps if she was lucky a more vital piece, a rook, or a bishop perhaps. Either way, she would be on the board.

No more freedom.

But then, she would do it. If it meant taking down those who had done such unspeakable things to others, she would be like the rest of them if she had to. She would play her part, and perhaps, knowing some version of justice had been done, would help numb the pain of yet again losing her own freedom. Of being part of a life not of her own choosing.

Perhaps...

Sighing, Angelique rolled slowly out of bed, the comforts of it lost. A dressing gown and some slippers had been laid on a chair by the side of the bed, and she slipped them on, tying the gown's sash as she went to the windows and thrust open the curtains. Outside, the overgrown park and gardens looked an idyll in all its rustic splendour with the warm spring sunshine basking it all in a fresh, glittering light. The light that came after a good storm.

One day my heart will be full of that light.

If she could not have freedom, at least she could have that.

Turning back to the room, Angelique's legs turned to jelly when she realized why she had woken enveloped in her mother's scent. It had not been merely a dream, or the remnants of one, but reality. For this, this had been her mother's room.

Certes, the floral pink, green, and cream wall hangings were faded, and that lace canopy was faded. Yes, the sage and cerulean rug was a little less plush, and the upholstery on the chairs and settee by the hearth had also been devoured by beasties, and torn from the frames in places. But still, it was the same. She remembered.

I remember.

She remembered how she'd sat at her mother's feet there, by the hearth, whilst her mother told her stories and brushed her hair. She remembered trying on her mother's gowns and jewelry whilst her mother readied herself for a party, all the gowns strewn across the bed for her to peruse, and she remembered sitting there, at the dressing table, whilst her mother taught her how to use powder and rouge. The tins were still there, coated in dust, but still there. With her mother's brush, strands of hair still caught in it, glinting in the sunlight.

Angelique's throat tightened, and she held herself, tears pricking her eyes, then falling down her cheeks. It was all still there, the good, along with the bad. And it hurt, yes, but how wonderful it felt too. To no longer feel disconnected from the past she'd locked away, but part of it. She remembered not only the happy times, but who her mother had been. Who *she* had been; who she'd been trying to become again all these years.

A girl who hoped, and dreamed, and loved, and was loved.

A girl who liked the feel of grass between her toes, and the taste of raspberry jelly.

A girl who was clever, and kind, and who feared nothing.

And no matter what came next, who she became next, she would not forget or forsake that little girl again.

∞

'I wanted to apologize, Mr. Warton,' Angelique said beseechingly as she stepped into the butler's rooms. The old butler who had chased after her laughing more than once, now seemed as old and tired as the house, though not quite as dead. He sat mending a sock at a little dining table set up in a corner of the front room, in which otherwise sat a desk, a shelf full of ledgers, and two armchairs. All simple, sturdy furniture, that suited him and Mrs. Warton.

After she had spent some time making peace with what she'd found in her mother's room, and cleaned, and dressed, she had made some decisions.

Resolved to face some final things before they left this place again.

Well, one thing, really.

Warton looked up from his mending, and set it down by a simple china tea set.

'For my behaviour when I first arrived,' she added. 'I was rather... Overwhelmed. But I should not have spoken thus to you.'

'It was nothing, Miss Fitzsimmons.'

'I also... I came to ask for the key to my father's drawing room. The red drawing room,' she said quietly. The butler's eyes flitted round and he shuffled uncomfortably on his feet. 'The secrets my father kept have been laid bare.' Warton's eyes widened, and she nodded. 'I need to see that place. Please.'

With no small amount of reluctance, he rose, and went to the desk.

Solemnly, he retrieved what she asked for, and placed it in the palm of her hand, concern, and yet admiration in his gaze.

'Warton, what happened to this house,' she asked softly as he went back to the table. 'I don't remember much, but I do remember enough to know it was once a splendid place. Full of life, and beauty.'

'Lady Fitzsimmons took you away the summer of your seventh birthday,' he began, gesturing for her to sit. He poured her cup of tea, and refreshed his own as she settled across from him. 'That very night in fact. Not a moment after your father told her what had passed. Barely had time to dress herself, and you. After that his lordship... Changed. He was as if a man sentenced by God himself to death.'

'So is that what this is,' Angelique asked bitterly, her rage and disgust for her father taking the forefront. *Safer that way.* 'Some pathetic attempt at redemption, living thus in squalor and ruin?'

'Pathetic, perhaps, but yes, it is his penance,' Warton conceded with no small measure of pride. Of respect, still, for the master whose despicable secrets she knew he shared. 'You would surely have discovered the sum of it when he is gone, but there is no sense in keeping it from you now. I do not think his lordship has told you, for he knows you would see it as you do now. Futile. You see, Miss, all the other estates are gone, sold, the ones that could be, let the ones which were entailed. Your father set aside enough to keep you and your mother in comfort, and the rest went to repairing all he had broken. All were dismissed save for Mrs. Warton and I. Though there is not too much for us. Only our quarters, the library, your mother's room, and your own. He goes there sometimes… To remember,' he told her.

And try as she might, she couldn't dismiss the pang in her heart.

She couldn't dismiss the man as entirely a monster; entirely something other from herself.

She supposed that was why Warton had put her in her mother's room.

'He has denied himself all comforts and pleasures these past fourteen years, for yes, though he believed he must survive, to ensure your protection, he died the day you left.'

'How do you know all this?'

'I have been a loyal servant to your father since his Oxford days,' Warton said with a sad smile. 'I was a boy myself then. Over the years, I bore witness to many of these decisions, and as he has weakened, helped him ensure all was as he wished it to be.'

Angelique fell silent, wondering just how far loyalty could take a man.

A man as good as she knew Warton to be, how it alone helped him live in this house, privy to all he was.

'It is not a servant's place to question their lord,' Warton said, as if reading her mind. 'But do not mistake me. I live with as much guilt as he for standing by without action, knowing all I did. But your father always had my loyalty. I saw how he tried to undo what he'd done, how he felt the magnitude of his misdeeds. And I could not abandon him. Not when I first learned the truth, nor now, in the end.'

Angelique nodded, and sipped her tea.

So many answers, so much knowledge, and yet, the truth of it all was not as comforting and liberating as she had once prayed it would be.

Only more confusing.

Give it time. Time... Heals.

'If you will permit me, Miss Fitzsimmons,' Warton said tentatively. 'I do not know what was said, but I can imagine things were not left as they should be.'

'I owe him nothing.'

'No, you don't,' he agreed. 'However, you owe yourself not to regret your final words to him. No matter his crimes.'

'Thank you for the tea, Mr. Warton.'

She set down her cup, and rose, and the old butler nodded.

There were some things, she simply did not have the strength for.

XXVII.

I think we can all agree, have agreed in some unspoken manner,' Percy began resolutely once they had all finished their breakfasts and the plates had been cleared. They had installed themselves in the old pink parlour, empty, faded, and decimated as much as the rest of the house, but which at least boasted chairs that could hold them, and a large table they could congregate around. They had eaten their breakfasts in silence, albeit not as tense a silence as there had been at the pub.

Now, it was more pensive, subdued, as everyone felt the effects of all that had come to light.

'Fulton must be stopped. Whatever he has built, must be destroyed. Burnt to the ground so that nothing may grow there again.'

Just as expected. You can do this.

Everyone including Angelique nodded, and murmured assent, though they were all thinking the same thing.

How?

What her father had said, the men he'd spoken of... It was no exaggeration to say it was a nigh-on impossible task they were setting themselves. If they were to survive whatever they undertook, they would have to be supremely clever, prepared, and united.

But we can, and will take them down.

'What do you suggest, Egerton,' Will asked, looking up from

his empty cup of coffee. Her father may have dispensed with most luxuries; but tea and coffee were not among them. 'If what Fitzsimmons said is true, he is more than well protected, and finding out scraps of information on those still masked could take us years. Never mind destroying it all. And as soon as he catches wind of what we're after, as soon as he knows Laramie has turned against him -'

'He won't,' Laramie declared, determination in his tone and features.

All eyes turned to him, frowning, and questioning.

It was as if the man had transformed overnight; no longer the surly, vengeful, spiteful Viking, but a man of pure stone and will.

A man who had nothing left to lose, if he had ever.

'Because *I* won't.' Surprise and fear flickered in everyone's eyes and hearts for the briefest moment, and Laramie chuckled. 'At least in his eyes,' he reassured them all, as if they were the daftest creatures for believing him capable of doing such a thing. 'I swore to avenge my mother,' he said, glancing over at Harcourt, who shrugged. Angelique got the impression the two had indeed found a sort of kinship, and spoken on the matter more than once now. 'And so I will. My father manipulated me,' he sighed. 'It is only fair I return the favor.'

'Richard,' Will protested.

'No, brother,' he said fiercely. 'This is what I was made for. I will return to my father,' he announced. 'And I will discover all there is to know about his business. I doubt however, that even he knows all of it now, it will have grown from him. So I will kill him, and I will take his place.'

A deafening silence overtook the room.

There was no arguing with him about it, it was a solid enough plan, and no one could truly say they would not be glad to see the day come when the Earl of Oster no longer walked the Earth.

And God will judge us all for that.

Me most of all, for it is the only way I shall be free of him.

'And then what,' Percy asked.

'Then, I shall need help,' Laramie conceded, looking to them all. 'To take down all those associated with him. To find them, to dismantle it all, piece by piece. I know what I ask,' he added. 'If you do not feel up to the risk, if you wish to reconsider your involvement in this, I understand.'

Percy sighed, and dropped his head into his hands.

No one would begrudge him stepping aside, not with Meg, and his grandmama, and his first child on the way. In fact, Angelique wished he would say no, that he would let whatever drove him to do such things as they were about to, go, dust on the wind. That the Ghost would rest, lay down his arms, and live a quiet, peaceful life for them all. That he would surrender before he crossed that line that surely he would have to now.

Only Angelique knew better.

Knew Percy better than that, and her heart clenched.

'Effy and I will help you in any way we can,' Harcourt said, taking Effy's hand in his. She smiled at him as he kissed her knuckles, and nodded. 'We have skills, and contacts that may prove useful.'

'And I have an army,' Percy said, raising his head, resignation and steel in his eyes. Laramie frowned, and surprise flickered in Will's eyes. 'Have you ever heard tell of the Ghost of Shadwell,' he asked, a hint of gallows' humour in his tone.

You,' Laramie asked, impressed.

'And others,' Percy nodded. 'But yes.'

My turn then. Show them you fear no more.

'I will -'

'No, Angelique,' Laramie said before she could continue. He turned to her, a softness she never would have guessed he possessed, and regret in his eyes. 'Thank you. But I am afraid, this is where it must end for you.'

'I can be useful, I can help -'

'Yes, you can. I need you to die,' he said bluntly, and Angelique froze. 'To the world, at least. I know, I ask much. But for this to work, my father needs to believe I succeeded in my pursuit. Perhaps, I got a little carried away with your... Punishment.'

'Oh,' she managed, her heart warring between relief, and

sorrow.

Relief, for she would be free.

To disappear, to live a life far from here, just as she'd set out to do. Sorrow, for she could not come back, likely for years. Not until they had completed their task. Her friends, her mother, Will… She would have to leave them all behind.

When not weeks ago that decision had seemed a worthy price to pay, now it seemed far too high to bear.

'It will not be forever,' Effy said gently, and Angelique nodded.

Raising her head, she managed a weak, but convincing, at least to her, smile.

'I know,' she said. 'A new life is what I wanted after all.'

'It is for the best, Angelique,' Percy said, and all at once a wave of sorrow washed over her.

How she would miss him, stubborn mule that he was.

She would miss them all. She would miss his child, who she'd never met, and might never. This task they undertook, it would be full of danger, and pain, and death.

And it might never end.

'We will see each other again,' Harcourt added, reading her mind it seemed.

'Excuse me,' she said, rising before anyone could stop her.

She left the parlour and ran back outside; hoping the air would help clear her heart and mind again.

You wanted freedom. Now you shall have it.

How bittersweet it would be.

∞

'I will make sure she is alright,' Egerton said, rising before Will could, an expression of fierce concern and intent on his face. Will clenched his fists, knowing it was best this way, but unable to accept the fact that Angelique was no longer his to protect. If she ever had been. 'I will speak to her of her plans, see what she wishes to do. No decisions should be made before then.'

Richard and the others nodded, and Egerton swept out of the room.

They all looked at each other awkwardly, a group of people with only tenuous, odd connections between them, but nothing really to say to each other.

Only Angelique it seemed, had the power to truly get them talking.

'We'll pick this up later then,' Effy said jovially, rising to her feet.

Will scrambled out of the chair as quickly as his brother, though Harcourt lazily drawled to his feet.

'A moment, if you would, William,' he said, just as Will went for the door, in a pleasant tone that was nonetheless menacing and unyielding.

When Will nodded, Richard and Effy continued on their way.

Effy shut the door quietly, shooting her partner a warning look that added to his unease. It wasn't that he was afraid of Harcourt, or rather, that he wouldn't have been before. The man was made of the same metal he and Richard had been forged from, and he understood that. In a fight, it would be anyone's bet who might win, only now, he would never be able to hurt the man. Any of Angelique's friends for that matter, for the simple fact that they were people important to her.

People she cherished.

Will crossed his arms and faced the man with as much mettle as he could, though Harcourt's eyes felt like they could peel flesh from bone. He felt like an animal at the tower, an exhibit, to be studied, and in time, dissected.

And completely at a loss as to what the man could have to say to him.

'It is strange, to think that I came to know Angelique because I sought to use her for my own ends,' Harcourt mused, trailing his fingers along the edge of the table lazily.

Will's eyebrows shot up.

He'd never really known nor questioned how they had all come together, this strange bunch they were, Angelique's friends. She had mentioned being involved in Mowbray's demise, but he hadn't really committed much thought to the matter.

A rake, a vixen, and an earl; such an odd collection.

'Oh yes,' he chuckled. 'I enlisted Effy to get close to her, to find a weakness of Lady Lydia Mowbray's... And so we did.' Harcourt's fingers stilled, in fact his entire body tensed, his features hard. 'She was never more than a pawn to me, that is, until after we left England. Effy and Percy have grown rather attached to her, and I admit, so too have I.'

'You don't have to worry,' Will said quietly, understanding what this was about now. Where Effy was a dreamer, encouraging him to believe impossible things could be; Harcourt was a realist. He knew what had to happen. 'Whatever her decision, it will be hers to make. I would never try to force her to do anything.'

'Again,' Harcourt asked with a wry grin.

Will sighed, and rubbed his jaw.

Of course the man would doubt him, his word, after all he'd done.

'I will let her go,' he said resolutely.

Richard and he had discussed what would happen to Angelique.

They'd both guessed her friends would want to join in the fun of destroying the despicable empire Fulton had built, but he had made Richard promise Angelique would be free no matter what. Safe, faraway from whatever they would do. She would have a chance at happiness. In fact he had been so concerned with that, he hadn't even thought to discuss what Richard had in mind for a plan beyond it, or even how to achieve it.

It wasn't much, yet it was all he could do for her. But now, saying the words out loud, for the first time, declaring that is what he would do, *let her go*, even after all he had come to realize these past few days, after all Effy had said to him... It felt as if the gavel of justice had sounded throughout the world, the pronouncement now law.

So it should be.

'I have, let her go. Richard needs her dead. And gone, faraway,' he added, hoping to lessen the magnitude of what he'd said.

Hoping to hide from this man at least, the truth that lay in every word, every action.

The truth that lay in his heart.

'Indeed,' Harcourt nodded, a strange smile on his face. Half pensive, half conciliatory. 'I am glad to hear you will not oppose her plans, whatever they may be. Angelique is strong, but she at least deserves to live a life faraway from all this... Filth. She deserves a choice in how to live her life.'

'She deserves so much more,' Will whispered, his grey eyes meeting black ones.

There was an understanding that passed between them then, the resoluteness in both their hearts meeting and recognizing itself.

'Good,' Harcourt said lightly. 'So long as we understand each other. I would hate to have to kill you.'

'I would hate for you to kill me,' he answered as Harcourt made for the door.

For he had no doubt the man would; no doubt it would be a terrible thing to endure.

Harcourt Sinclair would make him suffer the crimes he had committed, the sins he had committed, chief among which was hurting Angelique. Not that he didn't deserve it. Not that he wouldn't deserve every cut, every blow; not that he wouldn't endure them gladly if it would bring her peace.

Anything for her.

But before he stepped out of her life, they would have to speak. He had to...

Say something.

XXVIII.

'Angelique, wait, please,' Percy called. She glanced over her shoulder to find him running down the terrace steps towards her. She stopped, taking what little time she had to wipe away her tears, and compose herself. She might've avoided him if she could, but this talk they were about to have, she knew it was a long time coming. And truthfully, she owed him that much.

He expelled a long breath, and bent over, hands on his knees when he reached her, the image making her smile.

'La. You are getting old, Percy,' she chuckled. 'So out of breath in this fond chase.'

'Mock all you like, she-devil,' he pouted, righting himself slowly. 'But I am neither old nor decrepit. Simply unused to running now.'

'Soon you will be running all about the house, chasing after your children,' she said without thinking, conjuring the image before her eyes as she did.

Then the pain of realizing she likely would never see it hit her, and it must've shown, for Percy frowned, and looked at her with the same concern that had once felt smothering.

'Angelique…'

'Don't,' she warned, pushing away the swell of emotions as she'd been taught so well. 'Let us walk, for I cannot stand another moment in that house more than I must.'

They fell into step, and wandered about the wilderness that was the gardens for a while, through the skeleton of the box-green maze, then onto the roseraie, wild and untamed, but just beginning to bloom.

She remembered happy times here, remembered tea parties with her mother, and others in these very gardens, but somehow, it all seemed tainted now, by the rotten heart of the house, and her father, and all their life and comfort had been built on.

Once, she had felt something akin to pity for Lydia Mowbray, for having a father as terrible as she had. She'd been grateful her own father was not such as that. Only now she saw the irony of it; her own father a much more despicable beast than the duke had been.

But soon only new memories shall be yours to behold.

'There is a ship leaving Bristol in four days,' she said finally, tearing herself from her thoughts. 'It makes for Boston, and I shall be on it.' Percy frowned, and looked at her inquiringly. 'I memorised the schedules from all the ports,' she explained with a small smile. 'It was always going to be America, and you heard Laramie. It is for the best.'

Percy nodded, unable to refute it, even though she could tell he wished he could.

As do I now.

'I will go with you,' he said instead. 'To Bristol. Help make the arrangements.'

'I should like that.'

'Angelique...'

'I'm sorry Percy,' she choked out, her damned heart refusing to listen to its master. *But you are not its master, not anymore...* 'I am sorry, for everything. For running, as I did, for not trusting you...'

She stopped, shook her head, trying to beat back the tears.

Percy took her hand in his gently, and turned her to face him.

'*I* am sorry,' he countered. 'For making you feel you couldn't. I care about you so much,' he said fiercely. 'You are the best friend

I've had. You are my family. You understood me, stood by me, when so many did not. I only sought to protect you, but now I see, I did not listen when I should have. I got so caught up in the fear, and the worry, and Meg -'

'Understandable,' she chuckled, and he nodded.

'Still. I was not there when you needed me most,' Percy said gravely, and his hazel eyes shone with regret. 'I saw the fear in you, saw your drive for more, and I did not make it so you could lean on me. Only tried to conform you to what I thought you needed, just as everyone else did. I did not want you to feel such scorn as Meg and I have felt. As others have.'

'I am grateful for your friendship, Percy,' she whispered, placing her hand on his cheek, smoothing the lines of concern that had deepened so very much. 'You have been family to me too. A brother. And I think, I did not trust you because I was afraid of asking for help, not because I truly thought you would force me down any path I did not wish to go. I closed myself off to all I felt for you, and Meg, and your grandmother.' Percy chuckled, and she smiled. 'I closed myself off so that I wouldn't regret all I left. But now... It is the only thing I shall regret. I shall miss you so very much.'

'And I you,' he growled, pulling her into a tight embrace. 'We all will.'

Angelique nodded, her throat so tight she could barely breathe.

Percy's grip tightened around her, and a sob escaped her. Before she knew it, she was crying, crying as she hadn't in a very long time, weeping as every ounce of sorrow, and pain, and fear, and turmoil, was finally released from her heart.

They remained there, thus, for a very long time, until finally her tears stopped their infernal gushing, and her breathing evened. Finally, Percy released her slowly, keeping his arms on her shoulders, as he examined her closely. She was surprised to find tears of his own dripping down his cheeks, and though she felt light, she also felt that same pang of regret that she would likely never see him again.

It was as if she was grieving someone not yet gone; saying farewell even though the time for their final goodbye had not yet come.

'Please, I know it is rather useless to say, but be careful,' she sighed.

'I will. And so must you.' Angelique nodded, and Percy pulled her in a little to kiss her forehead. 'Effy and Sinclair always know best. We will see each other again.'

Angelique nodded, and he took her hand again, placing it on his arm.

Together, they wandered the grounds until sometime later Effy shouted at them to come have some food.

We will see each other again, Angelique told herself as they made their way back.

For I will it to be so.

∞

'I did not think I would see you again,' Lord Fitzsimmons said, astonished as she once again stepped into the library. If she had thought he looked broken, and diminished yesterday... Today, he seemed to have aged a century more. He set aside the book he'd held slowly, as if the weight of the thing was too much, and she wondered if she had the strength for this.

Only Warton had been right.

She needed more...

For myself.

All the other goodbyes she would have to say... She would not leave this particular chapter unfinished while she closed the book on the rest. If she was truly to begin anew, to leave it all behind, so she had to leave them as she wished to.

You are strong enough to face anything.

'Nor did I,' she admitted, taking slow, but steady steps towards him. 'But Warton and I had a... Conversation. He convinced me I should not leave things as they were. So, this will be the last time, father.' He nodded, and looked to the fire, which even on a sun-drenched day such as today, was the only thing to illuminate the room. She wondered if he was as cold inside as she had been not so long ago. 'I am going to America, but to the world, to Fulton, I shall be dead. I have written a letter to mama, it will be delivered by one of my friends, and burnt after it has been read.'

'Good. Good.'

'What I said before, of forgiveness,' she said softly. 'It stands. However you should know that I understand you. In time, I hope to find the strength to forgive you, for all of it, not only what was done to me. I have… Learned so much since I left London, since I came here. About myself. And the world. About what I wish to make of both those things. I hope it brings you some measure of peace to know that I will begin anew. I will have a good life, and I will find a way to be happy.'

'That is all I ever wanted for you.'

'What were their names,' she asked after a moment. Her father hesitated, not because he hadn't understood what she asked, but because he did. 'Do you even remember?'

'I remember all their names,' he breathed. And it was admittedly some small consolation to her, that beneath the monster still lay a man who knew what was right, and what was wrong, and what his soul was to bear. 'I say them in my prayers every night. Lucy, Esme, and Jean died here that night.'

'I hope you find peace, father,' she whispered. 'In this life, or the next.'

'I love you, Angelique,' he said.

For a moment, she tried.

Tried to conjure enough of the emotion to force her to say the words. Tried to recall enough of the man she'd known to feel it. Tried to say them even without meaning them, to give him something, anything. But the truth was, she never had felt love for him.

And not because it was more than he deserved, but because she refused to let one more lie leave her lips, one more lie be given life in this house, she did not say it.

He nodded, and she was sure she saw his heartbreak in that moment. She was sorry for it, but it could not be any other way.

So without another word, she left her father, forever.

God have mercy on you.

XXIX.

'A ngelique will be leaving for America in four days' time,' Egerton announced, a forced cheer not enough to dissimulate the sadness in his voice, or manner. They all sat in the faded pink parlour again, a measure of cognac before them all, save for Angelique who took whiskey. He'd never really noticed her aversion to the other liquor until now; though he could well surmise where it sprung from.

Will felt Egerton's mood across the room, as it was his own.

He felt the momentum of her decision, the weight of it on his chest, nearly crushing him; yet he felt the relief of it as well. She would be far away. She would fulfill her dreams.

She will be free.

'I will be accompanying her to the ship, which will depart from Bristol,' Egerton continued. 'We will leave in the morning.'

The same thought crossed all their minds, but Richard was the first to articulate it.

'There is perhaps someone you might introduce yourself to, whilst you are there,' he said, a calculating grin at the corner of his lips. 'As one business man to another.'

'Quite right,' Egerton agreed. 'Sinclair and I have been looking to expand our business, and an associate in Bristol would be most welcome.'

'I think that means we should look to acquaint ourselves with Captain Dunderville,' Effy said, glancing over at her partner, as though they were discussing the latest plans for society fun. 'Whilst Percy discusses expansion into Bristol, perhaps you can see what the Captain might be able to do for us in London.'

'We have been away from town so very long, dearest,' Harcourt grinned, taking Effy's hand in his, and kissing the knuckles in a gesture that seemed theirs and theirs alone though thousands of other lovers had likely done the same. Will felt a pang, of what he wasn't quite sure, and glanced to Angelique, who sat quietly, her finger tracing the edge of her glass. 'I think it is long past time we returned, and took an interest in the business. Particularly since Percy will be quite busy with his new family. We should certainly make some new friends.'

'Yes. I will go to Briar Hill once introductions are made, and I will return to Bristol when I can,' Egerton said. 'In the meantime, I have men I can send up from London.'

'We have time,' Effy said with a reassuring smile. 'In fact, I suspect this shall take a while. You should enjoy your family, Percy.'

'We will all need to tread carefully,' Richard said, shooting the others a glance, his gaze resting on Will, a strange look in his eyes, as though he were trying to decide something. 'Egerton, you cannot be in Bristol long alone. Or at all for that matter, not with your child on the way.' Will might've almost thought Richard was thinking of the man himself, had he not known his brother cared more of how suspicious it might look that a man everyone knew was enamoured with his wife, would abandon her at this particular time. 'Make the first approach, but we will need more allies, more eyes and ears everywhere. Especially when we begin to discover more of those involved.'

'I am sure as we uncover more perpetrators,' Effy said quietly. 'We will uncover more who have suffered because of them. With all that has been done, we cannot be the only ones searching to end these men.'

'There may still be those seeking to end you too,' Angelique said, turning to look at Effy and Sinclair.

Will and Richard exchanged a glance; neither of them had

truly thought of that.

But those the pair had taken down years ago were powerful, and some would not have been happy to see them toppled. Hence, why they had left to begin with he supposed. God, she was clever, his Angelique. Her mind working to protect others even in those darkest of times.

Not your Angelique. Never yours.

'And lest we forget, Percy, we still don't know who was after you last year, or why.'

'Whoever it was, they were not after me I think,' Egerton sighed, glancing around at them all. They all frowned; this was new information to them. 'I met with a solicitor last year, whose name I came upon thanks to one of my workers.' His jaw clenched, and he took a moment. Will sensed that he likely spoke of his old foreman, the inside man behind the attacks on the wharf. 'A Mr. Silverton. He informed me that the attacks had been those of his employer, and *born of misinformation; a grave miscalculation*. He promised so long as I did not look into the matter further, that I, and those I cared for, would be safe.'

Egerton glanced to Angelique, and she took his hand with a smile.

Everyone at the table had a good idea how much it must've taken to trust in that promise, to walk away from punishing those who had come after him. And yet, had Will been forced with a similar choice, vengeance, or someone he cared for, he suspected he would make the same choice.

Not that it mattered.

'Who the Devil were they after then,' Richard asked, breaking through the silence.

'I cannot know for certain,' the earl said, slowly taking his hand back, and downing his cognac. 'But I have given the matter much consideration, though I have been careful not to go poking about. I suspect it was another who operates in Shadwell, the leader of the largest, most proficient gang there is. Not even I could root out a name, though to be honest, I did not give it too much of a try. He kept the peace nearly as much as I, and was the least of my concerns when I served as the Ghost. His methods are, shall we say, less barbaric than others. Though his might, is steel, and his intelligence, unmatched. They call him St. Nick; that is all I know.'

'So another rival thought to take him down,' Richard frowned.

'A rival with quite some money and power,' Sinclair pointed out. 'Not many East-End gang leaders I know use solicitors from Fetter Lane to deliver their messages.'

'Quite,' Richard agreed.

They all fell into a pensive silence for a moment, as they digested all they had heard, solidified their plans, and prepared for all that was to come.

'Well then, I think we have decided it all,' Effy said with a determined smile. 'We should be wary if we correspond with each other,' she added. 'Never put details into writing, and use only our family name initials, I think. If anything goes wrong, we should have a place where we can leave a message, in London at least. You can arrange for one in Bristol as well, Percy. Check it, every day.'

'The statue of St Martin,' Richard said with a nod. 'In his church, in the Fields. There is a small hole beneath where his cloak is split. Enough to leave a small message.'

Effy eyed him carefully for a moment, then nodded.

'To us then,' she said, lifting her glass, urging the others to as well, which they did.

A sense of gravity, and kinship invaded the room, and Will felt his eyes yet again drifting to Angelique.

Toasting her friends, as if a woman wishing her husband well when going off to war. Perhaps it was harder, to watch others go and fight, whilst you had to keep on living.

But you must. And you must be happy, for all of us.

'To unexpected allies. And the sharp blade of retribution. May we meet again.'

'May we meet again,' they repeated in unison, clinking their glasses, and downing their drinks.

'We should begin making arrangements,' Sinclair said after a moment.

'Indeed,' Egerton agreed, rising. 'And we should speak.'

Sinclair nodded, and everyone rose, and slowly left.

Everyone, save for Will.

He watched Angelique go, watched her glide silently out of the faded old parlour, then stared at the doorway she had disappeared out of, neither seeing, nor hearing anything else, not even his brother's calls for him.

He remained there, for how long, he couldn't quite say, knowing that the time had come, yet refusing to acknowledge it by moving. Refusing to accept that the time had come for him to say goodbye, to break that final bond which remained, inevitably, inescapably, between he and Angelique.

Yet knowing, that setting her truly free, would be the best thing he ever did in his life.

∞

Once he did move, and go in search of her, it took time to find her. He finally found her in the last place he'd ever have expected. Standing in the foyer, before the closed door of the drawing room that haunted her nightmares. She was frowning, staring at it intently, perhaps a little paler than usual, but no paler than she'd seemed to be since his wretched betrayal. She was not shaking, nor lost to her memories as he'd seen before, and he approached her slowly, but loudly enough so that she would not start.

Giving her every opportunity to tell him to leave her alone and go to Hell.

'I spoke with my father,' she said quietly, and he wondered if she knew it was him, standing beside her, or if perhaps she thought him someone else. He wondered if she could tell him apart from every other being in the world as he could her. 'As much as I liked to think I could just leave things as they were, I couldn't. And I cannot leave without seeing that room.'

'I understand.'

'Did you ever go back,' she asked wistfully. 'To that place you were raised?'

'Yes,' he whispered, the memory of that day so vivid in his mind. He'd once thought it the most bright and beautiful day of his life. How utterly wrong he'd been. 'Richard bought it, first thing he did when he finished school on the Continent and took on his new life. Had it closed, and those responsible there... Well. He dealt with them. He kept it until he found me, and then, we returned there, together, to watch it burn.'

Angelique nodded, and he turned his attention to the door before them.

'Would you...' She inhaled a sharp breath, then shook her head. 'Nevermind.'

'Of course,' he said, his voice thick with emotion, answering her unspoken request.

He would do anything for her.

He would take all her burdens from her again, if only she would let him. Anything in his power to help her, to protect her, to make her happy. He'd always known that, somewhere in his mind and heart, but he'd never quite felt it as acutely as in that moment, when he knew he must also say farewell, for all those very same reasons.

If this was the last thing he did for her, so be it.

Angelique didn't look at him, merely reached out her hand until it twined with his. Such a small gesture. Yet such an intimate one. A simple representation of what they shared, *had shared*, would always share. Of the bond he wished he never had to break.

She closed her eyes for a moment, and he willed all the strength he had to pass to her. After a moment, she stepped forth, set a key in the lock, turned it, clasped the handle, and thrust open the door.

Immediately she reeled back a little, her hand on her stomach, and he tightened his hold, coming slightly closer so that she could feel his presence surrounding her. Tentatively, she crept forward, as did he, her eyes flitting about the dusky room beyond.

The shape gave away the room's original, intended use, but it had been stripped of everything else. The wall hangings had been torn and the walls presumably re-plastered as they were a stark white, even in the half-light provided by the paper-covered windows and French doors across from them. There were no curtains, no furnishings nor furniture of any kind, even the floorboards had been torn up.

They stood in the doorway together, examining the empty space.

'Angelique, are you well,' he asked gently.

'Yes,' she croaked, and he turned to find tears slipping down her cheeks. 'Their names were Lucy, Esme, and Jean,' she said, pushing down the emotion, and he longed to reach out, and hold her, but he knew that would be too much. So he squeezed her hand a little tighter, running his thumb against her skin, and she wiped away the tears, though more kept coming. 'The ones who died here that night. I asked him. He remembered them. I shall remember them too. Not as they were then, but their names, at least.'

Will nodded, and she closed the door.

On the drawing room, but not on her past.

Not ever would she be able to, just as he hadn't, but perhaps, it would not torment her so. Perhaps, she would be able to live with it.

Would that so could I.

'Thank you,' she said, releasing his hand, and turning to face him, her voice almost business-like. 'I thought I could do it alone, and I could've, only...'

'I was here,' Will finished, making it easier for her.

Easier for them both.

Angelique nodded, and began to walk back towards the stairs.

'So you are to America then,' he said before she could leave him.

This may not be the right moment to say what he had to, but

he had to say it.

And he wasn't sure he'd ever get another chance; have the courage.

'You heard your brother,' she said, turning back to him, her back as straight as the day he'd met her. 'I am to disappear. So please, whatever you have to say, don't.'

'I only wanted to say goodbye.'

'Oh.'

'I wanted you to know -'

'No. Don't try and make any of what you did better,' she warned.

'I'm not,' he soothed.

Well, he was, but not for himself.

For her.

This was it, his final moment of truth, the only thing he'd ever been able to give her along with strength.

Not that she needed it.

'I know what I did hurt you, and for that, I will always be sorry. But you understand that I cannot say, that dealt the same hand again, I wouldn't play it just the same.' Angelique nodded, slightly taken aback at the stark honesty. 'What I can say, is that I know now, with a certainty I did not some days ago, that what Richard asked... I could not have done so. Intentionally, at least. You said once, that you knew I could never hurt you. There was truth in that. I hope that perhaps one day, you will forgive me. And I... Wanted to thank you. For giving me a moment of peace. And happiness. For you did. You were the light in the darkness, and I... Do not wish things could have been different, for then, we may never have met. But I do wish they could end other than as they are.'

Angelique nodded slowly, and he took a moment to commit the vision of her standing there to memory.

For it would perhaps be the last look he would ever get.

And no matter that she was not smiling, or shining, or carefree as she'd been in Scotland, no matter that he would live forever with the image of her hurt by his actions, she remained the most beautiful, and precious thing, and this moment, would be enough.

To carry him through the rest of his life.

For it had to be.

He strode over to her, and took her hand, and she stared at him, with surprise, and what he would like to think of in the future as hope, that perhaps he wouldn't let go.

But he had to.

'You are free, Angelique,' he breathed, dropping his ring into her hand.

I love you.

He kissed her palm and closed her hand, then then turned on his heels, and left.

You are free.

Though I will never be of you.

XXX.

Packing. Again. The last time had been so difficult. She'd felt it a true ending, so bitter, and heart wrenching, but what had she known then? Nothing. She had known nothing of those things, and not truly known what finality felt like. What an ending, felt like. As she laid her meagre collection of things, to which she had added some of her mother's she wished to hold on to, to remember, she understood what an ending truly felt like.

Yes, it was heart wrenching, and bitter, but it was also, quiet. Peaceful.

Inspiring.

For no matter how bittersweet, it was also a beginning.

There was a little shuffle from her door, and she frowned, turning away from one of her mother's linen nightshirts, to the doorway.

Where Laramie stood at the threshold, waiting for permission to enter.

I suppose I must also bid him farewell.

'He was right,' she said softly, the invitation clear as she returned to her packing. Not that there was much left, just enough to keep her hands busy right now. 'You have your father's eyes.'

She should know, they had haunted her for fourteen years.

And it had been Laramie's eyes that had warned her to the

truth of it all.

'I wanted to thank you,' he said, clearing his throat and setting about wandering the room, his gaze and fingers travelling over every trinket, every painting and ornament she'd uncovered. She didn't mind; didn't mind him so much anymore. The truth really did have the power to set one free; though his eyes still unsettled her, and perhaps that was why he was making the effort not to look at her. 'For handling all that has happened with a fortitude, and grace, that puts us all to shame.'

'As I told your brother,' she sighed, unable to say his name at this particular moment. Needing to remind herself in some way of the bond of these two men; a bond stronger than any she might've hoped to claim herself. After what he'd said, *that* farewell… 'I did it for selfish reasons, for no one but myself. I wanted the truth, as much as the rest of you. I wanted my freedom.'

'Selfish reasons or not,' Laramie said, examining a tiny misshaped vase she'd not even noticed. One, that she had made for her mother many, many years ago, and which she'd never imagined had been preserved. She turned away, focusing on stuffing her petticoats a little further into her bag. 'Not many would have had the strength to face such circumstances, let alone, find a way to bring all those involved together. You fought, not only for yourself, but for us all. And whatever your reasons, you brought the truth to me. For that, I have no choice but to be grateful.'

'I hope you find the same freedom thanks to it that I have,' she said after a moment, closing her bag with that feeling of finality flooding her heart and soul. 'That you find a way out of the darkness, as I have. As the others have.'

Laramie nodded, gently replacing the vase in its place.

He turned back to her, and studied her carefully. Though his gaze was still slightly unsettling, she found the examination did not make her feel as nauseous, and afraid, as it once had. Perhaps, it was because she truly saw him now, beyond the resemblance to his father; beyond the mask of rage and bitterness, beyond the cloying need for revenge. Saw him for what he was, and had always been.

A man who is hurt; a man who is lost. A man who is not his father.

'If ever you were in need, you have only to ask. I wish you well, Miss Fitzsimmons,' he said. 'For what it's worth, I am sorry.'

With that, he left.

Angelique wandered to the windows, heaving a deep, relieved sigh as she gazed out onto the park, and the distant horizon that seemed to call her again. In a way, she was grateful to him too. For bringing her to the truth of her existence, that of her family, and most of all, even now, for bringing Will into her life. Just as she'd once told him herself. She had known the bond forged between them would change everything; and so it had.

Despite all that had happened, all that would, as Effy said, one had to be grateful for the gift of experiencing love. She had, for a brief moment in time, and so she was.

Fiddling with the ring now around her neck, she said a silent prayer for Laramie then, as she might've for a friend. She prayed that he too find peace, that this revenge, for no matter its other consequences, it remained thus, might not consume him. It had already, but in his eyes, in that last moment, she had also seen hope. Hope, that there was still a man inside, one who might have a chance.

After all, hope was all anyone had.

∞

There were some things which had always been a certainty to him. Things about himself, which, despite all he had endured, all that had transformed him over the years, remained a certainty. He was not an emotional man, though he had been a dreamer, in his youth; even when all hope seemed lost. He was strong, even in those moments when he had been terrorized by others, for he was a survivor. He was not wistful, and regretful; only rational, and pensive. Today, however, well, the past weeks, months, year, really, had thrown all of that into question; none so much as today.

As this moment, when he stood at the window of the old faded pink parlour, the only one with a clear enough vantage of what he wanted to see.

Needed, to see.

Angelique's departure.

Moments before, never carried such weight. He did not look on a particular moment, and think, *feel*, its significance, all it represented, all it did to him. Or perhaps, he'd simply forgotten. For he recalled that time when Richard had found him in the cellar, the time when he had relished those few moments, for all the hope and joy they brought him.

He'd forgotten, over the course of his life, how to *live*. He had survived, yes, endured, but he hadn't appreciated the moment a particularly pleasant scent wafted to his nose, or even when he saw a beautiful woman. He didn't taste food, didn't relish it. He didn't find something to see, truly see, when he walked out the door. He passed through the world, through his life, like a shade. Unseen, and unseeing. Richard did too, he knew. They were so alike in that way, moving onwards, fast and sure, towards a goal, without any notion of anything else. At least, he had been that way.

Until she showed you, reminded you, that you are alive.

He had known that, realized that, even told her as much. He had been grateful for that gift, until now. Until he remembered what a curse it was; when living meant pain. When you noticed how you felt as if you could never breathe again, as someone embraced their friends, and mounted their horse. When you noticed how bitter a promise could taste; realized how revolting spilt blood would smell now. When you realized food would never taste sweet again, nor the sun bring any warmth without her to share it all with you.

Ignorance of bliss and pain no matter the cost would be better than this feeling.

Will shook his head, clenching and unclenching his fist in the hope the gesture might help relieve some of the pressure in his chest, and stop the pricking behind his eyes.

He hadn't been able to go down there, to do so much as stand beside his brother and bid her farewell with the others. He hadn't been able to stand there and watch as she folded herself into the arms of Sinclair and Effy, and rode off with Percy, shooting one final glance back at the house.

Towards him, he liked to think, though he knew it was more likely she was saying her own silent farewell to her father, and to the house that had brought her so much pain. He had known he wouldn't be able to stand there, and not...

Beg her to stay. Beg her to take you with her. Beg her to...

So he'd come here.

Only, it wasn't any easier, watching it all unfold through the window, as one might watch a shadow play. In fact, he would argue, it was much worse, to be a mere spectator, but then, he'd made his choice.

And he had already said his farewell.

'I wish I could tell you it will hurt less in time,' came Effy's voice, tearing him from his lonely melancholy some time later.

Heartbreak, that is what this is, no sense denying it now.

How long he'd been stood here, staring at the empty gravel drive, who knew. Time didn't seem to matter to him anymore.

Which is something at least.

It had to at least be a couple hours, the sun was much higher in the sky now, not that it illuminated anything in this place.

'However, I'm afraid I have no experience in the matter.'

Will felt her come to stand beside him, but he couldn't turn to face her.

He was too afraid of what she might see in his eyes; or what he might in hers.

And what that might tempt him to do.

'I can only imagine what it would feel like to be parted from Harcourt,' she said gently, her hand coming to lay on his shoulder, and he bit back what he now knew were tears. 'And I am sorry for you.' Will nodded slowly, and took a deep, steadying breath. 'I am sorry this is how your story will end. But as I told Angelique, never curse the gift you were given, though the pain might tempt you to do so.'

Christ, the woman is a mind reader.

'I...'

'A moment, brother,' Richard said, interrupting him before he could finish the thought.

Will looked over to find his brother, arms crossed, a determined look on his face that never boded well, standing at the door.

He turned his gaze to Effy, who patted his shoulder gently, then shot him a reassuring smile as she left. He composed himself as Richard strode over, and mirrored Will's stance, his eyes studying the drive as if they held the secret to some ancient mystery.

The mystery as to why you are not focused on your goal, perhaps.

I will be in time, he longed to say, only Richard spoke first.

'We have travelled a long road together,' he mused, the light softening his features. Though perhaps it was all that had happened these past few days. A terrible light of truth had shone upon them all, and given them new purpose. 'And I would never have wished for anyone else to travel it with.'

'Why does this sound like a farewell,' Will asked. 'Am I not to come to London?'

He hadn't asked, they hadn't discussed it, but perhaps there was another task he was to be set to.

The thought pained him; Richard was all he had left now.

'Because it is,' his brother said simply, a strange smile at the corner of his lips.

It was a smile, unlike he'd ever seen on his face.

Not one of slyness, or mockery, or cruelty, but of quietude.

'I don't understand,' he protested. 'This isn't over, I swore -'

'I release you of your promise,' Richard decreed. 'I declare it served, a thousand fold. And I ask you to make me a new promise.'

'No -'

'Yes, brother,' Richard said, his hands on Will's shoulders, holding him in place, his eyes pinning him down. 'This next part, I must travel alone. Of sorts. And as for you... I want you to promise me you will live. That you will find even the smallest measure of happiness, and enjoy it, for both our sakes.' Will opened his mouth to protest, but Richard shook his head. 'You found something, something I never would have thought either of us could. I am not so cynical and dead, that I cannot see it. So please, swear to me, you will do everything in your power to grasp it tight. I am damned, but you, I think you found your redemption.'

'She will not have me. Even if she did, I have nothing to offer her,' Will croaked, the tightness in his chest from the unbearable mingling of hope, and loss.

Hope, that he *might* have a chance at that unfathomable thing he could not speak of for fear it would vanish; and loss, of his brother.

The only person he'd had his entire life; his mooring in the barren wasteland.

'I did not say it would be easy,' Richard pointed out, and Will half-chuckled, half-sobbed. 'But she is worth fighting for. And you, have so much to give. If she cannot see that, she is not worth it. Either way, a life, of your own, to live, for us both, is worth fighting for. So promise me.'

'I promise,' he choked out after a moment.

Richard clasped his neck, and pulled his head down so their foreheads were touching.

'Farewell, brother,' he whispered, before pulling away, and disappearing without another word.

'Good luck,' Will whispered to the air, praying to whatever powers that be, that he be granted the chance to see his brother again.

He stood there a long while, his mind a muddle of past, and impossible futures.

Not so impossible, perhaps.

XXXI.

My dearest Mama,

How long is it since I have called you thus? And yet, that is what you always were, and always shall be to me. There is so much to say, and not a hundredth of it could be written with all the ink and paper in the world.

I am so sorry for so many things, but sorry most of all that I must say what I will in a letter. That I will not be able to speak to you, explain all that has happened. That I will most likely never be able to see you again.

By the time you read these words, God willing, I shall already have begun crossing the ocean. I like to think that in the future, perhaps you shall cross it, and find me, living a simple, beautiful life. That we shall sit and speak of all we should have long ago, and drink tea, as mother and daughter; as we once were. Or perhaps, I shall cross the ocean again, back to you. Only time will tell I suppose.

You will not be surprised to learn why it is I must leave; the day you and father always feared came, and went. And thanks to God, to my friends, to a good man, I shall live to see another. You may rest safe in the knowledge that the man you dreaded so has not taken me, nor shall he ever have me. As my friend who brought you these words will tell you, I am now dead to the world. Until that wretched man, and the others of his business, are gone. If they ever are. Days, months, years, a lifetime, never... We do not know how long it shall be before they are victorious in bringing forth justice, or perhaps only retribution. Either way. They will fight, and that is all that matters.

I wish I could remain and fight, but they have given me a gift. The gift of freedom; and I am not so fool as to refuse it. It is all I ever truly wished for, and I think, all you ever wished for me, in your own way. I know now all you sought to protect me from, and all you did to keep me safe, and I am sorry I did not see before now. Sorry that I misunderstood every action you took; your entire being. I am sorry for thinking all the things I did of you, when truly, you only ever were, my mother.

I am sorry too, to have distressed you by running away. But I was remembering. I felt the shadow of that man though when I ran he had no name. I was safe; know that no harm came to me. I had quite an adventure in fact, and learnt a great deal about the world, about our family, and about myself. I dared, mama, to do things as we were always told we could not. I dared, to enjoy life, and to love. It was a painful journey, as I am sure you can imagine, but it was a great one. I have unshackled myself from the demons of our past, and I promise, I will live, joyously. I have brought people together who knew only hate and pain, and I like to think brokered a sort of peace that will chase darkness from the world, even in a small measure. My friends, old and new, know that they will be watching out for you, ensuring no harm comes to you. Help them, please, if ever they should ask. Do not judge them; aid them. They seek to right wrongs, in their own way. I will not debate here theologically on this, only remind you that sometimes the Lord works in mysterious ways.

I find myself wishing I could write books and books full of all that has happened, all I hope and wish for and dream of. I find myself wishing I could write forever for then I would never have to send this letter. I would never have to seal it, and give it away, and say what I must.

Goodbye, mama. Not farewell, God I pray not farewell. But goodbye. Until we meet again. Au revoir. I love you. I will miss you. I will think of you every day, and remember all the happy times I had until recently forgotten. I will remember you.

Remember me not as I was, but as I shall be so very soon. Happier than ever before, smiling as I gaze out onto the horizon towards England, and you.

I must go now, or I fear I shall never. My friend will tell you, but so will I. Burn this. Go into mourning. Stay safe.

Goodbye, mama.

I love you.

Yours, always,

Angelique

XXXII.

The docks here reminded him of his own wharf back in London. Of the place Sinclair had built, then abandoned to his own care. Of the place which had made him who he was today; the place that had brought him his wife. His love; his second family, Meg's. His only family. Well, along with his grandmother. And Angelique. The girl who was so much more than a friend; who was, as he'd discovered, admitted, only recently, a sister to him. And who now, was leaving.

It broke his heart a little.

His father's death had had an impact, there was no denying that now. Not after all that had happened since, which had forced him yet again to re-examine his life, and his heart. Not after the time on the road with Effy and Sinclair, speaking as they never had before. Getting to know each other as they never had before. Even these past days with Angelique, during which they had spoken to each other as family, and not as simple friends, dancing around truths, dancing to society's rules of what should and shouldn't be said and how.

He hadn't realized quite how much of an impact society still had on him, on the way he related to people. One had to, of course, follow some dictates, with certain people, in certain settings, but otherwise, they could be free. To be themselves. And he'd thought himself so free of society's shackles after finding love on a wharf.

Indeed.

He did regret not listening to Meg, not going to his father sooner; to speak, to understand, to say that which he'd held in the darkest corners of his heart for all too long. But he hadn't. He'd thought that he didn't quite have anything to say, that the old beast deserved nothing, not even acknowledgement of his existence in the end.

But after seeing Angelique with her own father, after witnessing her own fortitude, her own ability to confront the man who had made her... Well, he did regret it. Only he would not let it rule his life, or even define him.

He had made a choice, and he would live with the consequences. He would find a way to mourn his father, even if it was only mourning the man he wished his father had been. He would find a way in time to make peace with that final piece of himself.

In time.

Percy took a deep breath of the salt and refuse filled air, willing it to fortify him as the scent of the Thames always had, no matter how putrid the fumes. He stared up at the tall ship waiting to be guided out and onto the channel, from where it would then sail on to America.

Angelique, and so many others' promised land. It had taken all of his strength to let her go. To not try and force her into another plan, that would reassure *him* more. To simply enjoy the time he had with her, and purchase her a ticket, and send her off on her merry way, waving as she disappeared below deck to get settled. He had watched those bright golden curls of hers disappear, and he had known. It would be the last time he saw her.

For a time, at least.

He liked to think that despite all that awaited him, him, and Sinclair, and Effy, Laramie, and even Will... He liked to think they would all meet again, as Sinclair had said they would. That Angelique would meet his unborn child -

Oh Meg.

His wife was going to kill him before any villains got the chance when he told her all of it. Not that he would blame her. She would understand, but he was putting them all in grave danger, again. And regardless of the fact she had known danger might come for them in the future; he had made this particular decision without her. The others had given him an out, and he knew they would have understood.

But he would have been a different man if he had refused to help. Meg would see that, understand that, and still murder him when he finally found his way back to her. He hadn't been able to put any of that in a letter; simply scribbled a note to tell her Angelique had been found, and that he would be home soon.

Soon my love. I will not miss the arrival of our child.

No. He would see this ship off, and then attend to his *other* business in Bristol. And then when things were in motion, he would be back on his way to Briar Hill. To his family.

In truth he wasn't entirely sure why he was so determined to watch the ship depart. Angelique would likely remain below deck until it cast off, and even then, he probably wouldn't see her again. There was no reason really, to remain. Not even a silly sailor's superstition that he could think of. All he knew, was that he wasn't quite ready to go yet.

Sentimental old goat you're becoming...

Shaking his head and chuckling at himself, Percy let his gaze wander from the ship, across all the bustling business of the docks around him. Sailors, merchants, captains, passengers, cargo, moved to and fro like flotsam and jetsam on the waves; only perhaps with more purpose. It was dizzying, and soothing all at once, and he felt more at home standing there amongst it all than he had in crowded ballrooms and gilded tea salons. He wondered if he would be able to return to the simple life he'd built for himself when all this was over. If Sinclair would stay perhaps, and if -

What the bloody Hell is he doing here?

∞

Will felt Egerton's angry gaze before he saw the man. Stepping away from the gangway, he turned from the ship, and spotted the earl marching towards him through the busy crowds, anger, and righteous indignation in his eyes. Though he might've wished to avoid this, he knew it was a long time coming, and that he would deserve whatever Egerton had in store for him. He would endure it, welcome it, so long as he made it onto that ship.

Clasping the billet and bag tightly in his hands, he squared himself, ready to meet the man's fist.

Only, Egerton did not stride up and punch him.

He frowned as the anger in the earl's eyes faded, replaced with grim determination as he came to stand before him, as tightly coiled as ever, but somehow...

Relieved?

However unbelievable the notion, Will knew that is what he saw; and it was enough to completely throw him off balance. He stared at Egerton, waiting, questioning, as the other man drew slow, deep breaths, searching his face intently.

Egerton's fists unclenched slowly, and he sighed.

'What you did,' he began, menace still in his tone. 'I should gut you for it.'

'Yes,' Will admitted.

'And don't think it is just because I promised her I wouldn't, that I didn't,' Egerton continued, pointing a warning finger in Will's direction. He nodded, and the earl clenched his jaw. 'You betrayed me, and her... And I wish I could hold that against you. Sadly, I find myself unable to do that.' Will stared at him, and Egerton chuckled, running his hand across his stubbled jaw. 'Because I know, I saw, what you did for her. To keep her safe, despite it all. For some reason... For some reason I cannot comprehend,' he laughed, as a madman might, his eyes wild. 'She loves you. There was a time when I might not have been able to see it, or set any store to it. But she loves you. And you love her.'

'Yes,' Will breathed.

Egerton nodded.

'Just... Keep her safe,' he sighed. 'Give her the life she wants. Give her what the rest of us cannot have.'

'I swear it.'

'If we ever do meet again,' Egerton said after a moment, a spark of danger in his eyes once again. 'I will give you the thrashing you're owed. I would do it now, but you would miss the damned boat.'

'Thank you,' Will said gently, all that he felt pouring into those two, seemingly simple words. Gratitude, hope, joy, respect, and understanding. 'Godspeed.'

He offered out his hand, and to his surprise, Egerton clasped it tight.

'Off with you, now,' he ordered, nodding towards the ship.

With a crooked smile, a nod, and one last look at another man who had changed the course of his life for the better, Will did so.

There was not one moment to waste.

XXXIII.

The ship was finally underway. Having settled into her cabin, Angelique now stood on deck, watching England recede in the distance as they made their way from the channel into the open sea. What remained of that fear she'd lived with all these years, and of the weight she carried, floated away as the ship creaked and moaned all around her.

It disappeared into the wind that filled the now unfurled sails, and lifted the gulls high into the air. It misted away into the white spray that leapt from the sides of the ship, and sank to the bottom of the caesious waters around her. Only the weight on her heart refused to lift, but it would in time, hopefully. When the pain of heartbreak was healed by the memory of love, and the joy of a new life.

Closing her eyes, she inhaled deeply of the salty air, mixed with tar and hemp, which to her was now the scent of complete and utter freedom. She savoured every detail of that moment, which she declared would be the first of the rest of her life. Everything, from the feel of the worn but sturdy oak railing beneath her shockingly ungloved hands, to the music of the crew, shouting orders and acknowledging them, and the other few passengers, chatting and giggling all around her. All of them bound together, for a long voyage, and a new life.

I am as free as those birds crying above us.

'Did you know that a single man from Lincolnshire was the

first settler of Boston,' a familiar voice that made Angelique's heart leap from her chest out into the world said. 'Stayed there alone for about ten years or so, apparently.'

It cannot be.

Angelique kept her eyes tightly shut, afraid to turn, afraid to look behind her and see a man who was not the one she desperately hoped for. Afraid to discover her mind was playing tricks on her, and that she'd mistaken the voice. She would enjoy the dream, for a few moments more, because that is all it was. A dream.

For he couldn't be, wouldn't be here.

'Is that so,' she asked.

'His name was William Blaxton,' the voice said, closer now, and God, she must be dreaming, for she could swear she caught his scent too, there along with what was now freedom for her. 'Or so a rather dull but immensely edifying book on the city says. I would tend to believe it, for someone once told me William is the name of conquerors. And one could argue, that is what this particular one was.'

Her breath caught, and her eyes stung, filling with tears as they flew open, and found him there, standing just beside her, as always.

'Will,' she whispered, a thousand questions contained in that single syllable.

She searched his eyes, full of a light, and hope, that she'd never thought they could possess. Full of something she'd glimpsed, but never dreamed she could see in them, that which filled her heart now.

Love.

He looked so peaceful then, in the bright shining sun, strands of his hair catching in the wind, the weight he carried now gone too, a shy and tentative smile on his lips.

'What are you doing here,' she asked meekly.

She knew why she wanted him to be here, on this journey with her, but perhaps it wasn't at all like that. Perhaps he too was simply in search of a new life, or perhaps…

Really, there could be a thousand different reasons, and though she wanted to hope, was already hoping so much so that it felt as if her heart might explode, if she was wrong...

Please let him be here for me.

'I made a new promise to my brother,' he said, and her heart sank a little, that hope dying slightly inside of her. *Not for me then.* 'To live a free, and happy life, for us both,' he continued, quirking his head a little, his gaze inviting, and full of meaning. *Oh God, please, yes.* 'And I can only do that if I do so with you.' *Yes,* her mind screamed, and her heart, but the words did not come out. 'I understand, if you do not think you can forgive what I have done, if you do not want me, for I have nothing to offer you,' he continued, doubt creeping into his eyes, along with sorrow. Still, she couldn't say anything, her heart too full, and her head too dizzy with the prospects he offered. *Love, family, home.* 'I understand if you only felt, feel for me because I was there. Because I protected you so long. But I made promises to you too,' he said, his voice thick with as much emotion as was within her. 'To cherish you, to protect you, to love you. To be yours. And I will, I do. It took Effy and my own brother to see it, but I do, love you, Angelique. I never thought it possible, but it is the truth. You are my true north. And I would give anything, I will do anything if you will allow me to be your husband, and if you will be my wife. I -'

'Yes,' she finally managed to say. 'I told you once, all I wanted was you.'

Will's eyes widened, and he stepped forward, taking her hands in his as tears streamed down her cheeks.

He frantically searched her gaze, as if he couldn't believe it either, as if he too feared to hope they might end their story happily after all. She nodded, willing him to see all she felt for him, and he must've, for then she was wrapped in his arms, and he was kissing her.

And that kiss was unlike any they'd had, for there were no more lies between them. They were themselves, fully, uncompromisingly. The pain of the past still lingered in both their hearts, but there was a promise of healing, and trust, and companionship, and the pure light of love. There was forgiveness, in every touch, and understanding, and a thousand promises made.

They pulled away from each other, slowly, both breathless, and still dazed by the wonder of all they'd been given.

'I suppose I should return this to you, husband,' Angelique said quietly, releasing one of Will's hands to reach inside her bodice. She extracted his ring, which hung on a small silver chain, removed it, and put it back where it belonged, on his own finger. 'I do forgive you. I did, forgive you,' she smiled, tracing the lines of his face, committing those details to memory, adding them to everything else that would become part of this day. 'It might've been easier not to, but I forgave you as soon as I understood why you had done what you did, and that you hadn't lied. About yourself. You were never anyone other than the man I fell in love with. And it is the man I fell in love with; not what you did for me. All I need, all I ask for you to give, is yourself.'

'I don't deserve you.'

'Who are you to decide,' she said. 'We are together, we have something extraordinary, and who are we to question it? We are simply to begin anew, now. Together, Mr. Hardy.'

Angelique smiled, and Will nodded, before pulling her into his arms again, and tucking her into his side so they could both look out at the sea.

'As you command, little gremlin.'

'You may call me Mrs. Hardy,' she chuckled, shoving him lightly with her shoulder.

'Yes, that is much better,' he mused, kissing the top of her head lightly.

Much better indeed.

XXXIV.

New Cranston, Mass., September 17th 1824

The sun was finally beginning to set, taking with it the blistering heat of the day. Not even the fresh, salty North-Eastern wind had been enough to make it anything more than bearable. It was a different heat here, than anything he'd ever experienced before, and it had taken some getting used to, for both he, and Angelique. It was as if the sun sat higher in the sky, shone brighter, or perhaps, it was all simply in his mind, for it seemed everything was brighter now.

Wiping the sheen of sweat from his brow, Will raked back his damp strands of hair, and slid his cap back on before he undertook to trudge up the hill, which had seemed nothing more than a vole's mound when they had first moved here, and now seemed as much a mountain as any other.

He had never thought himself anything other than in strapping health physically, but this past month working the fishing boats had taught him otherwise. It was hard work, good work, which he enjoyed, but it was the kind of manual work that admittedly he'd not done in many years. Every muscle protested as he clambered up the steep hill, reminding him that guarding and fighting were one thing, whilst hauling crates of fish, crab, and lobsters in the heat of high noon was another. But it was worth it, it was honest work, which fed him and Angelique;

work he could be proud of, and which had helped bring his mind calm, and peace.

As had his wife.

Wife.

He still found that he held that word in the same reverence as when he'd first thought of making Angelique his, even more so now that they'd begun to build their life together. The two month journey across the Atlantic had helped them get to know each other, properly, to speak of things from their past more in depth, to heal, and to plan a future.

As soon as they'd docked in Boston, they'd been ready, to enact their plans, their dreams, and here they were, living them. He worked, as did Angelique, teaching the children of New Cranston, a small, but vibrant little seaside town whose quiet and industriousness suited them both. Together, they had a small cottage on the hill, which some day soon would include with its timber walls, simple furniture, and handmade quilts and rugs, the laughter of a child.

It was a terrifying notion, for them both, to be parents, to be father and mother to a being when neither of them had much experience to help them. But they would make it, together. They would make their child happy, and give it the life they had both been denied, a life of simplicity, peace, and love. They would give it all their hearts, and they would raise a good person, together.

Will stopped at the top of the hill to catch his breath, not from the walk, but from the sight that awaited him, which never ceased to impede his breathing. His little gremlin, full with another life though still only he could see it shining within her, tending to the small vegetable patch before the house, an earthly angel bathed in an orange glow, brighter than any celestial being.

He smiled to himself, and just as he did everyday, he thanked God, or whatever powers there were, for the sight. For this life, which he'd never dreamt of, but which had somehow been granted to him. He thanked his brother, and hoped he was well, and as safe as he could be. No word had come yet in response to his own letter. He prayed that one day he might see Richard again, perhaps here, and they might share a meal, along with all the others whom he now considered his friends. He could picture it perfectly, picture them all sitting cramped in the small room, around the wooden table barely big enough for four. There would be good food, and ale, and laughter, and everyone would be as at peace as he was now.

Soon, brother. Soon.

Angelique rose, a basket in her hand, and smiled at him, waving. He smiled back, something he found himself doing all too often now and went to her, his wife.

I kept my promise brother.
I am living for us both.
I am loving for us both.

EPILOGUE

E,

By the time you read this, I expect your primary business in Bristol will have been concluded, and that your secondary reason for visiting that city will be underway.

I write to tell you that here all is progressing rather quicker than we expected. Much has happened in our absence from town, things have been set into motion which will either favour us, or completely foil our own plans. My father is more reliant on me than ever, and I am taking on more and more responsibilities for him every day. I imagine you will receive further news from the others, but I could not rest without sending my own missive.

Shadwell has descended into chaos as the result of a gang war, and my own family's interests there have been decimated. I think I shall be sending some mutual friends of ours to find the saint who caused this upheaval as I believe it will be in all our interests.

Society is also buzzing with a rather scandalous series of events which occurred at a ball last Saturday, and I shall myself investigate the truth of some claims regarding my father which have come to light.

Things are changing, rapidly, so be sure of the ground you walk on.

Until we meet again, I remain faithfully yours,
RL.

AUTHOR'S NOTE

From her first appearance in *The Rake & The Maid*, I knew Angelique would be a crucial part of the series, though admittedly I had no idea just how crucial. Will & Angelique's tale is yet again proof that some stories have a tendency to run away with you.

I had originally intended for *Vixens & Villains* to be at most a trilogy; just as I had intended for Percy's tale to feature a one-book villain. However, the series has taken on a life of its own, and I have fallen deeply in love with the world and characters I first created in *The Rake & The Maid*. Every choice since then, has been made to ensure these books are both works of pleasure and fiction, as well as works which reflect the world we live in. Every choice has been made to honour the characters, and to give them what they ceaselessly demand.

Laramie for instance, began in my mind, as the central villain of the piece; you'll perhaps remember his appearance in *The Viscount & The Lighterman's Daughter*. Yet, as is often the case, I fell in love with the villain I created, and could not reconcile the man in my mind, with the man I originally planned to write. After I relented, and gave him only a central part to play, everything fell into place, and I had, instead of a trilogy, a sextet. And instead of a rollicking adventure for Angelique, I had a more personal, thoughtful tale.

It became clear as I began to write *The Bodyguard & The Miss,* that this would be the *calm before the storm* so to speak. This would be the book that set into motion the remaining three, and the one in which we would see all the pieces being set on the board. As I discovered Angelique's past, her story, and Will's, I knew this book would be extremely difficult, and delicate to write; and so it has.

Trauma has always been a central theme in my *Vixens & Villains* series, and that is admittedly because I find it important to give weight to actions and events we encounter in fiction. Murder, physical violence, sexual assualt, and so many other traumatic events; we find these often, in books or on TV, but often we forget that the effects of such violence are not temporary, but permanent. I sought to address difficult themes in my books, with care, and respect for all the repercussions these events have on a person's life.

Trauma is also an issue which affects me personally. In this book, more so than in others so far, I found myself exploring it more profoundly. Of course everyone experiences trauma differently; I chose to focus on two different types of trauma people can experience, to explore the different effects on one's psyche, and the lasting impact on personality and relationships. I sought to do so again, with care, thought, and respect.

It is in that vein that you will notice though Angelique has acquired fighting skills, those are not what saves her, and at times, she finds herself unable to employ them. This is something which can of course happen, and was not meant to be a Chekhov's gun of sorts. I also felt that though what Angelique learned, she gained strength from, it was important to show that like so many others, what enables her to endure what she does is her inner strength, her courage, and her heart, even in the most desperate of times and circumstances.

It is vital to remember that healing is a process, lifelong, and that there is a difference between healing with someone, and trying to heal because of someone. I would also like to remind you that if you, or anyone you know has suffered trauma, there are professionals and charities across the world that can help you.

On a historical note, the position of Fourth Sea Lord of the Admiralty was not created until 1830. Though I do try to keep my Historical Fiction as correct as possible, on this occasion I preferred to use this title as no name would have been associated with it in 1824.

I am also admittedly unsure of what routes boats took from Oban in 1824, but I did not think it a great leap to imagine some might've sailed to Ireland, even if not officially. You will, I hope, forgive the inaccuracy if this was not the case. I happen to know, and like Oban very much, which is why I set the Scottish part of the tale there.

In regards to the clubs such as that which the Earl of Oster creates, gangs, and trafficking, they are of course things which existed in 19th century London. Exploitation, in its various forms, has always existed, and I personally find it important to recall that with all the glitz and glamour, with all the bucolic beauty we find in the past, there is also as much darkness, and evil, as there is in our world today. I sought, and hope to represent, the scale of it; the intricate web-like nature of criminal enterprises which flourish still and are often the most difficult to bring an end to. For me, however, it will always be about finding love in the midst of all this; finding light, and hope.

Again, if you, or anyone you know has been affected by crime or exploitation, there are professionals and charities across the world which can help you.

Thank you for reading, and for those who are fans of the series, thank you for sticking with me. We will return to Shadwell next, to meet some familiar faces again, and I promise you more fun, adventure, balls, danger and love in the remaining books.

After all, as Effy Fortescue once said *revenge could be fun.*

ABOUT THE AUTHOR

Lotte R. James

 Lotte James trained as an actor and theatre director, but spent most of her life working day jobs crunching numbers whilst dreaming up stories of love and adventure. She's thrilled to finally be writing those stories, and when she's not scribbling on tiny pieces of paper, she can usually be found wandering the countryside for inspiration, or nestling with coffee and a book.

Be sure to keep in touch on Twitter @lottejamesbooks!

BOOKS IN THIS SERIES

Vixens & Villains

Set in Britain in the 1820's, the Vixens & Villains series is perfect for fans of historical romance with a dash of darkness, and danger!

Each can be read standalone, though there are stories which continue throughout the series.

The Rake & The Maid (Book 1)

The darkness in their hearts means they can never love - doesn't it?

Euphemia Fortescue fled an arranged marriage, and suffered the whims and trials of false friends and twisted lords. But as Harcourt Sinclair's housemaid, she found peace and purpose.

Harcourt Sinclair has been planning his revenge for twenty years against those peers of society who stole everything from him. But his single-mindedness will cost him, unless he can learn to trust his least expected saviour...

Redemption, adventure, secrets, desire, and love in Regency London.

The Viscount & The Lighterman's Daughter (Book

2)

They've hidden their true selves - but can they find each other?

Viscount Percy Egerton nearly lost everything in the wake of his friend Harcourt Sinclair's scandal. Not even taking over a shipping company and playing nighttime vigilante has helped him find what he wants most; himself. But when the daughter of one of his workers bursts into his life, he finds everything he ever wished for is within his grasp, if only he has the courage to reach out...

When Meg Lowell is dismissed and forced to return home to Sailortown, she is desperate to find the means to survive, and keep her family from destitution. Clever, and hardworking, she has no fear. At least until she meets Percy, and he threatens her with the most dangerous thing of all; love.

Redemption, adventure, secrets, desire, and love in the docklands of Regency London.

The Saint & The Madam (Book 4)

Love is a price neither can pay, and survive - isn't it?

For twenty years, Arthur Dudley has led a secret life as Saint Nick, the most powerful crime lord in the East End, perhaps even the city. But when an unlikely woman discovers his secret, he'll get far more than he bargained for.

Lily Fanshawe has been many people in her life, but she never expected to become a madam when she came to London looking for her sister all those years ago. Though neither did she expect to find love, and yet, she somehow has...

When a powerful enemy comes for them both, and those they

care for, they'll have to decide how far they're willing to go to keep their love safe.

Redemption, adventure, secrets, desire, and love in the docklands of late Georgian London.

BOOKS BY THIS AUTHOR

Liminal (Traversing Book One)

I'm pretty sure it's bad form to pick up a guy in a hospital.
Pretty sure it's even worse to show up uninvited at his brother's funeral.
Or let him…have you at the wake.
It's definitely not a smart move to let him into your apartment when he shows up uninvited after you made the reasonable choice to ditch him at said wake.
Still, I let him in.
Because… I'm messed up. And so is he.
Besides, he's also yummy, and we're both adults, and we have needs.
Needs that don't include getting attached, or telling each other our secrets.
Which I know he has. Then again, don't we all?
Except the longer we carry on with this arrangement, the harder it gets to remember the deal.
Even if I know that giving into our inexplicable connection will change my life forever.
And that Edward's secrets will either destroy us, or…
Open the door to a world I never could have imagined.

Rosemary & Pansies

When Flynn Carter is offered a job in Coombe's Cross, she can hardly refuse. Not even if that means working on Hamlet with temperamental director Clive Reid or movie-star heartthrob Jake Thornton. Her tough exterior seemed impenetrable armour enough until she met Jake...

No matter that he is here to save his career from scandal and ruin, his ego it seems hasn't suffered one bit...
But, they must learn to work together if they are to save the show, their careers, and whatever this is that is growing between them...

A sweeping and sweet low-heat contemporary love-story set in the magical world of theatre!

Printed in Great Britain
by Amazon

19181907R00154